num-
ber
One

CS

A Novel
by John
Dos Passos

CIC

HOUGHTON MIFFLIN COMPANY · BOSTON

The Riverside Press Cambridge

The Riverside Press
CAMBRIDGE · MASSACHUSETTS
PRINTED IN THE U.S.A.

Contents

c. 1

Contents

Number One

WHEN *you try to find the people,*
always in the end it comes down to somebody,
somebody working, maybe:
a man alone on an old disk harrow yelling his lungs
out at a team of mean mules (it's the off mule gives the

trouble, breaking and skittish, pulling black lips back off yellow teeth to nip at the near mule's dusty neck); it's March and the wind sears the chapped knuckles of the hand that clamps the reins; levers rattle; there's a bolt loose under the seat somewhere; it's hard to keep straight in the furrows as the pile of junk laced together with bindingwire lurches over the tough clods; it's March and the sun is hot and the dry wind rasps the skin and ruffles the robinsegg tatters of sky in the puddles along the lane that cuts straight from the mailbox under the roadside wires up to the house with blank windows that stands half tilted back on its haunches like a mule balking:

a man in his twenties, maybe, scrawny neck red and creased from the weather sticking out of the ravelled sweater, brows bent under the bluevisored cap, riding the jangle of castiron and steel over the caked clods (it's clayey land an' a rainy spell come on before he got shet of his winter plowin'):

a man alone with a team of mean mules and the furrowed field hemmed in on three sides with scrub and the sky full of blackbirds that wheel and scatter and light behind him to peck hurriedly among the new small furrows; when yelling he yanks on the reins to turn in a sweep by the fence trampling the brown silverpodded stalks of last year's weeds, the blackbirds take fright and soar in circling flight, specks that swirl black against snowtopped lumps of cloud drifting like ice through the blue windy rapids of the sky;

each time he passes his kitchen door there are more clothes out to dry on the line; sometimes he sees his wife with clothespins in her mouth wrestling with a flapping wet sheet or hears the whooping of the twoyearold or the weak squall of the new baby; harrowing towards the road he faces the wires looping from pole to pole and the shambling trucks and the shining fast cars and the old jalopies creeping like bluebottle flies cold on a windowsill;

each time he passes his kitchen door the radio fills his ears, voices bawling the price of fat stock in Kansas City, grains in Chicago, football scores, news of the fighting, smoothly a clause out of a government speech, swing moaning smokily from a late floorshow someplace where it's still night, the voice direct from me to you of a candidate who wants to be nominated,

voices talking bargains, threatening sickness, offering opportunities, wheedling chances,

voices from the gargled throats of announcers in glassedin studios beyond the sky and the clouds and the blackbirds and the wind,

that beat in the ears and fade into the forgetful coils of the mind intent on the edge of the furrow and the mean team of mules and the wife hanging out the week's wash and the kid with the whooping cough and the weak squall of the new baby lying wet in its crib.

Poor Boy

Tyler Spotswood was racking his brains. A trickle of sweat ran down between his shoulderblades to the wet place where the shirt stuck to his spine. Letting the yellow scratchpad drop from his hand, he leaned back in his chair and stared up at the ceiling. The drone of the electric fan in the hotel room made him drowsy. It was a hot night all right.

The stutter of the typewriter woke him with a jerk.

He started to go over backwards, but caught himself by jumping up and landing on the balls of his feet with the chair in one hand like an acrobat finishing a turn. Rubbing his eyes he crossed the room to where Ed James was hunched over a portable under a fringed standing lamp. Right away he saw what Ed had been writing was, over and over again: Now is the time for all good men to come to the aid of the party.

Ed pulled off his green eyeshade and mopped his bald head with a handkerchief. He looked up at Tyler, his eyes round and redrimmed in his moonface. 'Is it my fault,' he said in a whining voice, 'if a railroad boardin'-house ain't the right place for a presidential timber to be born in?'

'That's where you are wrong Ed,' said Tyler. He started to walk up and down excitedly. 'Why man alive Chuck Crawford was born right out of the middle of the American people . . . wait till you meet him . . . Of course I told you from the beginning I'm crazy about him . . . If I wasn't I certainly wouldn't be here in Washington. The thing I want you to understand about Chuck is that he's one of those fellers that wherever he was born it was just the right place for him to be born, see?'

'Well, politically Texarkola has some advantages . . . It's in two states.'

'Ed the trouble with you is you've been in the East too long . . . You've gotten cynical . . . You've forgotten how the folks feel back home.'

Tyler came to a stop behind Ed's chair and lit a cigarette. He stood frowning down at the bald head and at

[5]

the pink puckered face covered with little beads of sweat and at the fat freckled shoulders bulging out from the undershirt and at the hairless hands that hovered irresolutely over the keys of the typewriter. Ed's shoulders had begun to shake. When he turned his face up again Tyler could see it was drawn into a helpless knot from laughter. 'Why Toby you'd think it was me was the damyankee instead of you,' Ed whined as soon as he could get his breath. 'Boy I was born an' raised down there. I am those folks.'

Tyler couldn't help laughing himself. 'Well I am a kinder half and half proposition, I admit.' He yawned. 'The trouble with me is I don't get enough sleep. Nobody gets enough sleep who tries to keep up with Chuck Crawford . . . But I want you to get some kind of an outline down. You can fill in the facts from what Chuck has to say.'

Ed began to giggle. 'Facts did you say?'

'Ed . . . Chuck's a great man. He's going to be President of the United States some day.'

'I know. They all are.'

Tyler felt the ill temper rising up through him like the taste of a bad hangover. He went over and stood by the window to get hold of himself. A slithering noise of cars came up through the dense May night from roads along the creekbed below where headlights made a squirming green bright tunnel through foliage. Along with the choke of ethyl gas and scorched oil came a smell of sappy wilting leaves and trodden grass that made him think of women's underwear. He flicked the butt of his cigarette off his thumb with his forefinger and watched the red speck leave a trail of sparks as it spun out of sight.

'Toby,' came Ed's ingratiating voice behind him, 'don't you want me to enjoy my work?'

'I keep forgetting you haven't met the man . . . For crissake let's order up a drink . . .' When Tyler came back from the phone Ed was ready with a fresh sheet of paper in his typewriter. 'Well he was born in Texarkola in 1898 . . . went to public schools . . . What was his daddy like?'

'I used to know old Andrew Crawford when I thought I was in the lumber business with Jerry Evans . . . He'd been a pretty good small town lawyer years back but he was an opinionated kind of cuss and was always getting in wrong with the interests. The preachers said he was an atheist . . . you know the type . . . always up in arms for some fool cause or other . . . the tanktown agnostic. Poor Mrs. Crawford didn't have a very good break. I guess there were times when she expected the devil to come in person to carry the old gentleman off. He was pretty popular though with a certain element in the town. He took part in all the local political campaigns, and had quite a following. I can remember him now holding forth in back of Ed Seaforth's drygoods store with a dusty black hat on the back of his head and a streak of tobacco juice down each side of his chin.' Ed's typewriter was rattling now.

'That's great,' said Ed. '. . . A man after my own heart,' he added sourly.

'Mrs. Crawford was a mournful kind of woman. Her

[7]

mother came from an old plantation family from Georgia and had married a circuit rider. She read a great deal in spite of being so religious. Chuck got most of his schooling from her. They were about the best educated family in town I guess though their circumstances were straitened to say the least. There were plenty days when they didn't even eat. Chuck started making his own living from the time he was about ten years old.'

'Mother still alive?'

'She lives with relatives at Indian Springs. Chuck does everything in the world for her.'

'That's a lucky break. A presentable old mother's a mighty useful property if a man gets to be a national figure.'

Tyler's jaw muscles stiffened with irritation. 'Ed,' he started slowly in a solemn voice, 'if I didn't know you'd do us a good job . . .'

'Sure I'll do you a good job . . . But if I write an autobiography for a man that don't mean . . . Boy if I didn't see the funny side I'd been dead before this.'

'You wait till you meet him.'

'Anyway mom and daddy sound all right . . . I expect to have me a hell of a time writin' this book.'

'He'll tell you most of it . . . All you'll have to do is pull the paragraphs together.'

Ed gave a kind of snort, but he kept his eyes on his typing.

They had just taken a first swallow out of their highballs when the phone rang. Tyler found himself making a slight smiling bow into the receiver when he found the voice was Sue Ann's. 'Hello Tyler, how are you-all makin' out?' her voice rattled breathless. 'I tell you that was some dinnerparty. It like to scared me to death. The Chief Justice of the United States was there. You oughta seen Chuck . . . he was the cutest thing in his soup and fish . . . just like a little boy eatin' icecream with teacher. On the way home Senator Johns let us give him a lift in the car an' Chuck talked him into comin' up. Then there'll be some folks from back home. I'm comin' around to talk to you-all for a minute before we go in there.'

'We'll be expecting you, Sue Ann.' Tyler hung up. He walked over and stood behind Ed's chair. 'That was Sue Ann . . . I haven't told you about her yet.'

'Mrs. Crawford?'

Tyler nodded vigorously. 'She's a mighty fine girl. They were coeds together . . . They studied law together, passed their bar examinations the same week . . . She was the Jones in Chuck's first law firm . . . Crawford and Jones.'

'Where did she come from?'

'A little town in the Panhandle . . . If it hadn't been for her straightening us out when we needed straightening out Chuck wouldn't be where he is today and neither would I. She's coming here for a second before she takes us up to their suite. They got Senator Johns with 'em . . . now Senator Johns wouldn't be wasting his time running around with Chuck if he thought he was nothing but a hillbilly, would he?' Tyler was leaning over the bureau drawer reaching for a clean shirt as he talked.

[9]

With the shirt in his hand he drank off his highball at one gulp and went into the bathroom to wash his face. Ed went on typing. When Tyler came out to tie his blue bow tie in front of the mirror over the bureau he paused for a second to stare into his own gaunt yellow face with its straight black brows. There were puffs under the eyes and a beginning of sharp lines down the cheeks. He didn't like the way his face looked. The whites of his eyes were bloodshot. Drinking too much again, he told himself.

There was a tap on the hall door. Ed jumped up from his typing, snatching his shirt off the chair where he'd hung it in front of the electric fan to dry and scuttled into the bathroom. When Tyler opened the door Sue Ann was standing there looking cool and green as a cucumber in her frizzy green evening dress with sets of little ruffles on the sleeves and skirt. At the point of the sunburned V of her neck the dress was fastened by the big diamond brooch in the shape of a crown Chuck had bought her the day he had made his first big killing in oil leases. Her heavy sandy hair had been waved for the dinnerparty but it was already beginning to get out of hand. 'Tyler,' she said, drawing her eyebrows together like she did when she was making a point of law, 'we've got to get a photographer ... It's Homer's golden chance to get photographed with the Senator.'

Backing ahead of her into the room, Tyler pulled out his watch. 'Won't be easy, Sue Ann, not in this man's town.'

'But Homer is news,' squealed Sue Ann.

'We think so but they don't think so yet . . . Maybe Ed knows somebody . . . they're all on to me . . . say Ed.' Ed came out of the bathroom looking pink and neat in a pongee jacket. 'Sue Ann this is Eddy James.' Sue Ann had walked over to the dresser and was struggling with her hair. Bobbing her head at Ed's image in the mirror, she acknowledged the introduction. 'You must forgive me Mr. James,' she muttered through the hairpins in her mouth. 'We treat Tyler just like a brother.' She was hurriedly trying to poke loose loops of hair into place, and finally had to pull down the two long braids and coil them again round the top of her head. 'I reckon it would scare Senator Johns half to death if I went back in there in braids . . . Daddy used to say it would break his heart if I cut my hair off and now Homer feels the same way, but it gives me more trouble.' . . . She pushed in some final pins and turned towards them. 'Mr. James do you reckon you could raise us a press photographer?'

'They are shyer'n wild turkeys but I'll try.' Ed snatched up the phone and leaned all hunched up over it against the wall. Sue Ann walked across to the door with a skipping step like a little girl coming home from school. At the door she turned. 'Now I'm puttin' it up to you boys to get me a photographer. I don't care if you have to set the hotel on fire to do it. The Senator's goin' to eat a ham sandwich with us. He's just like Homer that way, can't eat at dinnerparties . . . Homer was too scared of the Chief Justice to swallow a bite . . . but we can't keep the Senator waitin'. He always goes home at ten-thirty . . . I don't want you boys to come in smellin' of liquor either . . . you know how the Senator feels about it . . . Now you hurry now.' As the door closed behind her Tyler went into the bathroom and sucked some pink mouthwash into his mouth from a bottle, gargled his throat with it and spat it out with some violence into the bowl.

When he came out Ed was putting the receiver back on the hook. He was mussed and redfaced and sweating. 'Kleinschmidt'll come but it'll cost you something . . . it's up to you to break a story.'

'Good boy Ed.' Tyler began to stammer a little . . . 'Sue Ann thought . . . there's a bottle of mouthwash in the bathroom. You know the Senator's savage against drinking.' Ed threw back his head and laughed crossly. 'You don't expect me to kiss him, do you? Hell man I've seen United States Senators before . . . I was born in this country.'

Tyler flushed red. 'We're so damned anxious to have Chuck go over big . . . After all it was his first really important speech in Congress today.'

Ed was mopping his face and neck with a towel.

'Speech was goddam good,' he muttered, 'but I wish he'd picked a cooler day . . . Come on let's go.'

They walked, slowly so as not to get into a sweat again, down the wide deepcarpeted hotel hall. As soon as they rounded the corner beyond the elevators they began to hear Chuck's voice coming from an open door some distance down. Outside the door a waiter was leaning over a serving stand mixing a salad. In the middle of the hall a gangling bellboy with a telegram on a tray in his hand stood looking up at the transom with his jaw hanging open. They began to make out the words:

'Why should one million people in this country have all the good things of the world while the other hundred an' nineteen million go naked an' hongry an' destitute? It's against common sense an' it's against revealed religion. Don't the Bible lay upon us the injunction, Senator, to spread the good things of the land equally among the people of the land? Leviticus 25, verse 23.'

At the sound of the familiar brassy twang, Tyler felt for a second the same warm musclerelaxing rush of belief he'd felt when he'd first heard it raised from a public platform. He was crazy about Chuck's voice. Right after, as always when he was hurrying up to meet Chuck, came the cold qualm of doubt as to how Chuck was going to be; would he look him smilingly in the eyes or would that hard bossy look come down like a plate glass between them? It wasn't that Tyler was touchy, but hell . . . The voice was going on quoting the Bible:

'"The land shall not be sold forever for the land is mine; for ye are strangers an' sojourners with me" . . . an' all the rest of that chapter.'

Pushing Ed ahead of him Tyler brushed past an elderly hicklooking couple who were hesitating in the doorway and looking in each other's faces with moist dog's eyes, and a second waiter who was frozen motionless in the middle of the room with a trayful of whitemetal coffeepots and covers balanced at shoulder height on his hand.

Homer T. Crawford, his face ruddy in shadow except for a flick of light that caught the bulge of his round eyes, was sitting between Sue Ann and the Senator behind a big round table with a stiffly creased cloth, loaded with a lot of shiny hotel metalware and big waterglasses full of glinting ice. The collar of his boiled shirt was open and his dark hair had a mussed steamy look.

'It's my profound belief, Senator, that there's more radical economics in the Holy Bible than those Roosian Reds ever thought of.'

Something about the way he said it made Sue Ann and the Senator burst out laughing. Chuck threw back his head and roared, and started ramming a section of a threedecker sandwich into his mouth with one hand, while with the other he stuffed in bits of ham and chicken that dropped from it at each bite. As he ate he kept his big bluegray popeyes fixed on the long creaseless countenance, so astonishingly like his pictures in the papers, of Senator Johns. The Senator had a plume of white hair across the top of his high forehead that shook as he laughed. Sue Ann, taking sips from a cup of coffee she held aloft with little finger crooked, was giggling like a schoolgirl.

The waiter took advantage of the pause to dart forward into the room, and the bellboy shambled in after him, staring at Chuck so hard that he tripped over a chair. Tyler took the telegram without looking at it.

Chuck caught sight of Tyler and Ed James and beckoned them up to the table with the hand that held the sandwich. 'Waiter,' he mumbled with his mouth full, 'bring these gentlemen some more sandwiches.' Tyler caught himself stifling a pleased feeling way down inside himself like a dog wagging its tail. As he drew up two chairs he had time to take a quick look at Ed's face to see what he thought of Chuck, but nothing got past that smile.

'In a land of too much to eat an' too much to wear an' too many dwellin' houses I don't see no explanation, Senator, for our naked an' homeless people, but usury an' greed . . . Daddy,' Chuck suddenly addressed the lanky old man by the door. 'Down where you come from, what proportion of folks who've had to leave their homes an' go trailin' over the land in search of work have done it because they was or'nary an' noaccount an' what proportion because the system jess druv 'em out?'

'It's right hard to say Mr. Crawford . . .'

'There ain't no Mr. Crawford here or in the U-nited States House of Representatives either . . . I ain't nothin' but ole Chuck Crawford that used to help you do your chores those cole mornin's while the missus was rustlin' up breakfast, an' now I'm here doin' chores for the American people. Senator I want you to meet Mr. an' Mrs. Price from Oklyhomy . . . They ain't my constituents, but they're genuine dirt farmers an' old friends, an' there's a million more like 'em. I want you-all to meet a great an' worthy public servant.' The Prices jerked their way forward and shook hands stiffly all around. 'Well thank you Daddy an' thank you ma'am for comin' in. I'm always glad to see real folks. You-all must excuse my eatin' but it's the only chance I git

. . . an' wearin' this uniform, that was because I had to meet the Chief Justice of the U-nited States . . . Now we've got to go into conference with the Senator on the state of the nation.'

The Prices began to edge their way out. Chuck took a big swallow of coffee and leaned back from the table with his cheeks puffed. 'You see, Senator, that's my life. Day an' night my door's never closed. I feel the people have the right of access to their representatives in Congress an' out of Congress. It has been the same thing ever since I entered public life. It was the same thing when I was on the road sellin' hardware. Look at Sue Ann here, if it hadn't been for a potatopeelin' contest I never would have met her an' she's been the greatest boon to me that was ever conferred in this world on a lonesome young hillbilly honin' for an eddication . . .'

'Why Homer Crawford I declare I never peeled a potato in my life . . . It was a wafflemakin' contest an' you were sellin' the worst old noaccount waffle iron I ever did see,' Sue Ann protested in her high voice.

Chuck threw back his head again and laughed until he began to cough and splutter: 'Well boys the drinks is on me,' he said. 'Senator have another cup of coffee.'

Suddenly a serious look came over his face and he turned to Ed James. 'Mr. James I understand you've come to see me because you want to write my life and biography. Well let me tell you somethin', my life ain't begun yet. My life's in the hands of the American people. It ain't goin' to be you nor any other single

man writes the life of Homer T. Crawford. The introduction was written by the folks back home an' if God
gives me strength the best chapters are yet to come.'

Little sparks of amusement appeared in Senator Johns'
glazy gray eyes. 'When I was a youngster,' he said,
'they called it hitching your wagon to a star.'

'Naturally Mr. Crawford I was thinkin' only of some
kind of portrait of the congressman as a young man.'

'You write it in the first person, do you hear?' roared
Chuck. 'I do everythin' in the first person.'

Tyler was getting worried for fear Senator Johns would
get the wrong impression. He never could get used to
Chuck's way of talking about everything in front of
everybody. He'd started to fidget with his cigarettecase
when the phone rang. He strode over to it relieved at
having something to do. It was the photographer in the
lobby. Tyler said to come right up. As he hung up the
phone he could see Sue Ann's eager face turned in his
direction. He nodded. She threw up her eyes and her
lips formed something that looked like 'Thank the Lord.'

Senator Johns was on his feet saying that it had been a
very pleasant occasion and that it was time he took his
old bones home. Sue Ann and Tyler exchanged worried
glances as Tyler started into the next room to get the
Senator's panama hat and stick. When he came back
with them Chuck had gotten between the Senator and
the door and was holding forth about what he'd done for
conservation of natural resources during his last term in
the legislature down in his native state. 'The American
people,' he shouted, 'have fallen heir to the richest

[17]

heritage in the world, an' they've run through it like a crapshootin' nigra cropper through his cotton money, an' the worst offenders ain't been the poor people . . . a poor man goes huntin' an' he won't kill him more meat than he kin take home an' eat . . . he knows how scarce things is. But these big corporations, lumber companies an' oil companies, all they think about is high finance an' gettin' em high falutin' homes in France or steam yachts an' the like.'

Three skinny sweating pale young men in black suits were in the doorway. Sue Ann, who'd managed to get behind the Senator, shook hands with herself in Tyler's direction. The photographer's helper started unpacking his traps. Already the photographer was advancing with the silvercrinkly flashlight bulb held up above his head. The Senator's mouth hardened into a peevish curve and he started for the door, but Chuck grabbed him firmly by the hand and began to carry on about how he'd been trying all day to get a dish of hog jowl and turnip greens, just the thing a man needed to freshen up his blood, weather like this, but he declared there wasn't a restaurant in Washington City where a man could get any plain old home vittles. The Senator gave up the struggle. A waiter was posed holding out the menu card and the Senator, with the face of a child who's been tricked into swallowing castor oil, let himself be induced to sit down at the table again while Chuck pounded with his fist and pointed at an empty plate and bawled the waiter out in dumb show because there wasn't any hog jowl and turnip greens to be had in the hotel. Meanwhile the photographers scuttled merrily around the room; the sourlooking little cub reporter's pale face loosened up as if he thought that maybe this time he'd hit the front page. Sue Ann got the giggles again. When it was all over Chuck led the Senator to the door and pumped him by the hand all the way so that the photographer could get final shots of the two of them shaking hands.

'Senator you must forgive me for layin' this little trap for you,' Chuck was protesting meanwhile. 'The boys do things for me an' I like to hand 'em a little somethin' nice now an' then . . . You got to forgive ole Chuck. He don't mean no harm. You're the hardest man to photograph in Washington City an' it means a raise to every one of these boys just gettin' a shot at you . . . A new photograph of Senator Johns is front page news any day . . . Ain't it boys?' The boys all nodded vigorously and Chuck and Sue Ann escorted the Senator off to the elevator.

Chuck came back grinning with his arm round Sue Ann's waist. 'We sure had the old goat over a barrel that time . . . Will they git the story past the city desk?' 'I wouldn't be surprised if they did, with all that hawg jowl an' turnip greens,' said Ed James.

Chuck turned and walked right up to him as if he were going to hit him. 'I know Mr. James you think that's all horsin' an' demagogue foolery . . . But lemme tell you jess why I do it. Down where we come from there's a lot of pore people don't eat the proper food . . . Those folks they listen to what I say because they know I'm their friend . . . That's why every time I git a chance I hammer away at turnip greens or pot liquor or sallets . . . a lot of those folks'll think if ole Chuck eats it it may be worth tryin', so they'll start to git the proper vitamins an' all that.' 'Mr. Crawford,' said Ed with his pleasantest smile, 'exception withdrawn.'

The photographer had packed up his traps and Ed James took his arm and the reporter's arm and walked with them down to the elevator talking briskly, first in the ear of one of them, and then of the other. Meanwhile Chuck was leaning against the door jamb with his cheeks sucked in listening to what two tall men in stetson hats had to say. Sue Ann let herself drop into an overstuffed chair and whispered smiling up at Tyler, 'Now at last we can relax.' Tyler nodded vaguely; he was wondering how soon he was going to get himself a drink.

Chuck came back in the room with a scrawled up paper in his hand. 'Here are some more names for the file, will you see to 'em Sue Ann?' Sue Ann got to her feet yawning and reached for the paper. 'You go to bed young lady,' said Chuck in a gentle voice and brushed her eyebrows with his lips. 'I'm goin' to take these boys out to paint the town.'

'Don't do anything I wouldn't do,' said Sue Ann giddily.

When they stepped out of the hotel lobby into the dense early summer night, Chuck shouted, 'Tell him where to go Toby,' and dove into a taxicab and stretched himself out with his panama hat tipped over his nose and his feet on the folding seat. Before Tyler and Ed James had time to fit themselves into the seat beside him he had started to talk in an even drawl: 'First thing I remember ever doin' on my own was sellin' newspapers. My folks never had a piece of change in the house from one week's end to the other. If I wanted any money, I jess had to go out an' make it. The newsagent back home at that time was an old feller with a wooden leg. He used to tell us kids he'd lost it in the river fightin' in front of Vicksburg, but I learned later he'd lost it by gittin' hot an' fallin' under a freight train; anyways he used to send me down to the train to git the *New Orleans Picayune* an' the Saint Louis papers an' sometimes he made me tend store for him. He had a little hole in the wall on State Line Avenue with a sign "Notions" up across the front . . . For the longest time I thought that meant the notions folks wrote down in all those books an' magazines an' papers . . . I declare I did.'

The driver slammed on the brakes and the cab stopped with a jerk just in time to miss a yellow streetcar that turned shuddering on its tracks into Connecticut Avenue. A hot draft of air puffed in their faces a reek of asphalt and grinding metal and overgrown foliage.

'Say brother you watch where you're goin'; you don't have to turn around to listen,' shouted Chuck.

'Sorry mister,' said the taximan. 'Sellin' papers is how I started in life myself. Ain't that a coincidence? But it looks like you'd come a lot further than me, mister, or else it ud be you drivin' the hack an' me sittin' up in back layin' down the law.'

'Don't you worry brother,' said Chuck laughing. 'We got room for all kinds of people in this country.'

'Sure,' said the taxidriver, 'and most of 'em waitin' in line for the poorhouse.'

'That's what we aim to change brother. Ever heard of Homer T. Crawford? Well he's the man that's goin' to change all that . . . Lemme tell you somethin',' Chuck went on, tapping Ed James on the knee, 'I guess I was the only kid in the U-nited States of Ameriky ever got a lickin' for goin' to Sunday School, not for not goin' but for goin' . . . You see my daddy was a mighty opinionated man . . . No he warn't no atheist, I'm sure of that, but he ran with Bob Ingersoll an' Brann the Iconoclast an' that gang . . . a preacher to him was a limb of Satan as much as he was to the preacher. As I look at it now he was a narrowminded man. My poor mother went to the Methodist Church. She used to say she'd given up everythin' in the world for Andrew Crawford an' she was durned if she'd give up her religion for him too; an' that was about the size of it 'cause my daddy was a right smart lawyer, but he was the arguinest an' the cussedest man in seven states, too stubborn for his own good. If he ever did win a case half the time he'd talk himself right out of court again arguin' the constitootion an' revealed religion with the judge. He paid out more in fines for contempt of court than he collected in fees in his law practice, an' most of his clients were pore people an' he never did press for payment . . . Well my mammy an' me we was set on me goin' to Sunday School. All the other kids used to go an' come home with little pitchurs for prizes an' go on picnics an' everythin' an' I used to feel terrible I couldn't go an' I used to

[22]

picture Sunday School like it was a barrel of monkeys. So I finally took to jess sneakin' out an' goin' to Sunday School anyway an' we told Daddy I'd gone fishin'. We figured a lie in a good cause like that couldn't be no sin . . . An' then one day the old man cotched me comin' home with the other kids with a clean collar on an' the scripture reader under my arm an' a blue ribbon in my buttonhole, kickin' out my toes an' stickin' my nose in the air, an' he took me out back of the house an' into the woodshed an' gave me the worst lickin' I ever had. He used to say that hurt him more'n anythin' ever happened in his life. It liked to killed me. My old man an' me we never was friends again from that day to this. But lemme tell you somethin', I sure cleaned up on Sunday School prizes memorizin' the scriptures . . . My, my . . . I could have memorized the telephone book in those days . . . I knew all the begats, an' the words of the prophets and the Song of Solomon; that came in right handy later when I began runnin' after the girls.'

Tyler was sitting up on the folding seat next to Chuck's feet pleased as could be; Chuck was going good and Ed James was taking it all in. This thing was beginning to click. Just three drinks of rye, he was telling himself, was what he was going to take to get rid of that limp dishrag feeling and then he'd go home and go to bed. It was pleasant jouncing this way in a cab with the pale streetlights and the shadows of trees brushing across his face through the broad streets muffled under masses of foliage that pressed down spongily on the lamps and the traffic and the empty sidewalks and the low brick dimly lit houses. The night oozed with that wilted summer smell that made him think of the smell of a woman's body under her underwear.

Chuck was beginning to tell about how he'd helped the preacher put stained glass windows in the First Methodist Chuch back home when they drove up to the brightly lighted curb in front of the restaurant and a doorman opened the cab door. Chuck shot out of the cab and strode in through the folding doors with Ed James following half a step behind him. While Tyler was reaching for his wallet to pay the taxi, the driver asked, 'Say mister, who is that guy?'

'That's Representative Crawford, Homer T. Crawford . . . We think he'll go a long way in this town.'

'Well he's a mighty sweet talker.'

'He's going to give some radio talks one of these days . . . you remember to tune in on him.'

Tyler hurried up the stairs into the stuffy cigarette-smoky chill of the airconditioned restaurant. He stood a moment in the door puzzled by the pink lights and the droning swing, looking around at the jumble of faces, mouths pursed round cigarettes, girls' bare shoulders, glasses, bald heads, napes of necks. Chuck and Ed were settled behind a big table in the corner. Chuck was talking. Ed already had a notebook out.

'. . . I jess went aroun' an' talked to folks all over town. I was right in with the feller made icecream because I'd run a little setup for him sellin' icecream to the highschool kids. They had me for cheer leader at the athletic events so I was able to fix up that we'd only sell his icecream. Old Dr. Wisdom's benefit for his stained glass windows was a big day for me I tell you; I don't believe I was sixteen yet. The man who ran the ice-cream factory was an old Eyetalian named Rosa, his boys got a big business all over the state now. I talked the old feller into givin' the icecream free for Dr. Wisdom's benefit, an' it took plenty. Old Rosa was a nice old feller but he'd never heard of givin' anythin' away free . . . He said it would be the ruination of him . . . well it wasn't. He found the more free icecream he gave away the more folks bought.'

'Sure,' said Ed James laughing comfortably. 'I remember old Rosa. He set up a business down in Horton years ago.'

'That was the same old Rosa. Well, before I got through I had every preacher in town comin' around to the benefit for that stained glass . . . Told 'em I'd git 'em all free icecream for their own picnics an' stuff like that. The toughest nut to crack was the Catholic priest, Father Scalise. But in the end I had 'em all feedin' outa the same trough like good Christians . . . An' the stained glass windows is in that church to this day . . . Say Toby is that waiter bringin' us some drinks? . . . I've talked myself dry . . . Thattaboy rye and setups, friend, an' please leave the bottle . . . The thing I learned in that Sunday School . . . outside the Holy Bible, that's the greatest eddication a man kin have . . . is that people's minds are full of mean lil barbwire fences . . . The thing to do when you are tryin' to talk folks into somethin' is to kinder fool around till you find a gate or a break in one of them fences . . . If you try to storm through a barbwire fence you'll git your pants tore. An' lemme tell you somethin' else I learned from readin' the Bible in that Sunday School; it was that the Children of Israel had to face a lot of the same kinder problems we had to face in this country an' the Christian religion is the final form of how they solved those problems. Now the ordinary man is a cussed an' narrowminded kind of a critter, ain't he? Mind fulla barbwire fences. But down where you an' me come from Mr. James . . . the wise guys in the Eastern magazines call it the Bible Belt . . . it's from the Bible most folks git all the little corrals an' fences their minds is filled with . . . I found as I went along the easiest way to git anywheres with 'em was to quote scripture to 'em for their own good. Helpin' run that benefit for old Dr. Wisdom's stained glass taught me more'n all the schoolin' I worked so hard to git afterwards . . . Been worth thousands of dollars to me. And once you've gotten through them fences, it's like breakin' a colt, you kin ride him easy . . . I was tellin' you-all about that ole priest . . . He sure thought I was a limb of Satan . . . I didn't know no Latin I guess . . . But lemme tell you somethin', when the time come for me to go away to school an' I was lookin' around for somebody who'd be fool enough to loan me some foldin' money, who do you suppose come across? It was that ole Catholic priest. He histed up his gown an' pulled out an old greasy wallet out of his pants, damned if he didn't. I didn't know they wore pants. I guess I thought they wore some kinda kilties like a Scotchman . . . an' he pulled out two one hundred dollar bills . . . they were the biggest bills I ever saw in my life up to that time . . . an' he said, "Take this son an' pay me back when you git a chance." Pleasantest thing I ever did was to pay the ole feller back. I didn't have no cash, so I paid him back in some oil stock I was interested in . . . He made a pretty sour face when he took it . . . you know what some people think about oil stocks . . . but before he died that old priest sold that stock for fifteen hundred dollars . . . If I'd knowed that stock was such a good proposition I wouldn't have given it to him.'

They all laughed and Tyler poured everybody out another drink. This was his third drink and he was beginning to feel more spring in him; Chuck's autobiography was his idea; it was going over big with Ed. Old Ed sure was the man to write it. 'My that story about the Catholic priest is a vote-getter,' he whispered to Ed while Chuck paused to take a swallow of whiskey. 'One election they voted a whole convent of nuns on the strength of it.'

'Of course I kinda dress it up some,' said Chuck, in a humble explanatory tone. 'Depends on what kind of audience I'm tellin' it to.'

Ed James' eyes were bright. He gave his glass a little circular shake to mix the ice and whiskey. 'This is great,' he said.

'I figure we can get a story out of Chuck's life millions of people will read,' said Tyler, pounding on the table with his fist until the glasses rang. 'We want the whole country to know Homer T. Crawford the way the people down home know him.'

'It's the McCoy,' said Ed James.

Before he knew it Tyler had poured himself another jigger of whiskey. He felt up to par for the first time all day. He drank it off straight. It was rotgut rye, but from the hot lump in his stomach it spread sweetly all through him. Pretending he'd just tasted that one, he filled up the glasses all around, including his own.

Chuck went on talking: 'I had a tough time eatin' when I went down to the state university, makes me feel hongry now to think of it. First I tried to introduce old Rosa's icecream, but the local icecream kings had the market all sewed up, so that didn't go so good. Then I got me a job clerkin' in a hardware store, but the trouble with that was I didn't have no time to study an' began to fall off in my grades. I was just about wore out an' the dean of men was carryin' me on the black books when they decided to have them a speakin' contest. Resolved: That national ownership of the railroads will react unfavorably upon the interests of the general public. The dean thought I was such a miserable little hillbilly he hardly would let me sign up for the contest. Well I borrowed five dollars to pay my board bill from a girl I knowed was kinda sorry for me an' I went in that library an' I read every book an' paper I could find about railroads from the first steam engine right on down . . . they assigned me the affirmative . . . an' I just recited those books an' statutes an' statistics right back at them off the platform jess like a goddam parrot

... I talked the judges blue in the face ... I was too goddam scared to stop talkin' ... Well sir I won that debate hands down ... one hundred dollars prize ... By the time I'd stopped an' everybody was clappin' an' stompin' I knowed I'd been talkin' on the wrong side. I been convinced we oughta have public ownership of the railroads ever since ... After that they couldn't do too much for lil Chuck down at school. They had me on the debatin' team an' out as cheer leader at the ball-games an' they rushed me for the frats until I thought I owned the earth. But it all cost me money an' nothin' came in to pay for my groceries, an' I ran up bills, after all what can a feller do? I tried to pick up a little change rafflin' off a typewriter, but it didn't go so good, so I had to git outa town real quick on a freight train one night. I went out to the Panhandle an' smashed crates in a warehouse for a while ... but from a kid I'd figured I wasn't laid out for that kinda backbreakin' work so before long I talked 'em into lettin' me go on the road an' demonstrate their line of kitchen appliances. Trouble was I didn't have no car ... you know a salesman's got to have a good lookin' car, an' I wasn't much more than nineteen an' didn't look that old for all I was tryin' to grow a mustache ...'

Suddenly it was closing time and the waiter was standing over the table with the check. 'Well where do we go from here, boys, where do we go from here?' chanted Chuck. 'We can't break up now, I got to hear the rest of the story,' Ed said earnestly. Tyler said he thought he knew a nice quiet spot.

Chuck winked. 'This feller Toby he's got an address book'll knock your eye out.'

They all roared.

Going down the stairs, Chuck brought his shoulder against Tyler's. 'How much of a roll you got?' he asked out of the corner of his mouth.

'I got plenty. Thought it might come in handy.'

'Better hand it over before you get too stinkin' drunk.'

'Not a chance . . . I only had three drinks.'

'Come on Toby I'm holdin' the stakes.'

Tyler peeled a couple of twenties off a fistful of bills and handed the wad over to Chuck without a word. The twenties he folded carefully and tucked into his wallet. His cheekbones began to burn. Then Chuck said gently: 'That way you'll have the expense account off your mind, see Toby?' Tyler didn't answer, but instead stalked stiffly across the sidewalk and stepped into a cab.

He sat hunched over his knees on the little folding seat, staring at the broad empty asphalt streets without listening to what the other two were saying. When the cab stopped he got out and stood looking up at the humming blundering swirl of moths and junebugs round the frosted globe of a streetlight overhead. The junebugs brought it all back: the stuffy loneliness he'd felt as a kid there these steaming Washington nights, the feeling of energy drained out, the feeling of emptiness behind the low brick housefronts under the sweating trees, nowhere to go, nothing to do. The feeling of wanting a woman. Well he'd gotten out, and he'd had plenty women. He'd made a mess of things and now he was back, working for that bigmouthed bastard. Here he was slaving like a nigger for that son of a bitch and what did he get for it? No one was going to tell him how many drinks he could have. He hadn't felt this way since he was a kid and Dad used to bawl him out for sneaking off to the ballgames. It must be this lousy town. The thing to do in this town was to drink plenty liquor. No he wasn't going to get plastered; he knew how to handle himself all right.

The cab had driven away. Chuck and Ed had gone on in. He rang the bell at the small entry beside the darkened plate glass window with 'Italian Restaurant' lettered across it. A fat man in an undershirt answered. 'Meester Spotswood, how you do? Your friends sit down a'ready . . . Please not for long . . . Very late.' 'Too goddam hot to sleep,' grumbled Tyler following the man back along a passage that smelt of garlic and stale wine into a little room with a square table covered with oilcloth embellished with red roses on a yellow ground. Chuck and Ed James were settled over a bottle of whiskey and a siphon of soda. There was nobody else there. They seemed to be getting along fine together.

'So this is your quiet spot, Toby? It's like ole prohibition times.' Chuck looked up at him with a friendly smile.

'You seemed deep in communion with nature, so we came on in,' Ed added with his whinnying laugh.

'Quiet spot's goddam stuffy,' Tyler answered morosely. Nothing could stop Chuck from talking: 'God a' mighty I could talk folks into doin' things in those days.

Old Ben Freeman was the manager of his hardware concern. He had the reputation of bein' a closefisted man
but I got him to go on my note for the down payment
on the car. It was a red Stutz roadster. Second hand.
We thought that was a mighty doggy-lookin' machine
in those days. Then I started to canvass the voters . . .'
Chuck started to laugh. 'Well it was the customers in
those days, but it's the same thing . . . that was when I
began my card index of every family rich an' pore I
canvassed.'

'I thought that was Sue Ann's idea,' interrupted
Tyler with his glass at his lips.

'The card index was Sue Ann's idea an' she's kep' it up
for me ever since. She'd taken a course in research down
at the university summer school. I'd started keepin' a
list of folks' names an' addresses every which way on
little bits of paper. At first I had it all in my head but
then it began to be too long even for my head . . . I was
jess comin' to Sue Ann . . . I used to be on the road day
an' night. Instead o' stoppin' in hotels I stopped in
farmhouses so's to git to know the folks, see how they
lived, see what they needed. I was always ready to
chop a little wood for 'em or help the misses light the
stove or clean the lamps or take the swill out to the pigs
. . . Wasn't a damn thing I wouldn't do . . . I got up
contests at county fairs an' all that crap. Took 'em out
of themselves a little . . . It's easy to git on the right side
of plain people. Folks were right glad to see me . . .
Well after I'd been on the road about a year I found I
was makin' big money for Ben Freeman, but not a nickel

of it stayed in my jeans . . . That's where Sue Ann
come in. Her old man, Mordecai Jones, was a wildcatter, sometimes he was in the money an' sometimes he
was broke. He had a lawyer, Lamar Parsons, was the
smartest lawyer in the northwestern part of the state,
but not a man you could trust with a plugged nickel, so
when Sue Ann an' me began to go together real steady,
ole Mordecai, he loved me like a son, he makes up his
mind I ought to study law an' gits Parsons to take me
in his office. There's a lot of law in the oil business an'
some of it's pretty tricky, an' ole Mordecai he figured
that if he had me in the office it would kind of keep his
attorney on the straight an' narrow, so far as he was
concerned. Sue Ann she started helpin' me read my
cases . . . she had a mighty long head for a girl . . . So
we thought she might as well study law too so that
between us we could do without payin' Lamar Parsons
all those fat fees. We got married an' the pair of us was
admitted to the bar, an' we started havin' a kid an' were
ridin' high wide an' handsome when Mordecai Jones was
burned to death when a well he was bringin' in caught
fire. The creditors come down on us like buzzards . . .
They took the oil leases an' they took the old Jones home
an' they didn't even leave us funeral expenses.'

Tyler drank off his drink and got to his feet. His
voice was louder than he expected. 'It stinks in here . . .
I'm goin' to call up Helen's place. We need the amenities
of life.'

'Not in Washington. They don't have such a thing,'
cried Ed.

Tyler was charging over towards the phone, fumbling in his pocket for a nickel as he went. After the phone had rung a long time a woman's voice answered shrilly. She said it was too late. 'Never too late for old Toby, Helen . . . It's jush a little quiet drinking party of three. Me and Number One and a big shot newspaper man . . . Sure . . . You call back.' He reeled a little as he came back to the table. 'Helen's occupay but she's got friends. She'll call back. I told her it's never too late for Toby. She laughed like hell. Helen's all right.'

'Say don't forget I'm a married man, at least a divorced man,' said Ed.

'Don't worry,' said Chuck. 'We just go around there to do a little high steppin'.'

'Need some action,' said Tyler . . . 'I hate this goddam town. I was raised here.' He poured himself another drink.

'Your quiet spot's too quiet for you is it? Me, I like a place with a band,' Chuck roared out. 'Down home I step out an' lead the band. Give the folks a time for their money, that's what I say. We'll all be a long time dead.'

When the phone rang Chuck got up and hurried over to it. 'It's a new address . . . sounds on the up an' up,' he said when he came back. 'We'll take over some liquor . . . Suppose you call a taxi, Toby ole sport.'

Tyler went into the kitchen to pay the bill.

'But Mr. Crawford, you haven't told me yet how you started in politics,' said Ed.

'There ain't no Mr. Crawford here . . . you call me

Chuck . . . I never did start in politics . . . I been fightin'
politics all my life. Me an' Sue Ann we picked up an'
went home to Texarkola. My daddy had passed on an'
my poor mother needed somebody to look after her . . .
an' we sure have looked after her, everybody'll tell you
that . . . We hung out our shingle in the Simmonds
buildin'. Our first case was against the utility company.
They'd cut off an old widow woman's lights unjustly an'
I sued 'em for damages. They got their dander up an'
brought in one of the highest priced lawyers in the
state an' be damned if the jury didn't award me five
hundred dollars damages. They've never let a case like
that go to court since . . . not when I was tryin' it . . .
always settled. Well come election time the feller who
was runnin' for county road commissioner on the Democratic ticket he gits run over by a truck so I nominate
myself an' be damned if they don't elect me. Little
Andy was a babe in arms then an' me an' Sue Ann an'
the baby jess drove around in the new car; we had a
Buick by that time, an' said Howdy to the folks I used
to be friendly with when I was on the road . . . When
they was real old we took the old lady along . . . We got
out voters hadn't seen the polls for fifty years . . . It
was a walkaway . . . Well those voters they ain't never
let me git outa public service since.'

Outside it was raining hard. Tyler lolled back on the
seat between the other two, as the taxi charged through
empty avenues shimmering now with reflections of
streetlights. There was a gleam on a wet statue of a
military man on horseback at a circle. Tyler drew him-

[35]

self up straight in the seat and saluted. They all laughed. 'Jess think of ole Chuck Crawford sittin' up on a bronze horse in the middle of the street . . . That ain't the longest shot in the world either.'

Ed James let out his whinnying laugh. 'Me I'd rather be a live dog than a dead lion.'

'Ain't no harm in bein' a live lion,' said Chuck. 'Easy as rollin' off a log if you've got the knack of gettin' around folks. Look at me . . . I'd hardly served my term as county commissioner when they had me on the State Utilities Commission, a dangerous job for a young man, full of temptations an' pitfalls. But the plain folks knowed I was workin' in their interests; why shouldn't I, when I was one of 'em? I come out of there after five years as clean as a hound's tooth.'

Tyler spoke up: 'All that time we were fighting one of the most entrenched political gangs in the country. I was in the lumber business with Jerry Evans . . . We ran into some trouble with oil and gas leases on the corporation's timberland . . . That's how Chuck and I met up . . . Then when the crash came and the business folded, Chuck gave me a job.'

'Ain't I treated you white, Toby?'

'Chuck you sure have.'

'I got the damndest bunch workin' for me . . . Every last one of 'em ud be in jail or the porehouse if it wasn't for Number One, ain't it the truth, Toby?' Chuck brought his hand down hard on Tyler's knee and squeezed it.

'Damn tootin', Number One,' said Tyler.

'Number One?' asked Ed.

'That's what they call me in the local political organization down home. Number One, that's the boss, eh Toby?'

'Yessiree,' shouted Tyler.

The cab had drawn up behind a limousine in front of a tallwindowed brick house that showed only a glimmer of light over the transom above the front door. All the windows were dark. 'Not what I call the bright lights,' said Chuck. They scampered across the uneven brick pavement through the downpour with the bottles clinking under their coats. A colored man in a chauffeur's uniform opened the door with a bow and held out his hand to take the bottles from them. Helen was waiting in the dim light of the hall that looked like the hall of an oldfashioned boardinghouse. She was a briskmannered woman with a turned-up nose, buck teeth and a shock of curly hennaed hair. She had thrown a man's raincoat over a purple evening dress. 'Well this is a pleasure,' she said in a highpitched society column voice. 'I just got Henry to drive me over so's I could introduce you to our friends . . . Right upstairs please.'

While Ed walked on up the steep narrow stairway covered by an oldfashioned flowered carpet, held down with brass rods that jingled with each step, Chuck and Tyler wrapped themselves round Helen. 'Good old Helen . . . Helen you look like a million dollars.'

'I declare boys I'm heartbroken . . . If you'd only called an hour earlier I could have had you at the house. But what could I do? But you won't be disappointed.

I never disappointed a friend yet . . . It's fifty dollars and everything paid for.'

Tyler started fumbling in his back pocket.

'I'm paymaster of the forces tonight,' said Chuck shouldering his way past Tyler. 'Toby goes an' gits hot on us.'

'Not hot, just congenial,' said Tyler making a pass at the front of Helen's dress.

Helen backed off sedately waving a handful of crisp bills in front of her. 'Well it's nice to have the business part all out of the way, isn't it?' She screwed her face up as she tucked the bills into her bulging black leather handbag and started up the stairs. 'I'll just slip out after the introductions. I've got to go back to my guests.'

'Let's see what they got up there Chuck,' said Tyler. He stumbled on the top step and caught himself with the palms of his hands against the wall of the upstairs hall. He sniffed. It was that oldfashioned boarding-house smell of stale cabbage.

He leaned against the wall a minute to pull himself together. Then he walked slowly placing his feet carefully, first one then the other, into a large oldfashioned room that had a black marble fireplace, with a goldbordered mirror above it that reflected a gas chandelier with dangling electric bulbs and clusters of little crystals that caught the light. 'Ain't this the funeral home?' said Chuck behind his hand. 'Toby we're seein' life.'

Under the reflection of the chandelier Tyler caught sight of his own head, his long face wearing a rather distant but gracious smile, not the face of a man who was cockeyed but the face of a man reconciled by a few drinks to the deceptions and disappointments of life, next to Chuck's curly round head, with its wellcurved eyebrows and its big bright popeyes that seemed to be looking in all directions at once. Chuck's cheeks were full of color; if it hadn't been for his heavy jaw and thick neck he would have looked like a boy of twenty going down the line for the first time.

There was an electric fan on the mantel on each side of the mirror that began to give Tyler the feeling that the room was moving like a barge under tow. Moving smoothly but moving. Somebody put 'Night and Day' on the phonograph. Solemnly, slowly, smoothly the room began to spin. He was dancing with a little redhead who knew all the words. She was crooning in his ear. He felt furiously happy. His life that all evening had seemed jerky and dull as an old local that stopped and shunted cars on every siding suddenly shot ahead like an express train. The fans whirred. The redhead crooned. The room was the cabin of a big roaring plane. He was bound for a destination. He was having one hell of a time on the way. He pulled the little redhead against him so hard she said, 'Ouch, no Tarzan stuff,' and pinched his arm.

Then they all sat down and had some drinks and the girls sat on the men's laps. The other two girls were both dark; one of them had a serious manner and a hooked nose and circles under her eyes and the third one, who was hanging around Chuck's neck, had a pageboy bob and remarkably big breasts. She went over to change the record and put on 'Andalusia.' Chuck said to hell with that, let's have 'Night and Day.' Meanwhile he gathered up the little redhead and started dancing without any music. Tyler found himself dancing with the pageboy bob. 'Isn't she cute?' he said waving a hand in the direction of the redhead. 'She's a darling,' the girl whispered. Her lips tickled his ear. 'It's the natural color. You can tell because her eyebrows and eyelashes is the same.' Then somebody else put on 'Andalusia' and Chuck said, 'No you don't,' and put back 'Night and Day.'

Tyler was sitting with the little redhead on his knee and he was crazy for her, and he was trying to get her to take a swig of whiskey from the bottle. Instead he took a swig and spilt it over his chin and she was dabbing at it with a handkerchief. And Chuck was dancing a double shuffle with the other two girls and there was Ed way off in a rocking chair smoking a cigar. The girls were all cakewalking with Chuck and Tyler was sitting on the floor just taking one more swig to keep his head from spinning, and Chuck was whirling the girls around and the room was whirling and swaying under that damn chandelier.

Tyler sat up on the floor with his back pressed against the wall to keep the room still. 'Come here redhead,' he shouted and grabbed her by the leg so that she tripped and fell down on top of him.

Chuck ran over to her with his face twisted up in an angry knot and picked her up by the waist. 'Cut it out.

Whose girl do you think she is?' Chuck yelled puffing hard. Then he set her on her feet and said in her ear, 'Don't mind him cuty he's drunk.'

'Who do you think you are?' shouted Tyler. He tried to get himself to his feet but there was no stiffness to his knees. 'I'd just as soon take a poke at you as at any other sonofabitch.' He waved his fists but he couldn't seem to get to his feet. Sprawling red in the face against the wall he heard Chuck's roaring laugh and could see his scowling eyes in different parts of the room and his mouth open laughing at him. The others all went on dancing without paying any attention.

That chandelier and all these damn fools dancing made him sick. He thought he'd better move along. He began to work himself carefully up to his feet. Leaning against the wall, he rambled round the room and out into the hall. 'They had cabbage for supper,' he told himself surprised at his own wisdom. He dropped into a chair. He'd been there a long time when some girl began to pull him up steep stairs past an open window where he caught sight of a faint grayness in the sky behind a shimmying curtain of rain. The stairs were steep. Upstairs it was goddam dark in the room. When a light suddenly went on he was reeling about in a bathroom. He tripped against a door padded with silky sachetsmelling wraps. The door opened so suddenly he fell flat, and a girl was giggling and he was struggling to his feet sweating and panting. He had hold of her. He was trying to undo some kind of a hook and there was a ripping of silk.

Tyler woke up with a start. He was suddenly wide awake. A streak of sunlight from the edge of the shade cut the room in two. He jumped up out of bed and started groping for his clothes. When he found them neatly laid out on a chair, his hands were shaking so he could hardly get into his drawers.

The first thing he thought was where's Chuck? Why the devil had he let Chuck come to a house like this with the amount of blackmail there was in this town?

He had a splitting headache. Water was dripping somewhere. He opened a door and found the bathroom and washed his face. Then he went back to see who the girl was. It was the little redhead. That made him feel better. Her face had a pasty look but she was young all right. Helen's girls were straight, he told himself, but you never knew. God what a risk to take. It would be just their luck to get blackmailed. What the devil happened last night anyway?

He stood there looking down at the girl's pasty sleeping face. She was asleep on her side with her turned-up nose in a crease in the pillow and her red hair over her eyes. Poor kid. He shook the girl's bare shoulder. As he turned her head up her eyes opened scared and sore. He tried to grin at her pleasantly but his face felt starched.

'Say cutiepie did the others go home?' he asked hoarsely.

She could barely talk she was so sleepy. 'Sure the Big Shot went home hours ago . . . Some Big Shot.'

'Jesus I'm sorry I was so stinking drunk.'

The girl yawned and turned over and went back to sleep.

Tyler had a tough time lacing his shoes. Every time he leaned over the pain shot through his head. He was trying to remember what had happened. Where the hell had they been? What a damn fool thing to go on a bat like this. He couldn't find his hat. His wallet was in his coat all right, but his suit was covered with dirt, still damp, all rumpled from the rain. He tiptoed down the dark stairs that creaked at every step.

The hot sunlight outside was like a blow on the temple from a baseball bat. The whole sky seemed to press the pain into his eyes. He had the longest time finding a cab. At the hotel his room had a neat soothing accustomed look. He shaved slowly and meticulously and took a hot shower and then a cold shower and got into clean clothes. Then, still shaking, he hurried down the hall to the Crawfords' suite.

The door was open. He walked in. The venetian blinds were down to keep out the sun. Chuck was sitting there at the big table eating breakfast in his shirtsleeves, looking cool and wellshaved and rested. Sue Ann fresh as a daisy in a starched blouse was typing at a desk beside him. 'We been lookin' all over for you Toby . . . We've had a right busy mornin'. Miss Jacoby's sick so Sue Ann's pinch hittin' for her.'

'Tyler,' said Sue Ann in a tense voice, 'Senator Stoat died in his bed at eight fourteen this morning.'

'That leaves an unexpired term of eight months.'

'I just had the Governor on the phone . . . He's goin' to appoint Mrs. Stoat to fill it.'

[43]

'Emma Stoat? My God.' Tyler let his breath out in a whistle.

'I was jess thinkin' . . . you know Toby I'm a gamblin' man.'

Sue Ann piped up: 'Homer's goin' to run for Senator. Ain't it grand?'

'Won't that mean resigning from the House?'

'Not till after the primaries.' There was a meditative rumble in Chuck's voice. 'After all we got some friends might like a spell in Congress.'

Tyler walked up to him and held out his hand across the table. 'Well, Senator Crawford, congratulations . . . the Senator's secretary regrets he got so goddam stinking drunk last night.'

Number One

W<small>HEN</small> *you try to find the people*
in the end it comes down
   maybe to a middleaged mechanic setting a bearing in the
back of a concrete garage,

(and outside the highway roars and rumbles with heavy trucks and hisses with the swish of cars passing at high speed,

and inside the radio all day long talks, croons, jingles, makes angel voices on the organ, sings sweet, sings hot, jangles, gyves, whispers the lowdown, prognosticates the outcome, inveighs, admonishes, exhorts: in one ear out the other);

he's a quiet man, lives in a boardinghouse off Main, has no children, his wife has left him, plays pool in the evenings or goes to lodge meetings or reads the tabloid smoking a cigarette in his narrow bed

taking down a gearbox, tightening a brakeband, screwing his eyes up to pick the right wrench off the bench of tools, laying the cotterpins by just where he can put his hand on them, leaning for a dreaming instant on the handle of the hydraulic jack;

muscles tighten, arms push three or four slow strokes as the rear end rises slowly off the floor;

(from the nerves meanwhile, in the throbbing blood, out of the lucid cortex of the brain irradiate the timeless enterprises of the mind:

one of some millionhanded gang, he walks in unison, wearing the badge, carrying the unioncard, belonging to the party, the party apart from the wrongheaded mass, belonging, pulling his weight; his is the knowhow), working alone inside concrete walls with smart fingers handling the bright familiar tools, the greasegun, the amusing intricacy of gears;

from everywhere the trucks on the road outside grind on to everywhere, cars slither into distance; from everywhere the radio out of its dusty box forms air into voices,

voices that lull, insinuate, incite the mind

to grow new tendrils of appetite, sow sets of words like seeds at random in the ears of a man alone with hands grimed with carbon and grease, trained muscles, a toolbench

and a couple of membership cards in the pocket of his pullover: from everybody everywhere the giant voices stir in somebody

embers of halfextinguished wants, old needs rancid under the deep lid of every day,

ambition maybe.

The Man Who

Through his halfsleep Tyler could feel the night's whiskey buzzing in his veins again. He was trying to think of nothing, but his brain went on ticking like a painful clock inside his head. And the timetable went round and round: eight o'clock, Pleasant Valley; ten o'clock, Oddfellows' Hall in Arrowhead Springs; noon, Poplar Fork, barbecue at the ball park, baseball game; three-thirty at the livestock exchange in Harmony, auction off prize mule; Eberhart in time to talk to the workers coming out of the packing plant; then Horton, the Mexican Market, Sam Houston Square, Technical High School, torchlight parade starts Sabine and 12th, then the big meeting at the Grand Opera House. Thank God tomorrow would be Sunday.

He lay flat on his back, keeping his hot eyelids tight closed. For an instant he had been able to let himself slide down under the surface of the dark, but already, through his eyelids, through the shades pulled down over the windows, through the skimpy frame walls of the house he could feel the sky overhead swell with light. In spite of him the bitter violet whiteness from the horizon was leaking into his sleep.

With the light sounds began. A rooster crowed, then another. Way off somewhere a Peter bird repeated his two notes endlessly. A mocker started off on a great gush of singing. From all around came a vague busy stirring and chirping, a rustle of impending commotion. From the barn came chomping and the noise of hoofs stamping on hollow wood. They were rattling dishes in the kitchen. A truck went into low gear on the highway and set off the rusty creaking of a flock of guineahens. Somewhere behind the hills a freight shunted cars. A locomotive whistled.

No matter how tightly he pressed his eyelids together the spreading light seeped through, showing up in awkward relief inside his head the outlines of all of yesterday's mistakes, the boners he'd pulled, the contacts he'd muffed, the names he'd forgotten, the damnfool gibberish he'd talked after he'd had those drinks at the Squaw Rock Country Club. He couldn't forget yesterday, he couldn't keep out today. If only it would stay dark. His head was going to burst from the pressure of the swelling white noisy morning.

He opened his eyes. It was a relief to see a plain ruddy shaft of horizontal sunshine cutting across the room from a tear in the windowshade opposite. He sat up. 'Gosh what a night,' he said aloud. 'Well I guess I'm up.' He staggered across the room to the cranky oldfashioned washstand and poured himself out a bowl of water and stuck his face down in it. Then he pulled off his undershirt and drawers and patted his skinny body all over with wet hands. The water drying on his body in the dry air made him feel cooler.

He went back to the bedside table, reached for a cigarette, stuck it in his mouth and tried to light it. It took him several matches before he could bring his shaking hand in line with his cigarette. He sat there with his eyes closed a moment dragging the smoke into his lungs. Already he could hear Chuck's voice from outside mixed with the clucking of fowls. Tyler grinned.

'Damn if he isn't in the henyard feeding the hens.' He pulled on his seersucker pants and went over to the window to raise the shade. He was surprised at the stillness outside. As far as he could see the land stretched in immense slow silent folds of bright faintly stirring green to the horizon. Low white farmhouses, with here and there a gray barn in tow, each anchored beside its slenderly tapering windmill, rode scattered over the slow smoothrolling contours, like fishingboats on a ground swell.

As Tyler stood yawning looking out of the window, Chuck's loud voice began to come nearer. There he was striding across the wet grass in his boots, looking cool and clean in his white stetson and his buffcolored silk shirt and whipcord breeches. Half a step behind came Tom Molloy trotting along with his neck stuck out of his denim shirt as red and creased and skinny as a turkey's. Then came a bunch of lanky ranchers and farmhands Tyler hadn't seen before, in overalls most of them, and after the men, having a hard time keeping up in her highheeled shoes, fat Mrs. Molloy with a pink poke bonnet on her head. They'd all gone past the window when Sue Ann followed, wearing a picture hat and a starchy navy blue dress, leading one of the smaller boys by each hand. Little Andy, the eldest, came last, all dressed up in a cowboy suit, taking sight on imaginary redskins with a toy automatic. Sue Ann caught sight of Tyler and gave him one of her quick grins that always made him feel good, and formed what might have been the word breakfast with her lips. He smiled and nodded and strode away from the window to duck his face in the washbasin again.

Shaving in cold water was agony, because he'd lost his shaving brush and couldn't seem to get his hands to quit trembling. To steady himself he had to take a deep swig out of a pint of whiskey he carried wrapped up in an undershirt in his satchel. He'd been trying to do without it. The whiskey tasted terrible. At first it made him feel worse, but his hand gradually steadied so that he could get through shaving. Dabbing at a cut on his chin that wouldn't stop bleeding he ran around outside the house to the kitchen. He was just lifting his foot up onto the first step of the latticed kitchen stoop when a big collie dog rose up from under it and nearly threw him. 'Toby my boy,' he said to himself, 'You've got to quit drinking.'

A blast of dry heat met him as he slipped into the kitchen through the screen door. Chuck's face, round and red and wet as a boiled beet, was bobbing from side to side as he talked from the end of the long narrow table. You couldn't see the oilcloth for the stacks of fried eggs and cornbread and the dishes piled with bacon and spareribs and fried potatoes glistening with grease. Among plates and coffeecups and glasses of milk moved brown hands at the end of hairy reaching arms. All the chewing sunburned faces of the men crowded along the benches were turned towards Chuck. Chuck's big jowls munched as he talked. His bright protruding eyes, blue in the morning light, rolled round the kitchen to take in every face.

Flattened against the walls behind the hunched broad backs along the table a row of men in overalls or wearing khaki pants tucked into high boots stood silently listening while they waited for their turn at the breakfast table. Way in the back was the range with its steaming pots and pans and the dim busy figures of Mrs. Molloy and the two husky blonde women in boudoir caps who were hovering over it helping her. When Tyler came in the men on one bench squeezed their elbows together to make a place for him at the end. As he sat down he tried to catch Chuck's eye to let him know he was on deck, but Chuck was looking every way except his way.

Chuck's voice was booming above the rattle of cups and knives and forks '. . . If we'd had a breakfast like this back home when I was a boy, I'd a thought I was dead an' gone to heaven. An' this ain't nothin' to the riches that could belong to the plain people in this country . . . it's the plain people that produce all the riches there is . . . if they'd only jess git together an' freeze out of our government the bankers an' usurers an' predatory interests that never did a lick of real work in their lives . . . that crucify mankind, in the words of the Great Commoner, on a cross of gold . . . an' the first step in loosenin' the stranglehold these interests has got on the produce of this country is to drive their willin' tools an' henchmen out of office. The first one we're a-goin' to drive out of the public trough is Mr. Fatty Galbraith . . .' a laugh went round the room; people were pricking up their ears . . . 'One of the dumbest an' bluntest tools that ever touched his hat to a banker, who's had the gall to present himself, in spite of what every man woman an' child in this country knows about his record, to the voters of this state for the Democratic nomination for U-nited States Senator. Here he's been eatin' an' fattenin' off the green things of this land worse than the crickets . . .' Chuck paused to let the laugh that had started down at one end run the full length of the table . . . 'an' now he's askin' us to send him up to

Washington to go sell out what's left to the big Eastern interests. Well what we're a-goin' to say to him is "No Mr. Fatty Galbraith it ain't good for your health to run for no nomination in this hot weather. Ain't good for your shortness of breath. You go back to your nice cool office an' go on representin' your wealthy clients in the courts an' not in the U-nited States Senate . . ." This time the people of this state is a-goin' to send up one of their own.' Chuck wiped his mouth and got to his feet amid cries of 'Attaboy Chuck . . . You tell 'em Chuck.'

Chuck made his way down the narrow space between the men standing along the wall and the broad hunched backs eating along the table, laughing and exchanging cracks and patting sweaty shoulders and grabbing arms and scruffs of necks and gripping hands. When he reached Tyler, who was managing with some difficulty to down a few sips of hot coffee, he laid hold of his coat collar and dragged him out through the screen door onto the vinecovered stoop. 'Meet me around in Mrs. Molloy's parlor,' he spat the words fast out of the corner of his mouth. 'Hell to pay . . . We gotto do some phonin'.' Then he turned with his wide mouth stretched into a grin again and yelled back through the screen door, 'Well boys we'll see you at the primaries . . . If Fatty Galbraith wants to go to Washington so bad he'll jess have to pay his own fare . . . The people of this state ain't a-goin' to send him there.' Then he plunged down the steps and was gone around the corner of the house.

Tyler stood in the shade on the stoop for a moment

shakily lighting himself a cigarette. Then he leaned over and scratched the shaggy head of the dog that had rubbed up against his legs and, straightening his shoulders to pull himself together for the day's work, followed slowly after Chuck through the flailing sunlight.

It was cool in the shuttered parlor draped with white summer covers. Chuck was stretched out full length on the settee telling the towheaded squarefaced young man who ran the sound truck what records to play. 'All right, son, git goin', I want you half a mile ahead till we hit town, then stick with the peerade . . . Let 'em know there's somebody comin' an' don't you git lost now.'

'Okeedoke, Chuck.'

As soon as he had gone Chuck rolled his head back on the pillow and said to Tyler in a low peevish tone, 'Steve Baskette's reniged on the meetin' tonight. Says he's too damn busy to come to Horton. What's eatin' him?'

'Well, as Governor of the state . . .' started Tyler doubtfully.

'Governor, shit . . . He's fixin' to endorse Galbraith.'

'Galbraith's ratpoison to Steve.'

'Ratpoison can be sweetened up so's anybody'll eat it . . . What'll Jerry Evans do for you, Toby?'

'Well, you know Jerry and I have been pretty good friends.'

'Jerry's done a lot of favors for Steve . . . He wouldn't be where he is today if it wasn't for Jerry.'

'Jerry don't like to do something for nothing, Chuck.'

'I know he don't trust no politicians. But this here

ain't politics . . . this is savin' the country . . . He'll trust you if he don't trust me . . . Call him up. You can still git him at his home.'

'Jerry's tough, but he's square, Chuck.'

'I know, I know, they're all honorable men . . . Brutus was an honorable man; still he stuck a knife in between the boss's ribs . . . If I don't have Steve Baskette's endorsement I might as well go home right now.'

Sue Ann ran in with her skipping step with the three kids romping after her. 'Well, Homer, I got poor Mrs. Baskette outa bed at the Governor's Mansion and talked her ear off about what interestin' people I was goin' to have to dinner an' how Mrs. Gibbs Cunningham was goin' to be there an' Miss Everitt an' what kind of favors I was goin' to have an' the flowers an' everythin' . . . The poor soul almost broke down an' cried when she said maybe she couldn't come because Steve was so busy.'

'He's damn well got to come . . . Git outa here, you little devils . . .' Chuck squalled at the three little boys that had started to crawl up over him. 'Pappy's busy . . . Toby, take this white trash along an' turn 'em out to grass. Me an' Sue Ann's got to have a talk.'

Tyler grabbed three little hands in one of his and dragged them shouting and giggling out into the wide hall. He started them off playing tag in the shady grass space back of the house and went frowning to the telephone.

He gave his number and stood there, first on one leg, then on the other, while country people who had come to get a look at Chuck went drifting in staring groups through the hall. Outside the sound truck had started and was off over the hills playing 'The Old Folks at Home.' Chuck hurried out of the parlor with a face like a thundercloud. 'Toby,' he shouted, 'you come along when you've made your call. Sue Ann's car'll wait for you. At Oddfellows' Hall I want you-all up on the platform.'

A colored girl's voice had already answered.

'Hello . . . I want to speak to Mr. Jerry Evans, please . . . Say, Duke . . . this is Toby . . . Tyler Spotswood . . . Yes siree. How's yourself? Well, I'm out on the warpath with our next United States Senator . . . a great little old campaign . . . Sure . . . I know . . . But Duke, you know how it is on the stump . . . Well, wasn't he reasonable when he was on the Utilities Commission? All he wants is to protect the public interest. . . . Sure he was, Duke. Why don't you slip over an' meet us at Poplar Fork? Chuck's speaking at a barbecue at the ball park . . . There are some things I want to talk to you about . . . About Steve . . . We'll have to work fast. Anyway you'll enjoy the show . . . We're a regular traveling circus. The band'll be there . . . Steve's just about made up his mind, but you know how much he relies on your judgment . . . It's not eight o'clock yet. The way you drive you'll be over there before noon . . . Fly? Better yet. Flying time oughtn't to be more than an hour and a half . . . You'll enjoy the show . . . Chuck's making the best speeches of his career and you oughta hear those hillbillies play "Every Man a Millionaire." Well, Duke,

I'm counting on you. We'll have to work fast. The big meeting's in the Grand Opera House at Horton tonight . . . so long Duke.'

The sweat was pouring down Tyler's face when he put down the receiver. His heart was pounding. He slipped into the bedroom to get his panama and his satchel and ran out the front door of the house. Sue Ann was sitting back comfortably in the creamcolored Zephyr exchanging recipes for upsidedown cake with Mrs. Molloy who stood there talking into the car panting and exclaiming, holding the sun off her face with a palm leaf fan. The porch was crowded with silently staring men and women.

The car was full of bags and the little Crawford kids were all over everything, so Tyler slipped into the front seat beside the elderly colored chauffeur: 'Morning, Sam,' he said. Sue Ann said there was plenty of room in back, but Tyler gasped out that he'd be cooler in front. The car started to move slowly and smoothly away from the low white house. The women squeaked goodbyes. The men waved their hats. The car jounced down the dusty road that wound between ranks of tall cornstalks round the contours of the gradual hills and clanked across a cattleguard out onto the smooth highway. The first thing Sue Ann asked in a tense little voice was how Mr. Evans seemed.

'I dunno . . . Maybe he's willing to be shown . . . he's going to fly over and meet us at Poplar Fork, he's got his own plane now . . .' Tyler twisted himself around on the front seat so that he was facing Sue Ann. 'My,' she said. 'He must be piling up money.' 'His oil properties alone net him a hundred thousand a year . . . Jerry's a comer all right.' 'What's he goin' to ask Homer to do for him Toby? You know there are some things Homer can't do.'

Tyler pursed his lips together. 'Maybe somebody else might . . . So many of the boys owe everything to Homer.'

'They sure do.' Sue Ann's voice dropped.

For an instant Tyler caught a look of fright in her narrowed gray eyes. Then she brought her brows together and gave him her schoolgirlish grin. 'You-all kin talk Mr. Evans around,' she said. 'Remember that banker who wanted to give all his money away after Homer had made that speech on "Every Man a Millionaire" at Little Rock?'

'We've damn well got to,' said Tyler. He settled back in his seat again and started looking out the window at the pale yellow dazzle of a field of wheatstubble. Small dust whirls moved sedately across it towards a parallelogram of green cornfield that rose up against the bright horizon. Beyond the corn the hills smoothed out into flat wheatland again as the car started to speed up along a straight road between telegraph poles and wire fences. Overhead white cotton clouds spread out in even rows with patches of steel-blue sky between.

The morning too was gathering speed. The sun was already high when they caught sight of the glitter of the watertank at Pleasant Valley poking up above a bunch of pale green trees at the end of a long straight shimmering reach of the road. A couple of board shacks, then a cattle corral rose into view beside the right of way; then a set of dusty billboards advertising Mother's Bread, Perry's Garage, the Alamo Tourist Courts, the Mayflower Restaurant, the Old Stockman's Dining Room; then, among treetops, the low red and white and aluminum roofs of the houses floated above the horizon.

At the edge of town Chuck's white car and the sound truck were parked in the midst of a string of other cars beside a small frame dwelling that was overshadowed by a huge aluminum cowbarn and a silo that flashed bright in the sun. Tyler looked at his watch and the muscles of his jaw tightened. The morning was speeding up all right. It was a quarter of nine already. Sue Ann leaned forward from the back seat. 'You better take charge, Toby,' she said. 'We're behind on our time-table.'

'Yare, I'll read the riot act.'

Before the car had come to a full stop, Tyler had jumped out and was striding towards the group of men crowded shoulder to shoulder round Chuck's white stetson. Shaking hands with a couple of men he knew, Tyler managed to worm himself into the middle of the crowd. In the center of a ring of grinning faces, Chuck was standing with his feet apart and his mouth pursed up listening gravely to an old man in weatherbeaten black with a face as brown and wrinkled as a walnut shell.

He had the look of a man who'd been talking for a long while. In his knotted brown hands that had ragged nails black with dirt, he held a long slender peeled stick that jiggled up and down at the end. 'You-all ought to be interested in this witchybitchy business. I been able to find water sence I was ten years old,' the old man was saying with his watery blue eyes fixed on Chuck's face. 'Now if you-all want to make every man a millionaire you-all got to learn to make the earth give up its treasures. My daddy was the seventh son of a seventh son and he learned me the witchybitchy business.'

Whenever the old man took his eyes off him, Chuck shot a rapid wink at the men behind him, but he kept his face straight.

'They's been treasures in the earth sence the time of Solomon. If you know the business you can find gold with a hazel stick.'

'How come you ain't rich, Pop?' piped up a chunky man in undershirt and overalls.

The old man looked him straight in the eye, stiffening his bent back, and, moving his cud of tobacco from one side of his face to the other, said firmly, 'How do you know I ain't?'

'What we do know, folks,' shouted Chuck, 'is that every man who's put in a lifetime of hard work ought to have something to show for it.'

The old man wrinkled up his face and spat out a long jet of tobacco juice on the ground between his dusty boots. 'I ain't never done a lick o' work in my life,' he said simply. ''Tain't fittin' for a man what can dip a hazel wand to work like a nigra.'

There was a laugh all around. Chuck began to get red in the face. 'Don't the Bible say, as he sows so shall he reap? The secret I want to get into the heads of the people of this country is that if every man who sows in a field or store or a business got the full value of his production back we could all have a standard of livin' like a millionaire's today. That means livin' better than Solomon lived in all his glory.'

'Who's got a piece of gold?' barked the old man in a peremptory voice. Tyler pulled out his gold watch and held it under Chuck's nose so that he could see the time. With one hand stretched out like a tightrope walker the old man held his stick over the watch. The tip jiggled up and down like the end of a fishing rod that's had a very small bite. The watch flashed in the sun.

'You win Daddy. You git the watch,' shouted Chuck.

'No you don't. That was my grandfather's,' said Tyler, hurriedly putting it back in his pocket.

He was wondering how to break things up when he caught sight of a tall longnosed man in riding clothes walking over towards the crowd from a lowslung European racing car that had just drawn up in a big burst of dust at the edge of the highway. He plucked at Chuck's shirtsleeve. 'Here's Norman Stauch.'

'Toby shake hands with Frank Goodday,' Chuck said, waving one hand towards a shortlegged fat man in a gray alpaca suit he was towing behind him as he edged his way out of the crowd. 'Thank you folks,' he shouted over his shoulder as he left. 'Don't forget to go to the primaries an' vote for Homer T. Crawford.'

Tyler had run back to meet Stauch. 'Norm how did you get up so early . . . you prompt old bastard.'

He grabbed his hand and pumped his arm. Norman Stauch had a long face and a long nose and big ears and a sharppointed Adam's apple that jiggled up and down when he talked. He stuttered a little. 'I r-reckoned I'd b-better let you know I was fixin' to handle that n-n-note.'

'Five grand,' said Tyler narrowing his eyes without smiling. 'Can I bank it today?'

Stauch nodded. 'Well how's Number One?'

'Goin' strong, Norman, goin' strong,' said Chuck who had just gotten in earshot. 'Gentlemen Mr. Goodday's offered to show us through his new hundred-thousand-dollar cowbarn.'

Tyler's lips had begun to form the words 'No time,' when a glare from Chuck stopped him. He and Stauch fell into line and followed along obediently while Chuck inspected in endless detail the cleanscrubbed concrete stalls, the monel metal milking machinery, and the ranks of sweetsmelling Jersey cows with big clean udders and large pencilled dark eyes with long lashes like Hindoo ladies.

When they started in on the separators and butter churns, Tyler drew the line. 'Mr. Goodday this is a magnificent installation you've got,' he shouted, 'but I've got to take this man away from here.' He pulled out his watch to make his point. 'Downtown and all over the state people are standing out in the sun waiting to hear what he's got to say.' Deaf as a post, Frank Goodday just stood there and nodded smiling.

Several neatlooking young men in white overalls with

'Goodday Dairies' printed in blue on their backs had gathered round. Chuck, who had been looking at everything with open mouth and round eyes like a small boy at the circus, raised his voice so that they could hear him. 'Looks like we kept our cows bettern old Solomon was able to keep his concubines . . . We sure have come a long ways from the old cowshed where I used to set on a stool an' milk ole bossy down home those cole mornin's.'

'Well sir I certainly appreciate your comin' . . . me an' the old woman would certainly be honored if you'd stay an' eat with us,' said Mr. Goodday.

'Frank,' shouted Chuck, grabbing his hand and leaning towards his car. 'Why don't you-all come down to Horton tonight? I'm bringin' up some points ought to be mighty interestin' to a dairyman. Fatty Galbraith . . . Fatty Galbraith, he looks like a cow but he don't know nothin' about 'em.'

'That sonofabitch,' said Frank Goodday at last catching a word. 'He got a judgement against me for five thousand dollars. We'd vote for a Republican before we voted for him around here.'

'Ma ole man was a Republican,' Chuck yelled and poked Tyler in the ribs with his elbow.

Then suddenly Chuck was off with his short trotting step down the lane towards the cars. 'We'll save you a seat on the platform, Mr. Goodday,' shouted Tyler breathlessly and followed along. As soon as they stepped out into the sunlight from the shade of the avenue of cottonwoods that led from the cowbarn, the boy on the

sound truck struck up 'Every Man a Millionaire.'
They fell into step with the jiggy tune. 'Is that the
c-c-campaign song?' asked Stauch. 'I heard one of those
c-c-commentators tell about it over the radio.' 'Sure . . .
Mrs. Crawford wrote the words and Chuck made up the
tune,' said Tyler. Chuck was crooning as he walked:

> . . . 'And every farmer in the land
> Up on his hind legs will stand
> And the laborer at his job
> And the soldier and the gob.'

Norman Stauch stopped in his tracks to listen. His
shaky lips were struggling with a remark. Finally he
got it out. 'Hot damn,' he said. 'Hot dickerty damn.'

Chuck was waiting for them beside the big white four-
door Lincoln. 'You and Norm better ride with me,
Toby,' he said. 'Boys,' he shouted at the two young
men in the front seat, 'here's Norman Stauch the
gamblin'est white man west of the Mississippi River . . .
Norm shake hands with Herb Jessup.'

'We've met,' said a slowvoiced softlooking young man
with the beginnings of a double chin oozing through the
gap in his wing collar, as he reached a pudgy white hand
into the back of the car. 'An' that's Jackie Hastin's
drivin'.' Chuck went on. 'We couldn't do without
Jackie. He handles my gorillas for me.' Hastings was a
stocky silent young man with a turned-up nose and tow
hair cut in a brush. He nodded over his shoulder and
said 'Present' in a crisp rasping voice. 'Mr. Stauch is
also one of the luckiest . . .' added Herb Jessup in a
welloiled tone.

'Well, Toby, what's the report of the finance committee?' asked Chuck as they shot out of the line of cars and followed the sound truck around the curve into the town.

'Norm's going to have something to say about that,' said Tyler.

'Norm I always knew you were a public spirited feller.'

'G-G-Galbraith's stinkin' with dough they tell me,' Stauch said looking down his nose. 'Is he buyin' many polltaxes?'

'He's too wise to mess with me. They won't none of 'em mess with me in the courts,' said Chuck.

The highway curved into the settlement between two rows of scaly frame bungalows that had once been painted white, with sagging porches and uncurtained windows and sunscorched patches of grass in front of them. At the railroad track the concrete road curved again, past the yellow sheds of a coalyard, a small concrete grain elevator, and a passenger station of dusteaten yellow brick. Then it rounded the corner of a boardedup factory building into the business section. The short street of flyspecked hotels and dingy lodginghouses widened into a square surrounded by onestory feed and implement stores. In the shade of the corrugated iron porches in front of the storewindows motionless men in workclothes leaned against the walls and posts and stared out in front of them. A few more were draped limply on the benches round the bandstand in the middle of the square. As the sound truck blared out its tune driving slowly round and round citizens in shirtsleeves came out of stores and lunchrooms. On the bandstand itself two small barefooted colored boys in torn overalls were hurriedly tacking up a piece of lettered bunting that read *Every Man A Millionaire. Homer T. Crawford for United States Senator.* As the Lincoln came to a stop at the curb Chuck jumped out to meet the members of the local committee who, spitting and stretching and hitching up their trousers, were slowly unfolding themselves out of a row of parked cars. The first thing he said was, 'Where the hell's the hillbillies?'

'Had a blowout . . . They phoned in they'd meet up with you at the Springs.'

Chuck made a spurting noise with his tongue against his eyeteeth: 'An' where the hell's the population? Is this the best you folks kin do to put somebody in Washington who really wants to look after your interests? What this burg needs is government money.'

A fat man in a pongee suit came up red in the face sponging his forehead with a big handkerchief and said, 'This here town's liver than you think Mr. Crawford . . . It's live enough to give its votes to the best man.'

'Hold your horses Mr. Fredericks,' said Chuck soothingly. At the mention of his name the fat man smiled. 'This is a great little town I kin see that. But lemme tell you somethin'. It won't be doin' me no favor to nominate me for this job . . . All it means for me is hard work an' loss of earnin' capacity . . . You jess think how much assistance you're goin' to get from that highbrow corporation lawyer. He don't know anybody's alive in a town like this except the railroad. I know how things are. I lived in towns like this all my life an' I know the magnificent future that lies ahead for the American small town once its productive capacities are released . . . Toby for crissake tell that guy to quit playin' that tune. Tell him to take a powder. Tell him we'll ketch up with him.' Tyler felt the sweat running down the small of his back as he ran off to intercept the sound truck. A voice in his head was snarling: If he don't stop treating me like a messenger boy, I'll quit him cold.

Chuck had climbed up on the bandstand and, with his head on one side, stood looking into the faces of the men scattered around on the hot asphalt paths and the trodden yellow grass plots. As soon as the sound truck was quiet he began to talk: 'Folks,' he said in a low crooning voice, 'I ain't askin' you to elect me to the U-nited States Senate. I ain't got the high toned eddication for the job to tell the truth. You all know me I'm jess a small town salesman with a smatterin' of law. All I know's how to keep my hands outa the other feller's pockets . . . To tell the truth I ain't really well enough off to keep up appearances like I'd oughto in a capital city like Washington D.C. A position like that's likely as not to be the ruination of our kinds of folks . . . All I'm askin' you-all to do is to think of your own interests. You vote against Fatty Galbraith. For thirty years now that man's been suckin' the blood of the people of this state an' helpin' the bankers an' usurers an' moneylenders, an' their sinful usury an' foreclosure an' exorbitant rates of interest, them that our Lord Jesus Christ chased outa the temple with his own hands, helpin' 'em to make themselves rich in this world's goods an' poor in the real wealth the Bible talks about that comes from honest labor an' sweat an' a day's work well done. Why if I was Mr. Galbraith's best friend, an' I ain't, nor of none like him, I'd be up here on this platform a-beggin' you to vote against him, jess for his own good. You know a man's heart can't stand too much fat. Up there in Washington City Fatty Galbraith'll have twice the chance to fatten himself up that he does down here where honest folks kin keep an eye on him. If you send him to Washington he'll git himself so fat rootin' in the public trough it may ruin his health . . . I shouldn't wonder if it cost him his life. I know you folks think very highly of Mr. Fatty Galbraith an' his high rates of interest but that wouldn't be a friendly act, now would it?' The blank faces rippled with laughter. Yips and shouts shot up like streamers. Chuck's voice started off again loud and confident.

'Ain't he g-g-good?' whispered Norman Stauch, laughing his mirthless snicker in Tyler's ear. 'Hot dickerty damn he's good. Toby if it's radio time you're worryin' about . . .'

'I thought you were the guy to do it Norm but I didn't just like to ask you . . .' Tyler whispered back.

'When you think of the stacks of real foldin' money I've blowed in on racehorses, what's the harm in askin' me to buy a little piece of a politician . . . Toby your boy's a comer.'

'Don't forget Chuck's different. He's given up a good business to devote himself to the public service.'

'Congratulatin' a racehorse for givin' up the plow eh,' said Stauch without cracking a smile.

In five minutes they were back in the car and speeding down another straight road between long rows of freshly cultivated cottonplants, that spread pale handshaped leaves endlessly over the sootblack earth until the rows blurred in a silvery haze on the horizon. They were an hour behind time. 'It's going to be hot,' Tyler kept saying, 'if there's a crowd in that hall.' Chuck sat mum in his corner with his jaws clamped together and his lips stuck out.

When at last they caught sight of another speck of a watertank gleaming far away across the steamy shimmer of the plain, Chuck leaned across Norman Stauch and said to Tyler in the clipped voice he used when he gave orders, 'This time Sue Ann an' the kids sets right up on the platform, see? What do you think we brought 'em for?'

His tone made Tyler's dander rise, but the minute the car stopped in front of the yellowbrick pointed blind arches of the Lodge Building on the main business street of Arrowhead Springs he jumped out and yanked open the door of the Zephyr just coming to a stop behind them. 'Why the Spanish cavalier?' Sue Ann asked making her eyes very round. 'Number One wants the happy family group on the platform,' Tyler said in a sour tone. Sue Ann laughed a rippling laugh that sounded tinny in Tyler's ears that time.

In the dusty entry a sloppy limplooking man, in a blue shirt with an ancient yellow straw hat stained by the dust and sweats of many seasons pushed back on his head, was explaining something to Chuck. As Sue Ann swept past him he took off his hat and revealed a round pale bald head with a few strands of spiky hair stuck to it. 'You see Senator it was this way,' he said, 'when you-all didn't come at ten o'clock I just turned the folks away an' told them the Senator had been delayed an' they might just as well go on over to Poplar Fork where they'd be sure to see a ballgame anyway . . . To tell the truth they was right few come . . . a fact which was surprisin' to me specially as I dreamed last night as I lay in my bed . . . I dreamed . . . I guess I had the Senator on my mind because my ole barbershop's been right much of a center for the Every Man a Millionaire movement in this town. The other parlor is in the hands of a noaccount Bohunk can't barely speak English an' he's come out for Galbraith . . . You can't imagine how many throwa-ways an' litrachure we've distributed . . . I was tellin' you gentlemen about my dream. Well last night as I lay in my bed I just dreamed that the Senator was nominated but it wasn't like an ordinary primary it was in a great enormous convention hall an' I told my wife about it an' she said of course what I was dreamin' about was a presidential nomination an' I guess that was about the size of it.'

Chuck's lips lost their pout. His mouth broadened into a smile.

'I hope you didn't tell her before breakfast,' said Herb Jessup in his singsong voice. Everybody laughed.

'Well, gentlemen,' said the barber raising his voice,

'I'm real sorry to disappoint you but Saturday ain't the most fortunate day for a meetin' to tell the truth. Of recent years folks has been goin' over to Poplar Fork right smart to do their shoppin' an' the likes of that. Some of 'em even gits shaved over there. Meanwhile if any of you gentlemen would care to step around the corner to my place of business I'd be right honored to pay you any sort of tonsorial attention free gratis that may seem in the order of the day, haircut, shave, shampoo, anythin' you say.'

'Mr. Waldensperger I kin see we don't have to worry about this district,' said Chuck.

'Thank you sir. Thank you Senator Crawford . . . Senator I sure would love to show you what I can do. A little trim or a hot towel would be refreshin' perhaps.'

Chuck shook his head grinning, pumped Mr. Waldensperger's hand warmly and threw himself back into the car. Meanwhile Sue Ann in the dark entry had been beckoning mysteriously to Tyler. 'Help me find a ladies' room,' she whispered. 'The boys can't wait much longer.' Tyler whispered in Mr. Waldensperger's ear. He nodded vigorously and they all set off down a plastered corridor that smelt of dust and cockroaches.

When they came back they found Herb Jessup leaning against the entrance door with a cigarette drooping from his flabby lip. 'Number One's gone on,' he said. 'He said for us and the missus to step on the gas. Live town, ain't it, ma'am?' he added as he handed Sue Ann into the Zephyr. 'You wouldn't think,' said Tyler, 'this district cast forty-four hundred and fifty-seven Democratic votes in the last election.' 'And with the Lord's help we'll cast em again,' said Mr. Waldensperger briskly from the curb. 'And every one for Senator Crawford.' He took off his antique straw with a flourish. 'A pleasant journey to you, Mrs. Senator Crawford.'

When they had driven off Sue Ann gave a low 'Whew' . . . She added with a little giggle: 'Are we crazy or is it just the rest of the world?' Herb Jessup turned around from the front seat to talk. 'Let me tell you somethin', Mrs. Crawford,' he said. 'There's one man in this state who's doin' a good job for this organization an' that's Clyde Galbraith.' Tyler didn't say anything. He sat with two of the little boys wriggling around on his knees looking sourly at the rows of unpainted negro shacks that dwindled in size and grew more dilapidated as they neared the edge of town. The road dove into the pebbly bed of a river, followed along under a bluff beside a string of stagnant pools full of green slime, then crossed on a new white concrete bridge and began to wind up through clay cuttings into a green stretch of tall pines and gumtrees. Beyond the woods was a region of small hills with peach orchards on them. There the road straightened out again across wide pasturelands fenced into enormous squares with herds of whitefaced cattle grazing as far as they could see towards the horizon. Way ahead tiny on the white ribbon of road they caught sight of the sound truck followed by a string of other cars. 'Catch up to 'em Sam,' said Tyler tapping nervously with his foot. 'Mr. Toby I don't like to speed with the kiddies in the car.' 'Go ahead Sam,' piped up Sue

Ann, 'don't be an old stick in the mud.' 'All right ma'am what you says I do.' 'We're behind time already,' said Tyler bleakly. 'Looks to me like we'd wasted our time this morning.'

'Tell me Toby who's your friend Norman Stauch?'

'Why Sue Ann he's just a natural born gambler. He'll bet on anything, snapping turtles, horned toads, racehorses, hounds . . . The first time I met him he went out gunning with Jerry Evans and me . . . we were shooting partridges along the edge of a patch of timber, Jerry had just bought to cut. Stauch took one look and bet him a thousand dollars he'd get more'n a million feet out of it and damned if he didn't win.'

'A man like that lives on hunches,' said Sue Ann sitting up straight with her eyes sparkling. 'I bet he's got a hunch.'

'And his hunch is correct, ma'am,' said Herb Jessup.

They were catching up with the sound truck so that they already could hear the faint chortling of 'Listen to the Mocking Bird' coming through the whir of their own tires over the smooth road. The little Crawfords all began to sing the song and made so much racket that nobody could get in another word. The small bodies wriggling on Tyler's knees made him feel sticky hot and were rumpling up whatever freshness there was left in the seersucker suit he'd put on clean that morning. To keep them quiet he started telling them a story about the last Longhorn and how bad that Longhorn felt when he saw the Herefords come in.

At a traffic circle all the cars were parked in front of

an ornate blue and white semicircular stand that had a big sign: *Chickenburgers* in red letters across the top. As they drew up beside Chuck's Lincoln, Tyler caught sight of Number One sitting back with a pleased look on his face with a big round bitten roll in one hand and a cocacola bottle in the other. 'Hay Toby,' he called, 'come here.'

The kids raised a chorus of 'Mom gimme a chickenburger . . . Mom gimme an icecream cone.' Tyler and Jessup slipped out of their seats and walked around to the window of the other car. 'What d'ye think of this for curb service?' Chuck shouted. The drinks and the round rolls stuffed with chopped chicken were being served on an aluminum tray by a barelegged girl in a pale blue and red drummajor's uniform. On a bench waiting sat a row of girls in the same uniform. They were slender and had pretty knees and their blonde heads were curled to the last hair. 'To hell with the hillbillies,' shouted Chuck. 'Next time I campaign I'm goin' to have girls in uniform.'

Stauch was all for hiring them right now so that they could come to the meeting that night in Horton. The girls smiled archly and said wasn't it just too bad they were under contract with the chickenburger company.

Tyler had his watch out. 'It's quarter past one,' he said frowning. 'We're getting pretty late for the barbecue.'

Chuck made a sucking noise with the straw in the bottom of his bottle. 'If I waste three quarters of an hour with a man, that means he's somebody,' he said emphatically. He had a handful of indexcards with names and addresses on them in his lap and was shuffling through them as he talked. 'How come Frank Goodday ain't listed as Chairman of the Fairhope County Dairymen's Association? That's what he is.'

'I guess we slipped up on that one,' said Tyler in a dull voice.

'Well, you get these girls' names and addresses . . . Pretty girls in uniform, that's somethin'.'

'You can turn their phone numbers over to me,' came Norman Stauch's highpitched kidding tones from the other side of the car.

At last Tyler got his caravan back on the road again. Far ahead there began to appear a green blur of trees and among them the glint of aluminum painted roofs; then the fat silver dome of the courthouse and several watertanks, a couple of white church spires, black chimneys. Then the oblong shapes of a factory ranked with flashing windows began to rise up out of the trees that banked a range of low hills at the edge of the flat land.

Right after passing the factory they reached the ball park. The sound truck was blaring loud. The first crowd was round a swimming pool under trees at the edge of a riverbed. Dripping heads yelled from the water and a cluster of boys in bathingtrunks all shouted together from the top of the high diving platform. They passed booths and a jingling merrygoround, and then followed a carful of local committeemen through a crowded parking lot into an open space behind a platform covered by an awning. Over the awning was stretched a transparency that read 'CRAWFORD FOR SENA–

TOR' and showed in the middle a pink round face with black curly hair. As they worked their way out of the car they got a whiff of the greasy spicy scorched meat smell of the barbecue.

'I declare,' said Sue Ann, 'I never saw such a crowd out in the middle of the day in my life.'

'If they haven't got a first rate public address system nobody's going to hear him,' muttered Tyler under his breath. He went off in a hurry to find a phone booth to call up the airport to see if Jerry Evans had arrived yet. He was beginning to wonder how long he was going to be able to stand all this business without a drink.

The phone booth was in the back of a hotdog stand. All around him people were laughing and talking, trucks were rumbling past with farm families sitting in rows of chairs, kids were shooting off firecrackers. There was a man selling long sausageshaped balloons in red blue and yellow.

Tyler was trying to keep hold of himself in the heat and the dust and the noise and the bustle. Christ, he needed a drink. Already the hillbilly band on the speakers' stand had struck up 'The Wreck of the Old Ninetyseven' and the music was jigging out from loudspeakers all over the grounds, so that Tyler could hardly hear the voice on the other end of the line. For an instant Tyler couldn't remember Duke's name. The voice was saying hello. He must say something. 'Say has a private plane come in yet?' 'Evans' monoplane, just signalled for a landin',' the young man's voice answered.

Tyler slammed down the receiver and rushed back to the cars. A big reception committee was milling round Chuck. Somebody had given the little boys each a small American flag. As they waved they kept up their racket yelling for balloons and icecream cones. Amid all the introductions and handshaking it was a while before Tyler could get through to Number One.

'I'm off to pick up Evans.'

'Ever saw such a crowd?' cried Chuck, slapping him on the back. 'Who says I don't attract the folks?' Then he brought his fist up to his chin the way he sometimes did. 'Half these crackers come to see the carnival . . . When I git through with 'em every last one'll think he come to hear Homer T. Crawford.'

'I'll take Stauch along with me.'

'Be sure he gits plenty barbecue an' beer.'

Tyler got Norman Stauch away from the little Crawford kids. He'd bought them eskimo pies and was starting off to buy them rides on the airplane whirlaround. Sue Ann was having a time keeping them herded up in the crowd.

When Tyler finally got Stauch back into the car, he said in a drawling voice, 'You know, Toby, I often thought if I had some kids I wouldn't do so many damn fool things.'

'You can't say you don't make money out of the damn fool things you do,' said Tyler. 'Me, I haven't any kids and I do plenty damn fool things and I don't make any money.'

'How about you an' me gettin' us a drink, Toby?'

Tyler shook his head: 'I got a long day ahead.'

They turned their heads to look back at the ball park, the scattering of women sitting under parasols in the bleachers, the mess of people moving around in front of the glittering ranks of parked cars, the booths and the whirling circling machines of the carnival. Long lines of cars were arriving along converging roads. A dun-colored streak of dust hung in the hot slatecolored sky overhead.

'Toby,' cried Stauch. 'This is the b-b-biggest thing since William Jennings B-B-Bryan.'

For a long time before they got to the airport they could see the big low-wing cabin monoplane all pale blue and aluminum shimmering in the wavy heat in front of the hangar. The ranks of small red and yellow training biplanes looked like children's toys behind it. Jerry Evans, a huge man in white ducks, was standing out in front with a panama hat on the back of his head framing his big red face. He was waving a cigar as he talked to two young mechanics in blue jeans. Tyler and Stauch got out of the car and walked up to him.

'I was beginnin' to think you'd hung me up, Spotswood,' he shouted. 'Why you old son of a bitch you.'

'Duke, shake hands with Norman Stauch . . . Norm, this is one of the biggest men in the state.'

'Don't worry,' said Evans laughing and showing two regular rows of large perfectly white teeth. 'The doc's sendin' me to Hot Springs to reduce. What the hell is this, a fat stock show?' he went on as he doubled up to get into the lowhung car.

'Naw. This is just a little impromptu rally of some of Chuck's constituents.'

'They tell me Galbraith's got the nomination in the bag.'

'You just wait . . . We don't want to talk you into anything . . . But after you've seen what you are going to see and heard what you are going to hear, if you feel like it, Duke, I want you to go over and tell Steve what you think about this business.'

'Ain't Steve up for reelection next year?' Stauch whispered in a mysterious tone.

'Sure,' said Tyler.

'What's the odds in Horton?' Stauch asked Evans.

'They're offering two to one on Galbraith.'

'Hot damn . . . lemme git to a telephone. They'll be even money after this afternoon.' Stauch started off at a run for the airport building.

'That bugger lives up to his reputation,' said Jerry quietly to Tyler, when he'd gone.

Tyler laughed. 'He's a gambling man . . . Jeez it was swell of you to come . . . Honestly I think we've got something big here.'

'Wouldn't be so bad if Crawford wasn't puttin' all these damn fool notions in people's heads.'

'You wait till you hear what he's got to say . . . He's got it figured so that the big fellow gets a break and the little fellow gets a break.'

'Well I'll stick around a few minutes . . . Steve can see me any time this afternoon. There are some things in this man's country you have to buck and there are some things you have to ride . . . The trouble with you,

Spotswood, is you are always fallin' for what the preacher says at campmeetin'. You're all alike . . . But this boy's got a crazy streak a yard wide.'

Tyler made a sour face. 'A man's got to have a crazy streak to appeal to the American people . . . I guess that's why I can't keep away from Number One . . . Let's keep track of old Norm. I don't want him to get too drunk to put his John Henry at the bottom of a note.'

'Toby, I locked my checkbook up in the safe before I left home . . . You know me, Toby.'

'Duke, I don't want one cent of your money, honest to God . . . All I want is for you to go over to see Steve and take him out on the back porch of the Governor's Mansion and tell him your honest opinion of what you'll be seeing and hearing this afternoon.'

'Ain't he kinder committed to Galbraith?'

'Hell no. Steve Baskette can sit on the fence longer than any man I ever heard of.'

From where they stood looking across the airport with their backs to Evans' plane they could see across the mile of lightbrown grass the parked cars at the ball park, the ferris wheel going round and the big umbrellas of the parachute jump moving awkwardly up and down in a yellow blur of dust, and hear the snap snap snap of the shooting gallery and the amplified jigging of the hill-billies playing 'The Old Maid.'

Norman Stauch said solemnly when he came back from the telephone, 'Well boys I'm in up to my neck. . . How about somethin' to eat and a pickup?'

'There's a soft-drink stand right opposite the plat-

form,' said Tyler opening the door of the car for him.
'Get in, Norm, or we'll miss the speech.' When the car
came to a stop among the crowds of the ball park, he
sent Sam off to get them some of the barbecue while
they stood in the shade of the awning over the rough
board stand. 'We can hear as well here as anywhere and
we won't have to mess with the crowd,' he said.

'Toby,' snarled Evans truculently, 'I thought you-all
loved the people.'

'Have a heart, Duke . . . If Chuck's said it once he's
said it a hundred times: the people is all of us.'

Evans laughed and made sniffing noises with his wide
nostrils. 'Let's eat,' he said.

Behind them a young fellow in a white gob cap, with
long white bony arms sticking out from a purple silk
shirt rolled up to the armpits, was slapping hamburgers
on a hot metal plate and frying onions in a skillet along-
side. Tyler ordered up a hamburger for each of them
and a tall cardboard cup of cocacola. 'Let's make this
a Cuba libre,' said Stauch. 'I got a spot.' He brought
a thin silver flask out of his hip pocket.

The steam piano had quieted down. The hillbillies
had broken off in the middle of 'The Hoot Owl Trail.'
Across the straw hats, stetsons, sunbonnets, palm leaf
fans, newspapers held over women's heads, Tyler, as
he stood there sipping his drink, could see the stand with
a white awning over it, and in the pinkish shadow panama hats, women's light dresses, stout men in shirtsleeves. Chuck wasn't there yet. A voice started coming from all directions blaring and blurred, it rose into

a shriek (Damn that public address system, thought Tyler), then gradually it came into focus . . . 'needs no introduction from me . . .' The voice went off into a vague braying but cleared up in time to enunciate: 'Homer T. Crawford the man who is going to represent the people of this state in the U-nited States Senate . . .'

There followed a roar of cheering, clapping, whistles as an open car moved slowly out from behind the parking lot past the rows of sitting people huddled in the shade of the bleachers and moved slowly through the crowd towards the stand. Above the heads and hats of the local committeemen stood Chuck waving his white stetson and Sue Ann holding Andy up in the crook of her elbow and the tiny heads of the other two little boys sitting on men's shoulders. They disappeared behind the platform and in a second there was a new burst of cheering amplified by the loudspeakers as the people on the platform pushed away from the center to let Chuck through. He looked small and boyish. Tyler winced when the public address system caught a peevish aside: 'Say pass the kids up. Let the folks see the kids.' A titter went through the crowd.

'Folks,' started Chuck, balancing himself in front of the mike with his head thrown back and his fists dangling on limp arms.

'Folks,' he began, 'my opponents in the kept columns of the reptile press . . . my opponents say that I'm goin' up an' down the highways an' byways of this greatest state in this great union of states tryin' to tear down everythin' that men have tried with patient care an' toil to build up to make their lives dignified beautiful holy . . .

'They lie.

'Fatty Galbraith lied in that speech he made over in Judson City last night . . . Whenever he wants to take it up I'll tell him so to his face . . .'

Chuck paused and tore off his coat. Then he yanked at his necktie and unloosened it at the throat.

'. . . in the face of God and man' he yelled '. . . I can't stand these store clothes . . . these lies,' he added in an everyday confidential tone, 'make me so hot under the collar . . .' A friendly laugh started along the front rows and rumbled across the field. Chuck stood there grinning boyishly in his bright blue suspenders as he finished untying his necktie.

'. . . Anyway you kin see my shirt ain't red like they say it is. Folks they say that under the white shirt of civic respectability I wear the red shirt of anarchy, socialism, communism, discord. They lie in their throats. What I'm a-tryin' to do with the help of all the decent Godfearin' people is save the home an' the little white church where we gather together on the Lord's day to worship the Lord of all harvests an' blessin's in whatever way our conscience tells us is right . . .'

Old Sam came tiptoeing over towards Tyler through the crowd with the expression of a deacon passing the plate in church. He was carrying a tray with three plates of barbecue covered with sauce on it. Tyler felt his throat tighten at the sight of it. 'You eat mine, Sam,' he whispered. 'I'm too busy.'

Tyler began to look around him. Norm was enjoying himself, eating and drinking, no use worrying about him. Jerry on the other side of him had put on the face of a man determined not to be sold on any proposition. He caught Tyler's eye and whispered, 'Why the hell don't he save the bloody shirt for the end?' Beyond were two ruddy young farmhands giggling and tittering with two towheaded girls, one in a pink and one in a yellow wash dress. Next was an old dirt farmer in overalls with a black lantern jaw who stood listening with one work-twisted hand cupped behind his ear and his ragged straw hat pushed back on his gray head.

'When you folks send me to represent you in that august assembly my first act will be to introduce a bill to protect the small homeowner whoever he may be.' 'Amen,' sighed the old man. The crowd yipped and cheered . . .

'Everythin' we have is founded on the home . . . Now right here an' now I'm goin' to answer this lie of my opponents. There are probably a hundred people in this crowd who've known me personally campaignin' for office or travellin' up an' down the state to serve the public in one capacity or another, or in the old days when I was a pore boy tryin' to git myself an' eddication sellin' hardware an' kitchen fittin's . . . if any of all those people who've had me in their homes have ever seen me say or do one subversive thing, I'd like him to speak up . . . I thought I saw Mr. and Mrs. Bill Jones from Morganville . . . Bill, have you got anything to say about me bein' subversive in the home?'

'You tell 'em, Bill,' yelled a voice. The crowd eddied around two distant figures. Some answer came that Tyler couldn't hear, followed by laughter, giggling, cheers. 'Judge Benton, what's your opinion?' 'I wouldn't trust you in ma home,' yipped a shrill voice. Chuck laughed: 'Folks, I'm a married man an' I got plenty to keep me busy in my own home.' Sue Ann was dragging the kids up to the edge of the platform but as fast as she did they disappeared among the legs of the committeemen.

'That boy's goin' to git him elected,' said Norman Stauch. 'Amen to that,' said the old man. 'If only it don't rain this afternoon an' spoil the ball game.'

'Ain't a-goin' to rain,' said Norm.

'I heard a rooster crow this noon. When a rooster crows at noon means hit'll rain before the day is up . . .'

Jerry Evans looked interested.

'Pop, do you think it's goin' to storm? The weather forecast was all right an hour ago.'

'No sir, I don't say hit's a-goin' to storm but what I do say is that when the roosters crow at noon that's a sign hit's a-goin' to rain within the day.'

'Well you may be right, Pop,' said Evans. He jogged Tyler's elbow. 'Snap out of that trance and let's get the hell out of here . . . Won't hurt to have a little chat with Steve . . . Come along, Mr. Stauch, I'd like to have you try out my new ship.'

Chuck's voice was booming all around them. It seemed hardly connected with the gesticulating little figure on the stand. Old Sam was working his way through the crowd with another trayful of barbecue sandwiches. 'Sam, you are stuffing us,' said Tyler. 'You lead the way over to the car, and drive us back to the airfield.' 'You-all won't have to miss the speech,' Sam whispered in his deacon's voice. 'I got the radio set for it. The boss sure is Number One this day.' Out of the corner of his eye Tyler caught the look on Jerry Evans' face. 'Jerry, you're scared to listen for fear you might fall for him.' Evans laughed. 'You mean easier for a rich man to go through the eye of a needle? . . . Hell, yes.'

'But don't forget that he's going to get elected.'

'Nobody ever said I couldn't recognize a fact when I saw one. Why the hell do you think I'm losin' a half a day?'

'Norm, how many people do you reckon there are here?' Tyler asked casually as they threaded their way through the crowd towards the parking lot.

'There's ten thousand people if there's a one . . . They must of come from as far as Hillsdale and Eberhart.'

The speech fell on them like rain as they followed old Sam to the parking lot. They passed people eating and drinking in the shade of farm trucks, young couples who'd come on motorcycles, two old people sitting under the canvas hood of a spring wagon. Their mules hitched to the back of the wagon were quietly munching at some forkfuls of alfalfa hay that dripped out from the open tailboard. They walked through rows of oldmodel dusty cars bleached into iridescent colors by the sun, with here and there a shiny new car of this year's make. Tyler noticed Jerry looking intently at the makes and license plates of the cars as he strode along. When they reached the Crawfords' car Sam opened the door for them with one hand and then handed in the tray of sandwiches.

'We'll eat these on the way over,' said Evans . . . 'Well Toby, you've got quite a crowd . . . but do they pay their polltaxes?'

'Never you mind about polltaxes,' said Tyler laughing. 'Sam, you take us past the back of that stand. I want to leave a message.'

Sam had to drive in a wide circle over the sunbaked earth before he could get near the back of the speaker's stand. All the time Chuck's voice filled their ears, out of the car's radio, talking prosperity, freedom from want, the even distribution of the products of farm and factory. Tyler hopped out of the car and threaded his way through the jam until he caught sight of Herb Jessup sitting sleepily on the steps in the shade of the awning. 'Hello Toby,' he said. 'You look kinder tickled with yourself. What's new?'

Tyler couldn't help smiling confidentially although he didn't like Herb. 'Herb, tell Number One as soon as he finishes speaking that I've gone over with Evans and Norm Stauch to pick up the Governor. We'll meet you all in Horton down at the hotel. You better put this down. I've engaged room 1503 and suite for Number One. Don't let 'em put us anywheres else. And for God's sake help Sue Ann keep him to the timetable.

They're fixing to start that torchlight parade at Sam Houston Park at eight sharp and Number One's got to have time to eat and for a conference with the Governor.'

'Any more orders?' asked Herb, yawning in an insolent kind of a way. Tyler felt his anger rise suddenly, stinging in back of his eyes. The muscles of his jaw trembled. For a second they looked at each other hard and then Herb's cupid's bow lips smiled his syrupy smile. 'Your orders shall be obeyed, Mister Spotswood.'

Tyler tried to smile but his face was stiff.

'O.K.,' he said and turned away sharp and climbed back into the car.

'Folks . . . What I'm advocatin' today on this platform, before this characteristic assemblage of the American people, the real people whose work an' brains on farms, in factories, in millions of small businesses throughout the land, have made this country what it is, ain't red anarchy like my opponents say, whose heads is turned by usurious interest rates, an' plottin' an' connivin' as to how they kin git the last dime out of the producers of this country; it ain't nothin' like red anarchy; it's the good old American doctrine of equality an' justice for all.' Applause rattled and barked in the shiny dashboard radio.

'Sam, turn that damn thing off,' said Evans. 'Toby, if I had my way I'd string you boys all up . . .'

Stauch abruptly started to talk. 'If somebody had sat up an' told me I'd miss a perfectly good ball game to go an' talk politics I'd a said he was crazy . . . Mr. Evans, I hope your skyliner's got a bar in it. This is one of the days I feel like drinkin' Cuba libre forever. What do you say, Toby?'

'Got too much on my mind . . . Ask me about eleven o'clock tonight.'

At the airport Stauch kept them waiting while he made another phonecall. He came back rubbing his hands. 'What did I tell you? The odds are four to three.'

'Your bet did that,' said Jerry Evans. 'Well gentlemen, we're off.' They climbed into the cabin and Sam handed the sandwiches and a set of cocacola bottles in after them. Evans introduced them to Babe Sisson, the redheaded frecklefaced young man who was his pilot. 'Have a sandwich, Babe.' 'No thanks sir, I've eaten.'

'We'll mix the drinks after we take off,' said Evans. 'What about the weather, Babe . . .?' 'All right for four or five hours yet,' the pilot called back as he climbed up into his seat.

'We won't need belts, just slip your arms through the leather thongs.' They sat stiffly in the monogrammed seats of pale blue leather as Evans set up the folding table across their knees. 'I guess I ought to have a steward aboard,' he said. 'This is the life,' said Stauch and stretched his legs out in the aisle.

The motor roared. The cabin shook as the plane started to taxi across the rough field. After a turn the motor speeded for the takeoff. They felt the air grow resilient under the wings as they got a glimpse of the bleachers and the baseball diamond and the roofs of the booths and stands of the carnival scattered like little fancy caketins here and there among the black and brown and white tweedy patchwork of the crowd.

'Hot dickerty damn, there are twenty thousand people there if there's a p-p-pissin' man,' said Norman Stauch. He pulled out of his pocket a big silk handkerchief that filled the cabin with a smell of toilet water as he carefully rubbed off his long nose and long thin face and the red ears that stuck so far out from his head. The plane was bucking in the hot air over the littered squares of the town. The bump when they crossed the highroad nearly threw them and sent the cocacola bottles rolling around the floor. Tyler spread himself out to hold the sandwiches down on the table and just managed to keep the bottle of barbecue sauce from spilling. The plane banked and took a halfcircle. The air smoothed out as they climbed. Evans came back from the pantry with three highball glasses full of cracked ice and a bottle of rum under his arm.

Tyler was on his knees on the floor retrieving the little scampering bottles.

'This is the only drink I'm going to take today,' he shouted. 'At least till after the big rally.'

'Steve won't give us anything . . . don't worry about that,' Evans shouted back.

'Will he come over to Horton?' asked Stauch.

Evans nodded his head vigorously.

Rags of cloud were going past the window. Below through the haze the plain glowed with sunlight like an enormous brass plate. Through the ventilators fresh cold air hissed into the cabin. Along the horizon they began to see ranks of motionless cumulus clouds lit as if from inside by a secret rosy light.

'Duke you lucky devil,' whispered Tyler filling his lungs, 'this is something like.' Evans hadn't heard him but he answered with a roar:

'If you'd stuck in the lumber business instead of scatterin' all over the map all the time, you'd have come on as fast as I have . . . you've got as good a head and a damn sight more education.'

'He's got a bear by the tail, though, this time,' shouted Stauch.

'Do you mean it how I mean it?' shouted Evans. He took a deep swig of his drink; then he turned to Stauch and talked close to his ear. 'You wouldn't think it but I'm fond of the son of a bitch. Him an' me was overseas together in the war. Then it was me that was raisin' hell and him that was tryin' to straighten me out. But how times have changed . . .'

Tyler couldn't hear the rest. He shook his head.

They'd eaten up all the sandwiches and drunk down a couple more drinks before they saw the river and the green trees and the white and red and yellow checkerboard of houses and the creamy dome of the state capitol go circling past as they corkscrewed down to the airport. As the hot soupy afternoon air poured in all around him Tyler suddenly felt squeamish and had to take a last straight pull out of the rumbottle to settle his stomach.

The old colored man in a white coat who was waiting for them at the open door of the Governor's Mansion when they drove up in a taxi said: 'This way please gentlemen,' and led them around the broad verandah to a little shady back porch cut off by a vinecovered lattice. There the Governor was sitting in a rocking chair with his feet on a small cane table dictating to a young man at a typewriter. He was a tall man with sloping shoulders and black hair that grew low on his forehead. He unfolded himself like a jackknife to get out of the rocker and shook hands with each of them: 'Gentlemen at your service,' he said. 'Won't you be seated?' They all sat down in silence. There was no sound but the dryflies on the lawn beyond the vines. Evans took a leather cigarcase out of his inside pocket and offered it to each of them. Without saying a word each man took a cigar. Tyler had his lighter out. He lit the Governor's first, then Norman Stauch's. Evans had lit his with a match. They sat silent puffing at the fat Romeo and Juliets. Inside the house somewhere somebody was practising scales on the piano.

'Steve,' said Evans at length, 'it's about as pretty a day for flyin' as I ever saw.'

'My it was cool and nice up there,' said Stauch.

'How does Chuck seem to be doin'?' asked the Governor.

'Layin' 'em in the aisles,' cried Stauch. 'It's even money now down in Horton.'

Tyler tried to start a laugh. 'Stauch's the bettingest man alive . . . He'd lay bets on the hearse that was taking him to his own funeral.'

'Ain't that what we all do when we take out life insurance?' The Governor let the big lids droop over his eyes.

'I never thought of it that way,' said Evans.

The Governor cleared his throat. 'Tell me there's right smart of a crowd over there at the Fork.'

'There is twenty thousand people there,' said Stauch, 'if there's a one . . . I never seen anythin' like it since William Jennings Bryan was laid to rest.'

'Well even if they're ten thousand,' said Evans.

Tyler tried to keep the tenseness out of his voice. 'Poplar Forks isn't a large place,' he said. 'Folks have to come a long ways to make up twenty thousand people.'

The Governor cleared the phlegm out of his throat and got to his feet and walked slowly over to a brass spittoon at the corner of the house. He spat carefully in it and walked back.

'Hot, too,' he said.

'Now and then,' said Evans looking up his tipped cigar at the ceiling of the porch and letting the blue smoke dribble slowly out of the corners of his mouth, 'a feller like that turns up you have to reckon with . . . It's the mob appeal all right.' Tyler looked where Evans was looking and saw that he was looking at a small chameleon poised comfortably upside down on the ceiling.

'I'm right busy this afternoon, Jerry,' said Governor Baskette.

'I could fly you over to Horton in an hour Steve,' Evans insisted. 'Countin' the run to the airport each way.'

The Governor got up slowly from his chair again and pulled up one of the venetian blinds that shut in the

[94]

porch. Tyler jumped up to help him. The grass of the lawn was dazzling green in the sun between the huge dark magnolias that cut out the view of the street and of the statehouse. The Governor peered up at the sky with narrowed lids. Just a rim of a white cloudhead stood up behind a magnolia tree. 'Thunderheads ... No siree. I'll drive the madam over.'

'Great, Steve,' said Jerry Evans. 'Don't forget you're dinin' with me at the Alcazar Hotel ... I'll call up and see if they can scrape us up a terrapin ...'

'You won't fail us Governor, will you? You know when Jerry orders up a dinner it's something,' said Tyler.

The Governor let his lids drop back over his eyes.

'Mr. Spotswood I ginerally manage to git where I'm plannin' to be at.'

The taximan had gone to sleep in a shady place against the curb outside of the drive. 'Sultry,' he said when they woke him up. 'I reckon it's a-goin' to storm.'

'Well get a move on,' said Evans.

'Don't you go gettin' us airsick, Jerry,' said Norman Stauch. 'I want to enjoy that terrapin tonight.'

The plane had hardly hit the beeline after the smooth spiral of the takeoff over the broad airfield before it began to plunge and buck like a trick bronc at a rodeo. 'This is going to be great,' shouted Evans tightening his safety belt and bracing his feet against the seat opposite. 'Stirs up the liver.' 'Great ... hell,' shouted Tyler. 'If I lose my lunch I'll sue you.'

The plane was soaring through a ceiling of driving mist

up into a dazzling white region of tumbled clouds.
Through tatters in the cloud floor below they could see
dark stretches of forest, a twisting silvery bayou, green
and brown squares of clearings, salt marshes and, beyond, the streaks of silvery shimmer of the gulf. They
caught sight of Horton's creamy white skyscrapers standing up against the wide palegreen stretches of the flat
lands of the coast. The plane plunged into a swirl of
driving mist, and rain beat against the windows. The
air that came in through the ventilators was cold and
wet.

'Well I hope your chauffeur knows his job,' Tyler sang
out keeping his mouth stiff for fear of vomiting.

'Babe,' roared Evans. 'He'd fly from here to Poplar
Fork and back upside down without battin' an eyelash.'

'You're sure he ain't doin' just that?' yelled Stauch.

A batch of dark pines rose hugely to meet them. The
pilot flattened out his dive so that the plane seemed to be
bouncing bumpily over the tops of the pines. Then
suddenly they were out in the sun again and crossing
broad grassy plains. They hopped across a row of trees
along a highroad and over the straightruled diagonal
lines of high tension wires. The dry grass of the airport
was speeding past under the shadow of the wing. Tyler
felt the pit of his stomach still all twisted up as he
stepped out of the cabin door onto the rubber treads of
the landingsteps, and came out into the quiet heat of the
late afternoon that was full of metallic rattle of dryflies.
It was all he could do to keep his legs from wobbling.
The sky overhead was a deep blue. Only along the

horizon a halfcircle of great cloudheads stood up, the rounded contours of their peaks touched with pale yellow and pale rose, their bases drenched in blurred indigo.

When they came out of the airport building, the colored porter following them with Evans' alligatorskin suitcase on a hand truck, they found only a single taxicab drawn up to the curb. The driver was asleep. 'Looks like things were kinda dead in town this afternoon,' said Evans. 'Wait till Number One gets in,' Tyler answered briskly. 'He'll liven things up . . . Hotel Alcazar please driver.'

Evans stretched out his legs. 'This is the first afternoon I've taken off in five years . . .' he said. 'What we need now's a shower an' a nice long cold drink,' Norman Stauch yawned comfortably. 'What I've always said is do what you like an' make money at it.'

'You don't suppose Steve'll change his mind,' Tyler muttered.

'You're just an old worrier,' said Evans.

'When I drink I don't worry enough, when I don't drink I worry too much . . . Anyway we'll all have a rest after next Tuesday.'

'Toby,' said Evans crossly, 'you're all set, damn you.'

'There's nothing much more Galbraith can pull out of his hat that he hasn't pulled out.'

'How about negro blood?'

'He'll probably pull that one tonight. If he does we've got an affidavit from a respectable physician that three members of Galbraith's immediate family have been

under treatment at the state insane asylum, one of them
for homicidal mania.'

The pavement outside the entrance of the huge yellowbrick Spanishstyle hotel gave off a staggering amount of
heat as they hurried across it. In the cavelike amber-
colored lobby it was cool and dark. A pile of messages
was waiting for Evans at the desk and sent him hurrying
off to get his office on the phone. Stauch went out to the
liquor store to buy some whiskey. Tyler enquired about
the 'Crawford for Senator' suite and was told that
Miss Jacoby had been up there all day.

He went up in the elevator and peeked through the
halfopen door of the anteroom of 1503. There at a
table stacked with pamphlets and throwaways, sat Ed
James wearing his broadest smile pulling books with
bright red white and blue covers out of a carton.

Poor Boy to President had arrived from the publishers
at last. Pretty near too late to be worth the dough they
had put in on it, Tyler thought to himself, as he walked
fast along the hall into the other room. He wanted to
get a shower and to change his clothes before he talked
to Ed. He had a bone to pick with Ed anyway about the
book's being late.

In the next room he found Miss Jacoby typing away
at a table in the window with her eyes half closed and her
long sharp nose pointing at the ceiling. 'Uncle Toby,'
she cried and started tossing herself back and forth on
her chair in a funny way she had like a bird on its perch.
Her black eyes looked birdlike too and her coarse black
hair and exaggeratedly curved eyebrows and her re-

markably sharply hooked nose. There was an old-fashioned Kentucky screech to her voice. 'Do you come back with your shield or on it?'

'We've called on every farm and ranchhouse in a thousand square miles . . . I'm all in. Miss Jacoby you look fresh as a buttercup . . . Anybody call up? I came in by plane with Jerry Evans.'

'Herb Jessup checkin' from Eberhart. He said it was the biggest yet. The stockyard hands went wild for Number One.'

'Bigger than Poplar Fork?'

She nodded her head vigorously.

'Be sure to tell Mr. Evans all about it if you get a chance. He'll probably be in here during the evening. He's gotten up a little dinner for the Governor and a few key men. Is Mrs. Crawford's party all set?' Miss Jacoby nodded her head again.

'It's goin' to be wonderful: lobster Newburgh an' baked grapefruit for dessert. I've got half a mind to go myself but of course I can't leave this room.'

'One more thing, Miss Jacoby; will you call up that friend of yours at the state capitol and ask him if the Governor really did get off. If he didn't we'll have to act quick.'

'I had Elkins Cone on the wire five minutes ago. The Governor and Mrs. Baskette left by car at three minutes after four.'

'Miss Jacoby you are wonderful.' He blew her a kiss as he ran out of the room and down the hall to his room.

His own room was depressing with its stale smell of

old liquor and cigarette butts and its desk stacked with letters that ought to have been answered a week ago. He stood still a moment staring at the mournfully familiar pattern of the green hotel counterpane on the bed. He started to open a telegram but put it back in its envelope without reading it, telling himself he'd take a shower first. He stripped off his clothes and jumped into the bathtub and stood for a minute with his eyes closed and his face turned up under the cold shower. As he pulled the towel back and forth across his back he took a look at himself in the mirror over the washbowl. The sight of his face gave him a squeamish qualm like the air sickness on the plane. The thin jaw was quite black. He'd gotten up so early that morning he had almost forgotten whether he'd shaved or not. He scraped hurriedly at his chin with a safety razor and pulled on a fresh white suit. Then he scooped all the mail and telegrams off his desk and poked them into a manila envelope and hurried back down the hall to Miss Jacoby's room.

He found Ed James leaning over her desk putting his name in one of the copies of the book for her. Something about the attitude of the fat grayclad figure with its broad buttocks gave him suddenly a feeling of disgust. Why the hell wasn't he doing something? 'Hello Ed,' he said curtly as Ed turned and walked slowly towards him with his hands out and an amused impudent smile on his broad pink face. 'Toby old boy,' he said, 'you look like a ghost.'

Tyler shook one of his hands in an absentminded way.

'Miss Jacoby,' he said, glaring at her, 'has Jessup checked in again?'

'Number One will be arriving at Sam Houston Park in about ten minutes.'

'I've got time to go over there . . . Meanwhile, Miss Jacoby,' he gave her a helpless childish smile and laid the manila envelope on her desk. 'Do anything you want about this mail . . . just so I don't have to see it till next week . . .' Miss Jacoby shook her finger at him and made a little clucking noise with her tongue. 'Come on, Ed,' he snapped briskly. 'We can talk in the taxi.'

Going down in the elevator he felt a splitting tightness in the temples. I've got to hold on, the words were so clear in his head it was almost as if he had said them aloud. He forced himself to pay attention to what Ed was saying about the trip on the plane down from New York.

When they got into the cab, Ed, said, 'Well I dropped everything and came on down. What's my job?'

'First thing I want to know, Ed, is why the hell was the book late?'

'You picked a damn little shyster publisher, what can you expect?'

Tyler lit a cigarette. He was trying to keep his temper. 'Let's skip it,' he said in an unexpectedly agreeable tone. 'We figured you could do yourself a magazine article or some kind of a story that would make the trip worth while.'

'Meanwhile,' said Ed dryly, 'how do I eat?'

'For the three or four days you'll be down here suppose

we treat you like the government does its experts: twentyfive dollars a day plus expenses?'

'That won't make me a millionaire.'

'It will if you elect Chuck to the United States Senate.' Ed burst out laughing. Tyler went on with a straight face: 'Take this thing seriously for crissake . . . If I ask you to come someplace it's because I know there's something in it for you.'

The afternoon sky was beginning to cloud over. 'Just our luck,' Tyler grumbled, 'to have it rain on the torchlight parade. Ed, for crissake don't miss this stuff. Rub the noses of the press associations in it. This is news. We are putting on the most colorful campaign in years and we are going to all this trouble putting on the oldtime stuff just to give you guys something to write about. I expect you to break the story in the New York papers. I want you to get on the phone the minute this meeting's over. The minute New York handles it that'll split the local press wide open.'

The taxi let them out the wrong side of the park. Tyler was so engrossed in what he was trying to put over to Ed that he hadn't noticed. With difficulty he counted out the fare from the scattering of change in the palm of his hand. It was as if his head was full of cold molasses. It was only after the taxi had driven off that he looked about him. 'Where the hell's the crowd?' A twinging thought shot through him that this was another flop like Arrowhead. Ed was looking in his face with a puzzled smile. 'I can hear a kind of a mulish brayin' comin' from over yonder,' he drawled.

Tyler set out full tilt down a path wound between beds of cannas and dahlias and pampas grass. In front of the buildings along Gulf Boulevard across the golf course he could see, in the steel and russet light that filtered through fast piling heads of coppery cloud, vivid green trees, and, under them, the white shirts of men and boys and the light dresses of the women massed round an animated black speck. He cut across the grass in that direction, walking so fast he could hear Ed's breathing becoming wheezier and fainter as he dropped behind.

The crowd was big, lively, cheerful; people were out to have themselves a time. A local wardheeler in a dark suit was rambling on, sweating, stumbling over his words, saying, 'Lemme tell you' and 'I mean' a hundred times if he said them once. Tyler turned an eager smiling face to Ed when he finally caught up with him. 'Chuck hasn't come yet. But look at the crowd we got.'

When people laughed he found himself laughing too a little harder, when they clapped he clapped like hell. 'Who is this guy?' whispered Ed James. Tyler had never seen him before. 'He's a local leader,' he heard himself saying in a ponderous tone. 'These local boys carry a lot of votes.'

The guy was terrible, Tyler was telling himself. Just his luck to have Ed get off on the wrong foot. He was beginning to fret again when he heard the sound truck coming down the boulevard amid a great rasping of klaxons; he could make out the Hillbilly Band playing 'O Susanna.' Voices started yelling 'Here's ole Chuck.' The blaring truck turned and backed in towards the

[103]

curb in the middle of the crowd. The sliding panels in
the rear had been pushed back to leave open a little
platform where there was just room for the five hillbillies to huddle with their instruments. They started to
play 'Every Man a Millionaire' and some young boys in
the crowd started singing it. Tyler threw himself into it
hoping the people around him would start it up but most
of them stood around just watching the show.

Then Chuck and his family drove in beside the truck
in a small open convertible. The Crawford kids looked
pretty redeyed and jangled. They were all three standing up on the back seat making a feeble effort to wave
their flags. Their noses were running. They caught
sight of Tyler first and all began to yell, 'There's Uncle
Toby.'

Tyler worked his way through the crowd dragging Ed
after him. Chuck was in the pink. Sitting at the wheel
of the tiny car he looked like a farm boy. His cheeks
had a flushed plump look like red apples. 'Where's
Steve Baskette?' he asked first thing. 'He's coming,'
shouted Tyler. He felt drunk though he hadn't had a
drink since the plane. 'Why the hell did you let him get
out of your sight?' Chuck hissed at him in his dry impera-
tive voice. 'Take everybody to the hotel. I'll be over
directly.'

Chuck jumped out of the car and climbed neatly up
the back of the truck. 'All right, boys,' he shouted.
'Let 'em have it.' He grabbed an ocarina from one
player's hand and led off with the tune. Then he played
it through with the band accompanying him while the

people yipped and stamped. 'An' my opponents said I hain't got a clean conscience . . . I tell you folks it takes a man with a clean conscience to carry a tune on the sweet potater. Well I know you folks all come here because you love Fatty Galbraith an' you-all got so much stock in the big oil companies an' railroad bonds an' interests in the bus lines you jess don't know what to do with it. While Fatty Galbraith stands up there perjurin' his soul before God an' man to vilify my character, to tell you how I stole the state funds when I was on the Utilities Commission an' public property in the shape of flowerin' plants an' weeds from the park commission an' washtowels when I was in the legislature an' used to stay at ole Miss Mulligan's boardin'house . . . Tonight he's goin' to tell you how my daddy had colored blood an' how I beat my poor old mother out the money from his estate that was due her, an' when he tells all those lies the big usurers an' the commission merchants an' the bankers an' the big utilities concerns Fatty Galbraith works for are goin' to gloat over his discomfiture of poor little ole Chuck Crawford that ain't had no schoolin' an' ain't had no money an' is nothin' but a poorwhite hillbilly wants to serve his fellow citizens . . . The demons in hell don't gloat like they'll gloat. Let 'em, I say. Let 'em gloat while they can. We got the votes. All they got is the money an' the newspapers an' the big suites in the best hotels . . . Fatty Galbraith ain't got the chance in this primary of a celluloid cat in hell.'

'See how he's getting 'em.' You'll get the story of your life, Ed,' whispered Tyler in Ed's ear. 'So long, kid.'

Then when Chuck paused for applause Tyler stepped into the driver's seat of the convertible and put his foot on the starter. The smallest boy had started to cry. 'Billy's wet his pants,' chanted the other two. 'We better make tracks, Toby,' said Sue Ann. 'You oughta seen Homer auction off that mule . . . Even the mule enjoyed it.' A heavy gust of dry wind blew dust in their faces. 'I bet you're tired, Sue Ann,' said Tyler.

'I could lie down on the bed and howl like a baby.' For just a second she rested her head on his shoulder. Then she pulled the little mirror in the windshield around so that she could look at her face in it. 'My, I'm a sight,' she said. 'My face is all streaks.'

For a long time Tyler could feel in his nostrils a little whiff of her hair and a sort of tingling in the place on his shoulder where her head had touched him. By the time they got the car to the hotel the sky was heavily overcast and the streets were a whirl of winddriven dust. Dragging the little boys between them they ran, with their heads bent into a gust, across the pavement to the hotel entrance.

Tyler went straight to the desk to see if the Governor had checked in. They hadn't seen hide nor hair of him. On his way up to his room Tyler happened to glance out of the elevator door at the mezzanine and caught sight of a broad familiarlooking back in a light gray pongee coat bent over a writing desk. The car had already started, so he couldn't get out till the next floor. His nerves were taut as he waited for a car to take him down again. It was the Governor all right, and there was Mrs. Baskette in lavender tulle looking very large in the armchair beside him.

'Why Mrs. Baskette, Mrs. Crawford's been looking all over for you. I hope you didn't have any trouble with rain.'

'Young man, the Governor and I came in the side entrance specially so that I could have a little visit with my husband,' said Mrs. Baskette in her highpitched voice. 'I don't often get the opportunity.'

The Governor looked up and nodded and then went back to his letterwriting.

'Mrs. Crawford would be delighted to entertain you both in her suite,' said Tyler ... 'I'll let her know you're here.'

To find a phone he had to go down to the main lobby again. As he worked his way through the late afternoon crowd he ran into a fat man with a big creased-up face he knew very well. It was Pete Spencer, chairman of the Business Men for Galbraith organization: 'Well Pete, how's your champeen coming along?'

'In the pink,' said Pete, laughing. 'You look kinda tired, Spotswood. Tell me Chuck Crawford wore hisself out and couldn't speak above a whisper at Houston Park.'

'You wait,' said Tyler, 'till you hear him tonight at the Opera House.'

'Say, Spotswood, somebody said he saw the Governor drive into town.'

Tyler shook his head emphatically without moving a muscle of his face. 'Must have been somebody looked like him ... Come to think of it I saw a man looked kinda like Steve getting into his car when I drove up a few minutes ago . . . Well, so long, let me know if you hear of any Galbraith money around. I'd like to win me a couple of bets this election.'

He hurried over to the house phone and got Miss Jacoby. 'Tell Mrs. Crawford her uncle and aunt are waiting for her in the writing room on the mezzanine. Tell her to come right on down.'

Then he went up to Jerry Evans' suite. A long table decorated with red roses and asparagus fern and all the silverware the hotel could muster was laid in the center of the parlor. At a buffet in the corner Jerry Evans and Norman Stauch were inspecting an array of whiskey and gin bottles and the makings of various types of cocktails. 'Toby, do you suppose we ought to have champagne?'

Tyler was so flustered he could hardly talk. His voice came in a breathless screech. 'We've got to get Steve up here right away. Pete Spencer and his crowd's all over the lobby. I bet they got tipped off and are trying to get hold of Steve to talk him out of it. Duke, suppose you call up the desk and tell 'em you're expecting the Governor but as it's a little private dinner he doesn't want to be bothered. They can just say he ain't here . . . I'll go back and stand guard. Number One'll be along in a minute.'

Sue Ann was already on the job. As he stepped out of the elevator he heard her highpitched girlish voice declaring she'd have been down to see the Baskettes sooner if the kids hadn't gotten into a pillow fight. Mrs. Baskette said Oh she'd love to see them. 'All right, Mrs. Baskette, we'll go right up and we'll turn the Governor over to Mr. Evans' dinnerparty . . . I'd better get back before they take the hotel to pieces.' The Governor said suppose he came too, he liked kids himself. Tyler was grinning and nodding in the background without putting in a word. 'Come on, Toby, if they haven't piped down you can wring their necks.' 'Ours are all grown up,' said Mrs. Baskette. 'Worse luck.' As they were walking down the broad cool hotel corridor Sue Ann was exclaiming, 'I declare it's excitin' news that Governor Baskette's goin' to introduce Homer at the Opera House this evenin'. This has been a wonderful day for us anyway. People have just seemed crazy about Homer everywheres we've gone an' your comin' puts icin' on it.' She was ushering them into the children's bedroom. Two of them were tucked into a big double bed and Billy, the smallest, lay in a cot. A grinning colored nurse was hovering over them. They all lay quiet looking up at the ceiling with big round eyes.

The Governor cleared his throat. Mrs. Baskette began to chirp, 'Oh my, aren't they cunning? I declare, Mrs. Crawford, I don't know your husband, but I'm sure that any man who's managed to get himself such a sweet young wife and such pretty children must be all right.'

'I guess there's been worse Senators than Chuck ud make,' said the Governor.

'Well, Governor, shall we leave the ladies to their own devices?' said Tyler in a tone that sounded falsely chatty in his own ears. 'I think our friends are waiting for us.'

The Governor didn't say a word as they walked down the hall. Tyler's head was empty. For the life of him he couldn't think of anything to say. He caught himself starting to whistle. They walked slowly side by side with ponderous steps on the muffling thick carpet of the corridor. In the elevator it was a relief to be able to grin at the girl operator in a gray uniform who said: 'Good evening, Mr. Spotswood.' Tyler wished she'd recognized the Governor, but there was nothing he could do about it. On the fourth floor, still without speaking, they walked down another long muffled corridor to Jerry Evans' suite.

Tyler couldn't help puffing out his chest a little when he opened the door and ushered the Governor in. The room smelt of Havana cigars and roses and whiskey and angostura bitters. The men looked large and clean and cheerful in their fresh linen suits. Smells like money; the words said themselves fast in a tiny corner of Tyler's mind.

'Steve,' they all cried out. Jerry Evans advanced towards the door with his right hand stretched out and a glass of cocacola in his left. 'This is indeed a pleasure.' Tyler smiled a discreet smile and hurried back to the elevator again, a procurer's smile, said the voice in his head. Going down in the elevator he could still feel the place where he'd worn it on his lips.

He walked through the lobby to the telephone operator's desk. She was a pointedfaced girl with hair bleached to the color of new rope and pretty dark eyes with doll's lashes. Tyler leaned as far as he could towards her across the phone books and looked down into her face. 'Hello, sugar,' he whispered.

'Why, Mister Spotswood, is this the language . . .? Yes, they are paging Mr. Bromfield . . . Alcazar Hotel . . . Good evening . . . Mr. R. J. Higgins . . . Mr. R. J. Higgins has checked out . . .'

'Honest, Francie. You're pretty cute.'

She lifted dark eyebrows at him that were shaved to a thin newmoon shape. 'Call Room Service, please, this is the operator . . .' Meanwhile her hands were moving up and down on the board in front of her, plugging out and plugging in. Occasionally her red nails flashed when she brought a hand down to dial a number.

'Suppose you and me,' whispered Tyler, 'go drink some dinner and see a show one day after the primaries?'

'I don't drink, Mister Spotswood . . . Don't you wish you knew who I was goin' to vote for?'

'Well, we'll talk about it. You look so cute tonight I quite forgot what I wanted to say. Mr. Evans is entertaining the Governor and a few of us in room 465. We don't want any phone calls. Put anything through to Miss Jacoby in 1503 or else tell 'em to wait until nine o'clock . . . Do you get that? You won't forget?' Francie shook her pale curls and a little whiff of musky perfume reached Tyler.

'That Miss Jacoby. Don't she toss her head in the air,' she said scornfully . . . 'I've had some calls for the Governor already. I hung 'em up because you said he didn't want 'em.'

'You did right. Keep on doing that. You always do right, sugar.'

Francie let him look deep in her eyes for a minute. 'That's what you think,' she said. 'Good evening. Hotel Alcazar. No, this is not the information booth . . . Room Service, please . . .'

Tyler tore himself away and went back to the elevator, lighting himself a cigarette as he went along. No, he wouldn't have a drink yet.

On the way back upstairs he stopped off on the mezzanine and walked around to the private dining room where Sue Ann was entertaining her ladies. Through the halfopen double doors came highpitched laughter and voices that merged into a dense henyard cackling. Tyler hung irresolutely outside for a minute while waiters brushed past him. He was so dead tired he couldn't make up his mind how to get in touch with Sue Ann to check on the arrangements for getting the Baskettes over to the Opera House after dinner. Gradually it came over him that the girl in the big black scoopshaped hat beside him was his cousin Lorna Stockton.

They turned their faces towards each other at the same minute. 'Why, Cousin Tyler Spotswood, I was just wonderin' how long it would take you to wake up out of your daze. Is she in there? Who is she?'

'Lorna, I'm so dead tired from this damn campaign I don't know if I'm on my head or my heels. How are you, anyway? How's Aunt Harriet and Uncle Mat?'

'Cousin Tyler, you are just the man I wanted to see,' Lorna said with a quick giggle. 'I've just started doing the Tabitha Tattle column on the *News-Dispatch* and I want a scoop.'

'Lorna, why didn't you let me know? I'd have gotten you invited to Mrs. Crawford's dinner.'

'That would have gotten me fired. You know what Mr. Carey thinks of your Crawford gang.'

'But, darling Lorna, if I fix it up with Mrs. Crawford will you give us a break?'

Lorna nodded vigorously. 'I'll have to kid a little about a ladies' dinner. Whoever heard of havin' a hen party at dinnertime. I bet they're smokin' cigars in there.'

'Lorna, do you think that Mrs. Stephen Rogers Baskette is the sort of woman who would do anything unbecoming to the dignified first lady of the state?'

Lorna's eyes began to bug out like they used to when he told her tall stories in the old days. 'She sent her regrets,' she said.

'You go in and see,' said Tyler. He pulled out a pad and started to scrawl out a note. 'Now, Lorna, if I introduce you to Sue Ann you'll play this straight?'

'Cross my heart . . . honest injun . . . hope I may die . . . but isn't she kinder common?' Tyler felt the ill temper well up in him. He frowned. 'She's one of the most uncommon sweetest brightest women I ever met.'

Lorna was looking at him searchingly through her small black gimlet eyes. 'Why, Tyler Spotswood . . . You are at it again. Sweetie, I can read you like a book.'

Tyler's face began to get red. He turned away abruptly and handed the note he'd been scribbling to a waiter and asked him to take it in to Mrs. Crawford. When he turned back towards Lorna he had his poker-face again. 'Just for that crack, Lorna . . . I won't give you the real beat on tonight's meeting . . . My, it's nice to see you, though.'

'Oh, Tyler, I was just teasing.'

'You get it out of Sue Ann.'

Sue Ann herself was standing in the door in a green dress that sparkled with sequins like a tightrope walker's. She wore her hair piled up in curls on her head and held back with a band of green tulle that had a row of shiny stars on it. 'Mrs. Stockton,' she said in her cosy low voice, 'I didn't know you were kin to Toby. It sure was nice of you to come around. Any kin of Toby's is mighty close to us. Won't you come in an' have some after-dinner coffee with us?'

Tyler could see Lorna melting. 'Well,' he said, 'I hope you girls'll get along. I'm leaving you a seat in a box at the Opera House, Lorna . . . Let's have lunch next week . . . like old times . . .' There was something a little forlorn about Lorna's face as she shook her head.

'You come out and see us,' she said.

'O.K. Lorna, I will.'

Going up in the elevator Tyler lit himself another cigarette. He'd smoked so much his mouth tasted like the bottom of a hencoop. He was beginning to feel more cheerful. A couple of good drinks at dinner would make him feel real good. Poor old Lorna. Years ago, he used to think he was in love with her. Walking along the corridor he was remembering the tearful evening they'd decided they oughtn't to marry because they were first cousins and he'd gone off telling her he was going to sit down and drink himself to the demnition bowwows. Well, he'd kept his part of the bargain. Lorna announcing her engagement to Lieutenant Stockton right next day had kinda taken the beauty out of it. Still Lorna was a pretty good scout. Maybe she'd manage to give the Crawfords a break in the social column.

Tyler stood still in his tracks a second outside Jerry Evans' parlor listening to the voices and laughter of the men at table, trying to drive everything out of his head except what had to be done this evening. Suppose he just went down to the bar and got potted and to hell with it . . . The thought of a drink of rye was so vivid he almost felt it warm his gullet. When he pushed open the door he found they were just finishing their soup. The waiter was keeping a plate hot for him. He sat down at the empty place between Ed James and Frank Goodday and as he moved his spoon back and forth in his plate he let his eyes run appraisingly round the table.

At the head sat Jerry Evans, big and bulky in an unrumpled white suit, his round face beaming over the white cloth and the flowers and the silverware, like a big red moon. Next him sat the Governor, his black hair brushed up straight from the low forehead where it grew down almost to the eyebrows that met bushily across the bridge of his straight nose. Steve Baskette was eating slowly, taking a sip of icewater now and then, letting the thick lashes that fringed his heavy eyelids cover his eyes when he drawlingly answered a question some man put to him. Chuck sat opposite. Past Frank Goodday's pleased blank countenance, Tyler could see Chuck's creased brows and the mess of sour lines and wrinkles round his eyes and at the ends of his mouth. He looked tired and out of sorts. He was saying mighty little for him. Right opposite was a bigmouthed braying young man, with light hair cut in a brush, who held down the pulpit at the Baptist Tabernacle, the Reverend Chester Bigelow, chairman of the Horton Every Man a Millionaire Committee. At the end of the table Norman Stauch was having himself a time, eating and drinking and throwing back his head to laugh as he told Judge Banning, who listened with the too kindly expression of a smoothfaced Santa Claus, a long story about shooting a twentyfour-point buck out in Arizona that turned out to be stuffed already. Ed and Frank Goodday and Herb Jessup were keeping quiet listening to the talk at the ends of the table, but the Reverend Bigelow was sparring for a chance to take over the conversation. When the terrapin came on, Judge Banning got in ahead of him and held everybody down with a set of stories about catching terrapin, and encounters with cottonmouth moccasins out in the swamps at Shreveport when he was a boy. Champagne corks popped. Jerry Evans seemed to enjoy keeping the old Judge going, so that each time the Reverend Bigelow pulled the air into his lungs to take the floor he had to let it out again harmlessly.

Tyler tried to eat a mouthful of the thick spicy mess on his plate but he couldn't get it down. He had to tell the waiter to bring him a jigger of whiskey to keep from gagging over it. He'd promised himself he wouldn't drink until after the rally, but one drink wouldn't matter.

After the waiter had carried a Baked Alaska in a big silver dish round the table to show before serving it, the Reverend Bigelow, who had been pulling out his watch from time to time, got to his feet and said if you gentlemen would excuse him, he'd better be going over to the Opera House to get that rally started and that he hoped everybody would remember that they would be on the air from nine-fortyfive to ten-fifteen. Chuck got up and put his arm round the Reverend's square shoulders and walked to the door with him talking earnestly in his ear. Jerry Evans got up too and went along to shake hands.

When Chuck came back he lounged along the table, until he was leaning on the back of Tyler's chair. Then he yanked him up and drew him back with him to his end of the table. When he let himself plop with a satisfied grunt into the seat at the head of the table, he motioned to Tyler to sit down in the seat next him opposite the Governor.

Meanwhile Jerry had dropped into the place next to Judge Banning and had him off on one of his Scotchman stories. At that end of the table everybody was laughing and sitting up waiting for a chance to tell a story, or to poke a joke in sideways.

At their end, quiet as if they sat behind a screen, Tyler and the Governor and Chuck looked at each other without saying anything. Each of them had pushed back his dessert plate without tasting it.

Chuck started talking fast in a low voice: 'Honest, Steve, if I'd known you wanted to run for the Senate I'd a waited . . . I'm young yet . . . If you want to run for the Senate when you've completed this term, I'll put all my organization behind you . . . I think you're the best governor this state has had in fifty years . . . Ole Senator Height's a civil old fishface, but he knows more about feedin' mules than he does about the politics of this nation. His term has a coupla years to run . . . Hell, maybe he'll resign. Steve, if you want to go to the Senate I'll place you in the Senate. I might resign myself if things worked out that way.'

'It's troublesome for two fellers to try to agree to anythin' they can't put down on paper,' drawled the Governor.

'You don't have to trust me, Steve . . .' Chuck's voice rose to a shrill falsetto. 'Just trust Toby here. Everybody knows that Tyler Spotswood is all wool and a yard wide . . . What I'm tellin' you is that, from this night on, our organization is going to be heard from not only all over this state but all over this nation.'

Steve Baskette didn't say anything. They were laughing and whooping at the other end of the table. At length a remark rose to the Governor's tongue and seemed to crawl with difficulty out through his thin lips. 'Well, I never believed in tryin' to ride herd to a lotta commitments.'

Tyler put in his oar. 'Suppose we look at it this way,' he said cheerfully. 'Both you, Chuck, and the Governor here have real independent voter support . . . outside of

[118]

any votes that can be delivered by anybody's machine. We know that the Governor was elected by a plurality of nearly a hundred thousand. When our district sent Chuck to Congress he snowed Willy Green under three to one. My idea is that the same kind of independent intelligent voters gave Steve his plurality as are going to send Chuck to the Senate. Whether we like it or not . . . and I for one can say perfectly frankly that I do like it . . . we have to stick together because we've got the same voter support. If we break that up, we'll all lose out.'

The Governor beckoned a waiter and whispered in his ear. The waiter brought him a plate of rolls and a bottle of catsup. Without saying a word he broke off a piece of a roll, spiked it with a fork and poured out a dab of catsup on it and popped it into his mouth. 'I don't eat dessert,' he said. He sat there chewing silently with his eyes on his plate. From the other end of the table Stauch's whinnying laugh, set off by the low monotone of Judge Banning telling a travelling man story, snickered out abruptly. Everybody was listening now, to what Steve Baskette was about to say.

'Well, I wouldn't trust Clyde Galbraith, not if he was the last man on earth,' he said in a crisp voice that sounded down the table. Without looking at anybody he folded his napkin with slow care and pushed back his chair as if to indicate that so far as he was concerned the dinner was over.

The waiters were passing around cigars and brandy glasses. Tyler brought out his lighter and lit first the

Governor's cigar, then Chuck's. He was about to light his own when Jerry called to him down the table, 'Three on one, buddy, jamais de la vie.' 'O.K. Soger,' said Tyler and put his lighter out and lit it again. The three men got to their feet.

'What time have you got, Toby?' asked Chuck.

Tyler looked at his watch. 'It's just about eight-thirty.'

'Time we were over at the Opery House . . . Where the hell's your parade, Toby?' The Governor and Chuck had walked over to the window. The others straggled after. The waiters snatched away the chairs.

'Parade'll be along.' Tyler craned his neck to see down into the street. 'We're great believers, Governor,' he said, 'in getting some oldtime showmanship back into politics . . . Say, boy,' he called to a waiter, 'how do these windows open?'

'They can't be opened, sir, on account of the air-conditioning.'

'That's what you think,' said Chuck. 'Toby, you call up Jackie and tell him to bring his burglar's kit . . . He'll get 'em open.'

They could already hear snaredrums and the racket of the sound truck from the street below when Jackie Hastings came in followed by a lanky shambling over-grown young bruiser with several hairy moles on his lantern chin. Big hands like bunches of bananas hung loosely on knotted wrists at the end of his long arms. The fact that one eye was smaller than the other gave his blank face a lopsided secretive look. 'Well, if it ain't

Saunders, my old sparrin' partner,' said Chuck, and punched him in the ribs.

Saunders doubled himself up and grinned affectionately. He had a little bag of tools in his hand. In a jiffy he and Jackie Hastings between them had ripped off the weatherstripping and had the windows open onto the balcony over the main entrance of the hotel. Hot moist air poured into the room from the street along with a shuffle of footsteps and a distant sound of automobile klaxons and horns.

'These boys'll take to pieces anythin' or anybody I want taken to pieces,' roared Chuck, slapping them each on the back.

'They set up our public address systems,' Tyler added in an explanatory tone.

Suddenly the sound truck started up right below, loud enough to split their eardrums raspingly spouting a record of Chuck's voice:

'These are the years that will establish the victory of the common man, the reconquest of his government an' of his whole civilization by the plain or'nary citizen. This is the time to elect plain folks, who will stand up for the rights of plain folks an' who will see that government of the people, for the people an' by the people, shall not perish from the earth . . .'

Chuck hopped lightly over the sill out onto the balcony. 'Come on out, Steve,' he called back. 'Let's see how many customers we've got.' The Governor, stepping carefully so as not to soil his white linen suit, bent double through the window and unfolded his lanky shape outside. Tyler followed. Steve Baskette was sniffing the heavy air and looking up at the sky. 'Goin' to storm,' he said.

In the street below redfire lit up the white sound truck and behind it a string of cars draped with lettered bunting that fluttered in the gusty wind, and the heads and shoulders of marching groups that flanked the cars, and flickered in the blind windows of the buildings opposite and tinged with pink the lowhanging fringes of cloud overhead. The sound truck stopped and went quiet. Two spotlights from the tail of it lit up the men on the balcony and threw their sprawling shadows up the wall above the windows. A shout roared down the street. Ranks of faces caught the red glare as they turned up towards the balcony. The sound truck struck up the record of 'Every Man a Millionaire.'

Tyler noticed that the Governor gave a start as if he'd seen a gun pointed at him. Chuck had spread out his arms and started to jump up and down. Then he threw his arms around the Governor. He wasn't tall enough to reach his neck and only managed to hug him round the chest. The Governor's lips tightened to a short black line. With a free arm he waved gravely to the crowd below, then he ducked quickly, cautiously as a man who thinks he's being shot at, back in through the window.

Tyler, not wanting to be part of the tableau, had scrambled in before him. When he held out his hand to help him across the sill, Steve Baskette brushed past. For a second Tyler caught a rattlesnake look that bored into his eyes from lustreless black pupils. Then the heavy lids drooped again. Steve Baskette was addressing himself to Judge Banning: 'When we used to have torchlight parades in the old days, Judge, we used to light up a tarbarrel at every corner,' he drawled. 'Out in Tucumcari I seen 'em burn down half the town once.'

'And a barrel of whiskey, don't forget the barrel of whiskey,' said the Judge in his velvet voice.

Chuck bounced back into the room. 'What the hell . . . Put on a show, that's what I say.' He clapped one hand back and forth against the other to brush off the dust. 'Close this goddam window, Toby, we're stiflin' in here . . .' He stood with his legs apart looking round the room with a broad arrogant grin. 'If you'll excuse me, gentlemen, Toby and I have got to do a little work on my speech. We'll be over to the hall in half an hour. He tells me what to say an' I say it . . . Mr. Jessup has charge of the seatin' arrangements on the platform . . . Where are you, Herb? You been so quiet I ain't seen you all evenin'.'

'Present,' drawled Herb Jessup, drawing his limp bulk slowly out of a chair. 'Gentlemen, I reckon we better get a move on.'

Chuck had grabbed Tyler by the arm and drawn him out into the hall. 'Where are those damn gorillas?'

'Room 425 down the hall.'

They walked in without knocking. Chuck started right off shouting mad: 'Goddam your stinkin' hide, Jackie. What kind of a torchlight parade do you call that? I counted ten pieces of redfire. Didn't I tell you

[123]

to spend money? What the hell did I give you that grand for? What's the use of a show like that? A crowd ain't a crowd unless they call out the police reserves.' 'Number One,' said Jackie Hastings. 'Have a heart.' His blue eyes glared. His face that always had an unfinished look with its turned-up nose had turned the color and consistency of putty. 'I was tellin' the boys I thought they done pretty well.'

'Where are Saunders and Crummit?' Saunders and a bulletheaded thickchested fellow slouched in from the bathroom. 'I bet you're drinkin' corn liquor in there . . . If you boys git hot before that rally's over I'll fire the lot of you. If you bastards think it's anybody but me keepin' you outa jail you're very much mistaken. I wanted a traffic jam outside that Grand Opery House an' every seat filled by eight o'clock tonight. That bunch of highschool kids wavin' a little redfire ain't nothin'.'

'I might git me some colored boys and Mexicans but hit's kinda late,' whined Saunders.

'Goddam it, I want white people.'

'Rally's already started. The Reverend has been letting 'em have it for the last half hour,' said Tyler.

'How many boys you got you kin get word to in the hall?'

'We must have a hundred at least, Number One,' said Jackie in a wheedling voice. 'Honest, that opery's packed. I jess come from there.'

'Well, pass the word in they're to give the Governor a hand. Give him a great big hand when he comes in, when he starts to speak, all through his speech. Don't matter if they hear him or not. People'll give me hand anyway, but I want the Governor to go home feeling good. He's sore as a crab.'

A sound like a load of coal going down a shute came through the closed windows.

Chuck started nervously. 'What the hell's that?'

Jackie Hastings threw out his chest. 'That there's rain, Number One. Now ain't you glad I saved you some dough?'

Saunders hitched up his pants and edged a little to-wards Chuck. 'Even if we had a crowd they'd all been soaked an' gone home an' voted for Galbraith . . . Wait till you see the hall, Number One. Ain't it better to have 'em in the hall than out on the street catchin' their death of cold?'

'All right, boys,' said Chuck without smiling, 'git goin'.'

Jackie Hastings walked first and Saunders and Crummit fell in behind Chuck and Tyler as they strode over the muffling carpet down the corridor to the elevator, flattening a couple of travelling men against the wall as they passed. They all walked with short fast steps as if they had practised the formation. The elevator took them down to the basement garage. Chuck and Tyler jumped into the broad back seat of the white Lincoln and the other three crowded into the front. The streets ran to the curbs with swirling mudladen water. 'Anyway,' whispered Tyler with a little giggle in his voice, 'they can't walk out on your speech.' Chuck didn't laugh, but lay back as if he hadn't heard, staring up at the ceiling of the car.

At the stage entrance they had to run for it. Chuck was spluttering mad. 'Why didn't one of you bastards bring an umbrella?' They hurried, sweating, up the old dusty iron stairway to the wings. 'This is a hell of a stinkin' ole firetrap,' Chuck was muttering. 'We'll tear it down and build a new one.'

Before going out on the stage, Chuck stood behind a scaling flat painted with foliage until he could catch his breath. He was watching intently. Tyler stood right behind him, his heart pounding. Judge Banning was talking on and on in his smooth velvety voice. In front of them were the listening faces in profile of the men and women on the platform. Beyond was a segment of the hall, violet shadows evenly studded with little knobs of heads, blurred pinkish with faces. Chuck waited, his body taut, like a man about to make a high dive. He mopped his face and neck. 'Gimme a handkerchief,' he said in a gruff whisper without turning his head. Tyler poked a folded clean handkerchief into his hand. His hand was icy cold and shaking. Chuck was wet and trembling all over like a hound dog in a thunderstorm. Suddenly he shot out into the glaring spotlight, walking with easy short fast steps, his face rosy and boyish, his eyes very big and round, an impudent kind of grin on his full lips. The hall broke into a rattle of applause. The people on the stand left their places and swirled about him. Judge Banning turned and stretched out his arm from the shoulder in a togaed gesture.

Tyler came out a little into the light so that he could see better. Chuck headed straight for the Governor and grabbed him by the hand. The mouths out front roared, the hands clapped. Suddenly for Tyler it was all worth what he'd put into it. He was breasting the tape. The job was done. Now he could take a drink.

Everything was going off according to the book. Judge Banning was finishing his speech and introducing the Governor. The hall was giving the Governor an ovation with yips and shouts and tin horns, and the hillbillies were playing 'Oh bury me not on the lone prairee,' the Governor's favorite song. Steve Baskette looked sour enough when he began to speak but he was going through with it. 'Friends . . . and fellow Democrats of the greatest Democratic state in the Union . . . it is a great pleasure to be with you this evening . . .'

Tyler wasn't listening. Only an occasional word broke through all the other words of the day's speeches that still bumbled like flies around his ears . . . 'privilege to address you . . . honor to introduce . . the man who . . .'

They raised the roof. People were getting to their feet cheering and stamping. Tyler suddenly felt the bile rise in him. He turned his back and walked slowly away. By God, now he could have a drink.

On the iron stairs he met Ed James puffing in a leisurely fashion as he slowly ascended step by step. Ed looked Tyler up and down. 'Couldn't take it eh?'

'You shut up, Ed. Come on over to the hotel and have a drink.'

'That's more like it. I was afraid you'd got religion, Toby.' They stood a while in the rainslashed entrance waiting for a cab.

'Well,' Ed was saying, 'I got you your story. God knows how I did it . . . When I think that I gave up doin' publicity for the investment bankers and took up free lancin' in order to be able to tell the truth . . . It is, friends Romans and countrymen, to laugh.'

Tyler was tapping nervously with the toe of his shoe. Suddenly he found that he'd gone hoarse and couldn't speak above a whisper. 'For crissake,' he rasped pleadingly, 'wait till I get a drink.'

The hotel corridors had a dead stale soothing coolness. His room was quiet. The bed, the desk, the armchair, the telephone, the electric fan were in their accustomed places. He reached up onto the shelf of the closet that was full of a familiar reek of the cleaners' from his clothes, and hauled down a quart of whiskey. He was so tired he couldn't get the thick enamelled tin off the cork.

'Here, lemme have it . . . I got a corkscrew on my knife,' said Ed in a soothing voice as if to a baby.

Tyler pulled off his sweaty coat and his necktie and threw himself on the bed in his chilly wet shirt. 'Home,' he croaked, 'is where the heart is.'

'That's a hot one,' said Ed and handed him half a tumbler of tepid whiskey. Tyler raised his head and gulped it like an obedient child taking medicine.

'Here, I'll just take a nightcap an' make tracks. You need some rest,' said Ed. Tyler drank off the tumbler and lay back choking a little on the pillow with his eyes closed waiting for it to make him feel good. He raised his head.

'And let me get drunk all alone?' He could talk easier already. 'Damn you, stick around till I sign off for the night.'

He sat up grinning on the edge of the bed and held his tumbler out towards the bottle.

Number One

CHAPTER
III

W<small>HEN</small> *you try to find the people,*
it comes down maybe to a boy seventeen who's worked all
day in a chainstore; at last he's home (his old man's a
rummy, his folks don't understand him, his hours are too
long and his pay too short, he needs a new pair of shoes, he's
scared to pick up girls; he wants a sports model car, to own

a messjacket, to be manager and sit at a broad slick desk, somewhere dimly sometime to be President); he's nuts about radio;

he runs up four flights of stairs (it's an old dwelling converted to flats), he keeps his ears closed to neighbors' voices, phonographs, favorite programs, girlie doing the scales on the piano, somebody's steak frying, unlocks the attic door, slams it behind him, breathes happily the hot close air of old chests full of mothballs and dry dusty lumber and glue from busted tables and chairs;

under the dormer on a threelegged table securely propped by a packingcase nailed to the floor so that it can't jiggle stands his two-way set:

sending and receiving:

short wave; when he pulls the earphones over his uncombed hair that he ought to get cut (his pimples are terrible, he forgot to write for that cure for acne, nights in bed an agony of woman dreams): the switch is right, he's plugged in; his ears glow with the hum from the warming tubes:

he's on the air, resounding immensity, concave with voices, dotted with signals,

limitless sphere: his ears are everywhere, his tongue, trigger of wisecracks (Have you heard this one?), talks to everybody, to unseen hams, to unknown stations that fade roaring

on the horizons (last night he tinkered with that con-

denser until he fell asleep in his chair) of the power of his homemade set:

the policecars are talking, heavy cops' voices: three-alarm fire on Conduit Road, man abusing woman at Locust and State, fight in that bowling alley back of Freeland Street . . . it's George on Catalina Island, talks like a guy knows a lot . . . our little yawl . . . the race . . . she jibed . . . I cracked her over and she held . . . before we knew what it was all about she turned on a dime and we had about thirtyfive cents left . . . okeydoke on Long Point . . . had us a time . . . Joe (he sounds like a heel), he's going to a dance tonight, went downtown and hired him a soup and fish . . . that crazy galoot that won't stop talking he's a vegetarian, worked all week on his crystal set to tell the world about carrots, ain't hep to a thing . . . Fred picked up Melbourne last night, now he's shooting for Bombay. How's for some swing? . . . ears throb to a rumba band and a woman's small voice whining tangos in Havana:

up in the attic the window's dark, must be late; supper; when he pulls off his earphones

it's the universe gone

and left only the cramped restriction of every day, the worn soles of his shoes, the frayed trouser cuff, the spots on his only good necktie,

the crazy need for change.

Clean as a Hound's Tooth

Tyler tottered barefoot across the slick linoleum of the kitchenette. Scrambled green and violet shafts from the sunbeaten foliage outside stabbed his eyes through the bright bars of the venetian blind in the window. For once he didn't have a headache. He felt good and a little tiny bit drunk. Only his head felt large. And very delicate. His great skull, brittle as an eggshell, perched precariously on the tip of his fragile spine. His skull was transparent so that the horizontal bars of green and violet light beat into his tender faintly throbbing brain. He groped for the cords with shaky fingers and yanked at them peevishly to flatten out the battens so that only a few thin lines of light still stung his eyes.

He didn't have a headache but his legs were chilly. He only had the top of his pajamas on. He staggered back to the bedroom door and looked in uneasily. She was still asleep. All he could see in the blue dusk was a pile of mussed-up blonde hair on the creased pillow and a shape under the bedclothes. She was snoring. How in Christ's name was he going to get her to go home? How long had they been there? The inside of his head swirled blackly with confusion when he tried to think back. Who the hell was she anyway?

He caught sight of his clothes neatly hung over the back of a chair. With his tongue between his teeth he tiptoed into the bedroom that still reeked of cigarettes and whiskey and lifted the chair in his arms and carried it into the kitchenette. Then inch by inch he pushed the door to until the latch clicked. He let his breath out; he'd been holding it so long he felt dizzy. Now I got to get the hell outa here, he heard himself whisper to himself confidentially. He began to giggle softly under his breath, as he lifted the chair with his clothes up into his arms again.

The other side of the kitchenette there was a narrow livingroom with a purpleflowered carpet and a birchwood table and a settee with purpleflowered cushions. He set the chair down in there and settled down on the settee with his hairy chilly legs outstretched over the carpet in front of him to think. He sank into a vague so sorry for himself doze. Chuck's voice was full of static in his ears insisting: 'Toby, why the hell shouldn't they sell me the leases? I put 'em where they are, didn't I?' 'Chuck, we can't do it like that. No, Chuck, no.' Tyler's head was waggling from side to side. 'Ain't no harm in a profit. We sell out to the best businessman . . . The people gits the wells developed . . . the royalties lower their taxes. Ain't nobody goin' to squawk. It's clean as a hound's tooth.' They'd set off the burglar alarm. Tyler stiffened with panic. The alarm was ringing.

It was the telephone. It was ringing and ringing. It would wake that damn woman. He screwed up his forehead till it hurt trying to frown his head clear. He had the phone in his hand but he couldn't figure out which end to put to his ear. It was Sue Ann's voice shrill and excited so that the receiver kept jarring. 'Just a minute, Sue Ann,' he kept saying. She was talking and talking. She wanted him to come right over. Where had he been all this time, she was asking. Where was Homer? Suddenly he got control of his voice. 'Sue Ann, I can't see you now.'

'Tyler, you've been drinkin'. You promised you wouldn't.'

'I've been laid up. I'm under the care of a physician,' he heard himself saying. 'What time is it?'

'Tyler, it's two o'clock.'

'Sue Ann, I'll be over to the hotel at six.'

'Sober?'

[136]

'Without fail.'

She banged down the receiver and he found himself getting into his trousers in a great hurry. It took him a long time to get into all his clothes. There was no mirror and he was afraid to go through the bedroom into the bathroom for fear of waking that woman. A button popped off his shirt. His necktie got into a tight knot under his ear. He'd lost his vest. Suddenly he found that he'd opened the outside door and was staring at the glittering narrow radiator and the intent headlights of an automobile. It was like meeting somebody face to face in a dark hall. It was his car. Then he remembered that he was at the Sunnyside Motel. As he crept around the side of the car he stuck his head in to make sure the ignition was turned off. His key wasn't in the dashboard, wasn't in his pockets either, must have left it in his vest in the bedroom. He wasn't in any shape to drive, anyway.

Past the car it was windy out of doors. He was walking across the crackling sunlight of a cement court that had a sycamore tree in the middle of it. Overhead big handshaped leaves jigged in the wind. Scabs of bark peeling off the great straight trunk had left a green, white and pallid yellow mottling. All his insides felt like that.

At the entrance to the court a whiteboy in a blue shirt was sitting at a desk in the allglass office doing a crossword puzzle. 'Get me a cab, will you?' Tyler croaked at him in a froggy voice. The boy yawned as he reached for the phone. Tyler stood outside waiting for the cab, praying that nobody would come up to try to talk to him. The sun glaring on the cement hurt his eyes. He felt raw and skinless in the gusty wind and the driving dust.

When the taxi came he was just able to totter back and say to the boy in the office that if Miss . . . What the hell name had he given when he signed the register? . . . er Mrs. . . . er if the missus asked for him he'd gone to a business appointment. The taxi was bowling along down the wide highway lined with signs and tourist courts and restaurants. The driver was shouting over his shoulder, 'Where are we bound for, mister?' 'Take me to the bathhouse. I want a treatment,' said Tyler. 'I'm under the care of a physician.'

As he stumbled into the quiet dark reception room at the baths, a man in a white coat with a broad yellow greasy face and a mouth like a toad's strode in through the opposite door. 'Don't you worry, Mr. Spotswood,' he was saying. 'I'll git you straightened out in no time.'

'Go to it, Pelke.' Tyler let his shoulders sag. 'Got to be outa here ready for an important conference at five-fortyfive.'

'Don't you worry,' Pelke answered in a threatening tone.

First Tyler was put in a hot mineral bath. Then he was steamed in a box with only his head out and after that dowsed gasping under a cold shower. Then Pelke laid him out on a slab and gave him the works. While he was kneading Tyler's skinny arms with his big smooth hands, he began to talk. 'Took care of him yesterday . . . Him and Herb Jessup went through together . . . if there ain't a couple of wild Injuns, they had me in stitches so that I couldn't hardly do my work. That boy Herb, ain't he got a line? They talked about you real nice, Mr. Spotswood, they said you'd like to killed yourself an' they couldn't a won the campaign without you. They'd been hittin' it up down to Lunt's . . . Big men like that they've got to have relaxation. He tole me Norman Stauch owned that dump . . . That too hard, Mr. Spotswood?' Tyler grunted. 'It's circulation works the booze outa the system. You oughta seen him with that medicine ball . . . He liked to killed Big Joe in the gymn. He put on the gloves with Herb Jessup and had him blubberin' in two minutes, ain't got no stamina, but he's pretty tough, says it's choppin' wood does it. Won't be if he lets that belly git away with him. Says everythin' he eats an' drinks goes to his belly. Where else would it go? Ain't only the belly it goes to. Damn lucky for him Patsy Donahue keeps his girls clean. If one of them hookers gits sick, it's goodby to Lunt's for her. You know McGuire, the chief of police, well, he's Patsy Donahue's halfbrother, and when Patsy gives him the tipoff he runs 'em outa town . . . but it sure was a surprise to me that Norman Stauch owned the shack. I always thought Patsy an' the chief owned it between 'em. Wouldn't be surprised if Norman Stauch won it at a crap game. The stakes down here is out of sight . . . That shack's nationally known, would you believe it? I had two big shots from Chicago the other day came down special to try it out . . . What do you think of that? They said Eileen McCoy was the hottest little tramp east of Reno, Nevada . . . She's what they used to call flamin' youth. Tell me she's that uppity now she won't uncross her laigs for nobody but a U-nited States Senator . . . give you three guesses what Senator . . . An' 'tain't so long ago that if one of us fellers took her home she thought it was Christmas . . . Mr. Spotswood, what's a mandamus?'

'Nothing in the world but a court order. We had to get one out to force the Secretary of State . . . he's one of that Galbraith crowd . . . to certify Chuck's nomination.'

'It's all sewed up, ain't it? It's in the bag, ain't it? I don't want to lose that twentyfive I put up. The feller won't shell out till the nomination's certified.'

'Don't worry, Pelke,' panted Tyler. 'You'll get your money.'

'Well, after a campaign like that I don't blame you folks for hittin' it up a little, Mr. Spotswood, but if I was you I'd drink a juice of a whole lemon in a glass of hot water every mornin'. I do every mornin' of my life. Norman Stauch, you know his kidneys used to bother him until I tole him about it, greatest thing in the world to keep the blood clean. Well, I'll let you be now, Mr. Spotswood. Here's hopin' I'll be havin' you regular from now on so that you'll go away from here all healthy. I guess you'll be goin' to Washington with him like you did before, won't you?'

'I guess so,' sighed Tyler, as he stretched himself out on the cot in the stuffy little white cubicle. 'Don't forget, Pelke; five-thirty.'

'I don't forgit,' said Pelke and tucked a blanket around him.

It was white and far away in there like in a thick fog at sea. Vaguely, like the shape of a vessel becoming gradually solid and visible out of the fog, the outline of the last couple days' happenings began to form up in his mind. Of course the girl was little Francie, who ran the switchboard at the Alcazar. Francie was all right. Tyler yawned. She had to get back to her job. He was going to put her on the eleven-fortyfive train that night, thank God. Very tentatively, because his arms and legs felt so brittle, he stretched under the blanket. He yawned again cosily. There was still a painful jangled humming all through his body. His head was made of dough. He dozed off gently to sleep.

An attendant in white woke him pulling at his toe through the blanket. He sat up with a start, dashed cold water over his face at the corner washbasin and got slowly into his clothes that dangled neatly pressed from a hanger on a hook over the cot. His head was still thick from sleep, but he felt all right. He had a not disagreeable languid sensation of having been thoroughly laundered inside and out. The tiny thought of just one drink came coyly to the surface of his mind but he shoved it down again. He was through. Sue Ann needed him now. A benzedrine tablet would wake him up.

His heart was beating hard when he gave a timid rap on the door of the Crawfords' suite at the hotel. 'Come in,' she called. She was alone, walking up and down in front of the windows in the big room full of twilight, wearing a long hostess dress with tight sleeves. Her hair was every which way. First thing he thought was, she knows about that little tramp at Lunt's. He had an impulse to throw himself face down on the floor and grab her feet and tell her that he loved her.

'Well, you're on time at least,' she was saying in a bantering kind of way. 'Are you all right? Tyler, I bet your ears have been ringin' from what I've been thinkin' about you.'

She switched on an amber glass lamp on the round table in the center of the room. Her face was drawn taut and there was a look round her eyes as if she might have been crying. The long full dress was salmon color with white embroidery on it, expensivelooking and not particularly becoming. He stood staring at her with his arms hanging limp against his sides for some time before he could say anything. 'This time,' he said, 'I'm through. Naturally I don't expect anybody to believe me.' She wasn't listening. She took a step towards him with her hands halfclenched as if she wanted to wring his neck.

'Tyler, where's Homer?'

Tyler found himself stammering. 'I don't know, Sue Ann. I haven't seen anybody for two days . . . I just come from a treatment at the baths. He's probably out at Norm Stauch's. They had some papers to go over.'

Sue Ann had suddenly turned her back on him and walked out of the room. Tyler tremulously lit himself a cigarette but it tasted so terrible he crushed it right out again. The thin wisp of smoke that came out of the ashtray and curled in twisted green spirals against the amber glass of the lamp made him feel sick at his stomach. He was still tapping at the ashes with his finger to put it out when Sue Ann came back. She had put a lot of powder on her face and coiled up her hair. 'I ordered you up some buttermilk,' she was saying. 'That always used to fix up Dad when he'd been drinkin'.'

'Thank you, Sue Ann,' Tyler said humbly.

'Let's sit down at the desk an' try to use our heads,' said Sue Ann quietly. When she turned on the green-shaded reading light between the windows he could see that the desk was piled with legal papers in blue jackets. 'That's all over and done with,' she said. 'The nomination was certified this afternoon, but it cost us a whole lot more money than we expected . . . We got to make a loan somewhere quick . . . What about Mr. Evans?'

'You know Jerry, Sue Ann,' said Tyler. 'Chuck's working on a kind of a deal with Norm Stauch . . . Norm's our best bet. That's probably where he's been all this time.'

Sue Ann jumped to her feet and began to walk back and forth in front of the blue oblongs of gloaming in the windows. 'Oh you-all make me tired.' Tyler got up and stood in her path with tears in his eyes.

'Sue Ann, I'd do anything in the world for you . . . We all would . . . You know that . . .'

'My, I feel mean,' she said. 'If things go on like they've been goin' I'll be so meanlookin' I won't dare look at my face in the glass.'

[143]

She gave him a shove over towards the desk with her two hands against his shoulder. Everything turned into warm molasses inside him. To keep from throwing his arms around her he sat down at the desk again and began to read a writ of supersedeas. 'That's not the one,' she said pettishly. 'Let's act our age . . . Here's Judge Minnegerode's decision . . .' She sat down beside him and began to read in a firm courtroom voice: '"No act of qualification is required of a candidate nominated in a primary election. So when the vote has been canvassed and he has received his certificate, he is at once in possession of his quasi office in so far as anybody can be in possession of it, and entitled to its single privilege, namely the right to have his name put on the ballot in its proper place as against all the world . . ."'

There was a knock at the door. Tyler started up guiltily out of his chair. 'Come in,' called out Sue Ann, without moving. It was the waiter with the buttermilk. 'Thank you, just leave it on the table,' she said, without looking up, and went on reading . . . 'until in some proper action or proceedin' to contest his right it is decided that some other person was in fact nominated . . .'

Tyler was blushing like a boy in his teens. He didn't dare stay so close to her. He pushed back his chair and poured a glass of buttermilk out of the bottle, spilling half of it on the tray, and drank it down. As soon as he could get his voice to work he said, 'Is there anything in the last clause they could hang on to?'

'Not a thing in the world,' said Sue Ann. 'They've

been tryin' to get up some affidavits but they can't get anywhere with that. But we've got to have some money in the bank just in case. When we used to handle law-suits in the old days Homer an' me were on the receivin' end: now we're on the payin' end an' I'm tellin' you, Tyler, the cupboard is bare.'

'Gosh, I wish I hadn't thrown away every cent I'd ever had my hands on.'

Sue Ann looked at him and gave him a quick hard grin. 'Tyler, you're a sweet old thing an' I'm goin' to try to keep you . . . you know . . . like you promised. We owe you plenty all ready, an' neither one of us is goin' to forget it. Now you be a good boy an' drink up your buttermilk an' then get a car an' go out to Lunt's an' see if you can't round the boys up an' bring 'em in for dinner . . . Homer's been so kinda hotheaded recently I wouldn't wonder if he hadn't set out to try to win him that money in a poker game.'

'I wouldn't be surprised. They sure hit the high stakes out there.'

Sue Ann walked with him to the door. As he went out into the hall she stood looking after him with one hand on the knob behind her and one hand above her head against the doorjamb. He stopped in his tracks and turned back with his mouth half open to say something, but he couldn't find words. His mouth was dry. At last he heard himself lamely stammer, 'Things'll come out all right, Sue Ann.' She didn't say anything. He couldn't get himself to go. He stood there, without daring to look her in the face, feeling the pulse throbbing in his temples and his lungs breathing and his heart pumping blood. Without a word she slid back into the room and closed the door. He hurried with long steps down the corridor to the elevator.

Sitting in the back of the cab, driving out the highway past the neon lights of hot dog and root beer stands, and the floodlighted stage architecture of service stations, he tried to straighten out the thoughts that writhed confusedly in his head like a mess of angleworms in a baitbox. His heart thumped like an old onecylinder gasengine. Sure he was crazy about Sue Ann, but what was the use of all these feelings he'd had on ice so long suddenly thawing out and bothering him. Act your age, he told himself. He'd had his little party with little Francie. She was a cute kid and quite a snappy dresser, a girl you could take anywhere. All the same the thought of seeing her again to put her on the train tonight made him feel sick. Too decent a girl for him, he guessed. Well, now he was going to straighten out and attend strictly to business. He took another half tablet of benzedrine out of a little bottle in his pocket and swallowed it dry.

The car turned off the road through a grove of pines and drew up in front of a long low white building in Colonial style that had only one small blue sign reading *Lunt's* in neon script across the fancy pediment over the door. As Tyler felt in his back pocket for his wallet to pay the driver, he took a deep breath of the lemon scent of the tall pines all around and looked up at the sky that showed green beside the intense blue of the neon tubes.

The cloudless sky was darkening and already minutely perforated with stars. Bats flitted back and forth between the trees. Tyler walked in under the sign, nodded to the ceremonious old colored man who held out his gray hand for the hat that Tyler wasn't wearing, and walked into the bar. The smell of lemonpeel and bitters and whiskey and swabbed varnish almost broke him down, but he didn't order a drink. The barman wasn't the one Tyler knew but he asked him if he'd seen Senator Crawford or Mr. Stauch anywhere around. The barman shook his head blankly. Tyler frowned. 'Is Patsy in?' 'Won't be back till nine-thirty.'

Tyler turned away and started looking around on his own. A door in the back of the bar opened into a long corridor, with brightly lit whitewalled gambling rooms leading off it. Varnished chairs were arranged in neat order round green tables; racks of chips and counters and fresh decks of cards were set out; the covers had been taken off the roulette wheels; everything looked fresh and tidy, but it was too early for customers. The floor creaked underfoot under the red carpet. At the end of the corridor he poked his head into the empty washroom, that smelt of fresh disinfectant, before turning back towards the restaurant. No customers in the restaurant either, only a few blackjowled waiters hunched like a scattering of cranes in a salt marsh over a waste of empty starched tablecloths set with cutlery and bordered with napkins in the shape of bishops' hats.

Tyler went back to the old colored man at the door and started tossing up a quarter in one hand. 'Well,

George, I guess it's slack water,' he said. 'Have you seen Mr. Stauch?'

'Indeed I ain't this evenin', sir . . . They might be a few gemmen in the parlors.'

'I looked there.' Tyler tossed the quarter. Old George's eyes looked big and white as hardboiled eggs.

'I believe I knows you . . . ain't you sometimes been one of the Senator's party . . . ? Well, I wouldn't be a bit surprised if dose gemmen was all down to de bungalow. Mr. Stauch he often stays down dere.'

'Where's the bungalow?'

'I'd show you de way maself but I'm askeered of Mr. Patsy if I leaves dis here door . . . You jess go out back an' foller de lil' gravel path circlin' t'rough de trees.' Tyler placed the quarter neatly in the middle of the old man's pink palm, said, 'Thank you, George,' and started off out the back door.

The path circled all right. Tyler began to hurry. He was getting that feeling of senseless obstructions rising under his feet he often got in nightmares. The gravel was shifty under his thin soles. Tiny stones got in his shoes. It was so dark in the pinegrove that any minute he might run head on into the trunk of a tree. He was walking with an elbow raised in front of his face to ward off the blow. At last some bushes moved out of the way and let him see one yellow window streaming light, then a row of them. He heard a radio crooning a torch song, and men's voices laughing and the muffled thump of people moving around inside a frame building.

Without meaning to he glanced in the first window he

passed. It was a bedroom fitted up in gray and white with twin beds of light varnished wood. Chuck wearing pale blue striped pajamas was sitting on one of the beds with his back to the window and a tall highball in his hand. Something about the attitude of his thick shoulders and red bull neck showed he was talking to a woman. Tyler's ear caught ever so faintly the rustle of silk and the husky whisper of the woman's voice. He hurried on past until he came to a glass door that opened into a hall with buckhorn coat hooks and an oak settee piled with hats. At the top of the heap was Chuck's white stetson.

Tyler knocked, but as there was no answer he walked in. Around a corner an arch of stout knotty pine opened into a big livingroom lit from skulls of longhorn cattle with electric bulbs in them set in a row round the varnished log walls. In front of a fieldstone fireplace where a couple of small logs burned Norman Stauch stood with his legs well apart shaking a huge silver cocktail shaker. As soon as his eye lit on Tyler he opened his slit of a mouth and brayed, 'Well, if it ain't the for-for-forgotten man.'

Herb Jessup straightened himself up slowly from the panel of the radio cabinet he'd been monkeying with and took a step towards Tyler, holding out a limp hand. The other side of the room Judge Banning got up from a desk and stood peering at him over his glasses, leaning on a pile of typewritten sheets. 'Well, where the hell have you been?' voices cried in unison. A heavy hand slapped him on the back. It was Jackie Hastings drawling, 'I sent Saunders to dredge out every cathouse and blind pig in the county an' still we couldn't lay hands on you.'

'I been around,' stammered Tyler. 'Guess I kinda drew a blank.'

All their mouths opened at the same time as they roared with laughter. They all seemed to think everything was enormously funny. 'Number One was sore as a boil,' drawled Jessup with a queasy smile around his pale gills. 'Then it kinda tickled his funnybone.'

'Son,' said Judge Banning in smooth and fatherly tones, as he let his soft pearshaped body settle down behind the desk again, 'we like to left your name outa the incorporation papers, but the Senator he said he'd have to have you.'

'Anyways,' said Jackie, 'better late than never. Mr. Evans ain't here yet.'

Tyler turned away from them suddenly. Chuck was standing in the doorway with his head to one side and his fist against his chin. The height of the arch above him made him seem shorter and fatter than usual. The striped pajamas looked too large for him. His face was pale and puffy. He didn't smile. 'Tell Daddy,' he said coarsely. 'Was she pretty good?'

Tyler's voice failed. He cleared some phlegm out of his throat.

'All right, Judge,' said Chuck, without looking at Tyler or waiting to hear what he had to say. 'Now that the party of the second part or whatever goddam part it is has seen fit to turn up would you please bring him up to date on what's been done . . .' He made a gesture with his head for Tyler to follow him into the hall.

'Excuse me, gentlemen,' said Tyler, and walked slowly after him.

'Damn your hide, Toby,' Chuck whispered, drawing him back out of sight into the hall. 'I bet you ain't even been to the hotel.'

'Sure I have, I just came from there.'

'Sue Ann all right?' Chuck's bulging eyes were intent on Tyler's face. Tyler didn't know what to say. 'Kinda hot an' bothered?' asked Chuck with a confident smile. 'Well, you call her up and explain that we got business that'll hold us up till late . . . Dress it up a little. Tell her that we are havin' a meetin' with Jerry Evans and the two rankin' members of the Utilities Commission . . . I ought to know they're rankin', I put 'em there . . . on a matter that ought to be of great benefit to the people of the state.'

Tyler couldn't help smiling. 'Have a heart, Chuck,' he said. 'Sue Ann isn't a press conference.'

Chuck screwed up his mouth as if he had tasted something sour. 'Shit . . . Tell her anythin' you like. I got some unfinished business.' He jerked his thumb over his shoulder down the hall. 'Let me know when Jerry Evans comes.'

'Where's the phone?' asked Tyler gruffly.

'How the hell should I know?' Chuck opened a door at random as he went off with short quick steps down the corridor. 'Here's one in this bedroom; use that.'

Tyler closed the door behind him and sat down on the pink counterpane of the bed to talk into the phone on the nighttable. It was quite a while before he got a connection. The sweat was pouring down his face.

When he heard her voice sounding so fresh and sweet saying Hello, he found himself blurting out, 'Sue Ann, I feel like a skunk.' Her laugh rippled shrill in the receiver. 'Tyler, don't carry on so. This isn't the first time you've done a little crookin' of the elbow an' it won't be the last unless I manage to hang a blue ribbon on you. I'm aimin' to set the pair of you rootin' for the W.C.T.U. . . . I warn you right now . . . Is Homer all right?'

'What I mean is,' Tyler reiterated doggedly in a dead voice, 'that if you do things too often that make you feel like a skunk, then after a while you get to be a skunk, ever thought of that?'

'Tyler, you answer my question.'

'Chuck's in the pink,' said Tyler after a pause. 'He can't get home yet a while because he's got some business to discuss with Jerry Evans. Jerry's coming over for dinner here.'

'Money business?' asked Sue Ann.

'Uh huh,' Tyler whispered.

'I should think the Senator's suite at the hotel would be a better place than that Lunt's.'

'There's kind of a back room . . . I can't explain over the phone. He asked me to call and ask how you were and say he'd be in late.'

'You-all haven't gone to drinkin' again?'

'No, honestly, Sue Ann . . . It's going to settle what we were talking about.'

'Well, keep in touch, Tyler. I'll be worryin' my head off.'

After he had put the phone back on its holder, Tyler went on sitting where he was on the bed with the heels of his hands pressing against his temples and his sharp elbows gouging into his knees. He felt like sitting there all evening. He wished he could break down and sob like a baby. He lit a cigarette and forced himself to walk with long slow strides back into the living-room.

Judge Banning had started to talk in his creamy attorney's voice. He was sitting in a rocking chair, with a cigar that had a long ash on it held carefully in one hand. On a space cleared of magazines on the long oak table beside him typed sheets were arranged in neat stacks. 'Now if you gentlemen don't mind my refreshin' your memory on a few details of these transactions I will begin at the beginnin' by abstractin' for you the decision of the Utilities Commission in relation to the leasin' of certain subsoil rights, known as the State Park Bottoms, State leases 312, 313, 314 etc., specifically for searchin' and surveyin' an' prospectin' an' developin' by means of drillin's, etc., etc. . . . and/or the emplacement of gas or oil wells, etc., etc., and/or the construction or main-tenance of the necessary roads, railroads, pipelines, tracks or paths, etc., etc., etc., essential to the development etc., etc., of the mineral wealth of the aforesaid State Park Bottoms or sections of land adjoinin' not actually used for recreational, educational, scientific, cultural or other public purposes . . .

'Whereas it is greatly to the advantage of the people of the sovereign state of etc., etc., that they get some income from those state lands an' that they be protected from loss resultin' from leakin', tappin', seepage, etc., which might result from the development of adjacent areas in private hands, etc., etc. . . . Now whereas . . .'

'J-j-just let's tell T-T-Toby what it's all about, Judge,' Norman Stauch interrupted in a wheedling stutter. He gave his cocktail shaker a last clinking shimmy and set it down in the middle of a group of glasses with sugared rims on a hammered brass tray in front of the fireplace. 'Whew . . . I got to l-l-listening to those whereases so hard I forgot to stop shakin' . . . I like to f-f-froze my f-f-fingers.'

The Judge had put the papers down and had let his pincenez drop to the end of their black ribbon so that they dangled just over the rim of the large hemisphere of his gray vest. He looked slowly round the room, beaming at each of them. 'Well, boys, so that too much ice won't melt into Norman's cocktails, which certainly, so far as the olfactory senses are concerned, are very appealin', I'll try to put the rest of it in a nutshell. The Utilities Commission, in return for certain cash advances an' provisions for due payment of royalty, has decided to lease out certain sections of the State Parks. For the purpose of acquirin' those leases we are formin' a jointstock company known as the Struck Oil Corporation, to which sufficient funds have been subscribed for the purpose of makin' the necessary advance payment . . . to be incorporated accordin' to the laws of our native state with Mr. Norman F. Stauch as president, Mr. Tyler Spotswood as vice-president an' treasurer, an' Miss Eleanora H. Jacoby, whose faithfulness an' industry an' unfailin' tact we all so admire, as secretary. The articles of the incorporation are all made out an' signed by everybody but Mr. Spotswood.'

'Go ahead, Toby, let's have your John Henry,' growled Chuck, who had come to the doorway again and was standing with his hands on his hips looking into the room.

Tyler walked over to the oak table. The Judge's short breath wheezed in his ear as he pointed out with a short forefinger that had a squarecut carefully manicured nail the pencilled crosses at the dotted lines. Tyler shakily signed his name a number of times. Meanwhile a young colored man in a white coat had started to pass the cocktails around. 'This is what they call a green swizzle in Barbados, only I sh-sh-shake it,' said Stauch. He picked up a glass and brought it over to Tyler himself. 'You see, T-T-Toby, we want to be on the up and up in this deal,' he said soothingly. 'So that there'll be no chance for . . . c-c-criticism. That's why the Senator here wanted you for an officer instead of him.'

Chuck waved away the tray of cocktails. 'Naw, I'm drinkin' whiskey with the ladies in the other room,' he said. 'You-all know me . . . I want this thing as clean as a hound's tooth.'

Just a sip won't hurt me, Toby was thinking as he

brought the cocktail to his lips, a spot of absinthe clears the head. Delicate tendrils of the warmcool lime and absinthe tingled in his nose, climbed enticingly back of his temples. Then he remembered he might have to go to see Sue Ann later and put it down on the table untasted.

'The leases have been all made out to be turned over to Mr. Evans when he comes,' said Jessup blandly. 'All they still need is Toby's signature duly notarized to be ready for the transfer. We'll probably have to wait till mornin' to get hold of a notary.'

'I bet Patsy's a notary p-p-public and a justice of the peace too,' said Stauch, laughing. 'I'll give you f-f-five dollars if he ain't.'

'Lemme taste that stuff.' Chuck charged into the center of the room and snatched up the cocktail glass which Tyler had tucked out of sight among the piles of magazines. Then he hoisted his fat behind onto a corner of the table. 'Phew,' he said, 'tastes like a nigger whorehouse smells . . .' He drank it off and sat there swinging his legs. 'If the Judge goes on usin' all these long words I'll begin to think there's somethin' crooked in it . . . We all know that Jerry Evans is a business man an' that his Southeastern Development Company is a crackerjack concern . . . well, if Herb an' the Judge here representin' the sovereign people of this state turn the leases over to him it ain't turnin' 'em over to no flyby-night wildcatter . . . the wells'll be dug an' the state'll git its royalty. The rest of it's technicalities . . . We jess have to make sure our legal phraseology's right so that that Galbraith crowd can't sick their dawgs on us. Next thing on the program is a corporation that can buy that damn radiostation an' that can pay me for my services to the cause of the people enough to enable me to keep on servin' the people . . . Well, the profit resultin' from the transfer of the leases . . . an' why shouldn't there be a profit? . . . will be used by Struck Oil to buy stock in Every Man a Millionaire Corporation that will be all spick an' span an' aboveboard . . . I won't own a cent of it. It's up to you boys to fix it up yourselves . . . Old Norm here is throwin' that five thousand dollar note into the kitty and goin' to git stock in return . . . everybody'll have a cut in it includin' Evans. I'll be merely an employee of this corporation as I am of the sovereign people. I want you-all to git that straight. This thing's as clean as a hound's tooth.'

A girl's voice from the room at the end of the corridor called, 'Say, Chuck.' 'Comin' . . .' He rolled his eyes. 'Can't you wait even a minute?' The men sent up a roar of laughter. Chuck slapped his thigh. 'Well, the radiostation's all set so ain't it right I should pick me out a torch singer . . . Lemme know when Evans comes.' As he walked away down the corridor, Tyler sourly noticed the strutting waddle of his walk. The blue-striped pajama pants hung down baggy behind.

'Well, boys,' said Stauch. 'How about a c-c-couple hands of stud poker while we are waitin'?'

Judge Banning gathered up his papers into a pigskin briefcase and piled up the magazines at the end of the table to clear a space and they all sat down to play.

But there wasn't much life to the game. Tyler couldn't keep track of his cards. Stauch dealt from the end of the table, but he kept leaning back in his chair and talking about horses.

At last they heard the wheels of a car grind on the gravel outside. Stauch got up and went to the glass door in the hall. The others turned in their chairs and watched him. He was screwing up his eyes to look out into the darkness. Suddenly he held his hand out.

It was Jerry Evans all right, wearing a light camel's-hair overcoat, his face very red from driving in the wind. Under one arm he carried a heavy black briefcase. He was pulling off his gloves as he came in. A thickset man with goldrimmed spectacles and a bald boxshaped head followed a step behind him. 'Good evening,' Jerry was saying. 'I asked Judge Parsons to come over with me.'

Judge Banning jumped up as if a bee had stung him and hurried forward. The rest of them straggled to their feet. Judge Parsons acknowledged the introductions with a solemn nod of the head. 'Gentlemen, I'm very happy to meet you,' he said in an uncordial voice.

Jerry turned to Tyler. 'Well, Toby, where's your Number One?'

'He'll be right in,' said Tyler.

'I asked Judge Parsons to come along just to look over the papers . . . Is everything ready?' he asked curtly.

'Judge, this is indeed a pleasure,' said Judge Banning taking Judge Parsons by the arm. 'Over here, Judge, you will find all the papers in order.' He picked up the pigskin briefcase and named the documents as he brought them out, each in its blue jacket. 'First the leases Numbers 312, etc., duly signed and acknowledged by myself an' Mr. Jessup for the Utilities Commission, these bein' the two out of three members of the commission necessary to validate the lease accordin' to law, and second the assignment of the lease duly signed by the officers of the Struck Oil Corporation . . . Judge, wouldn't you like to sit down?'

Jessup with his weary smile was pushing up an easy chair. Judge Parsons was just about to settle into the chair when Chuck trotted into the room with his hair parted in the middle and combed into a curly wave over each temple. He was wearing a newly pressed double-breasted blue suit and a pink shirt with a starched wing collar and a blue bow tie. He held both hands out. 'Well, well . . . in the nick of time . . . I was jess about fixin' to turn over those leases to Standard Oil . . . An' if there ain't my old instructor an' highly respected opponent Lamar Parsons . . . Judge, I certainly do appreciate your comin' over to look at these papers . . . If nothin' else, your very presence proves that this transaction is clean as a hound's tooth.'

'Homer, I'm glad to see you,' Judge Parsons said with a glance up over his glasses and let himself sink back into the broad leather chair. 'As Jerry's attorney I thought I might better look things over a little . . . Well, Homer, when Mordecai Jones brought you into my office a gangling lad with pants too short and outrageous socks I said to myself . . . This boy will go far . . . I didn't guess how far . . . You sure have lit a brushfire under us old standpatters.'

'Lamar Parsons,' said Chuck, standing in the fireplace with his legs apart and thrusting his fists deep into the pockets of his doublebreasted jacket, 'you ain't seen nothin' yet.'

Judge Parsons didn't answer. With pursed lips he was reading through the papers in blue covers. Stauch was shaking up another cocktail. Tyler sat down at the long table again and tried to get the others interested in dealing out another hand of stud poker, but Jackie and Herb couldn't seem to keep their eyes off the black briefcase Evans still held under his arm as, with a cocktail glass in one hand, he leaned over the back of Lamar Parsons' chair. He hadn't taken off his overcoat.

The room was silent, except for Stauch's occasional thump into a piece of furniture as he went around filling up the glasses from his shaker. From the other end of the pinegrove came faintly the throb of the band up at Lunt's starting the evening off with the 'St. Louis Blues.'

'Very good . . . only one signature has not been notarized.'

'P-p-patsy's right here,' shouted Stauch. A short hairless man, who had a long horse face full of curious knobs and depressions, had tiptoed into the room so quiet on his rubber soles that no one had noticed him. He was wearing a redchecked necktie and a waspwaisted brown suit. 'Patsy, did you bring your seal?' Patsy nodded with a shamefaced smile as he drew the stamp out of his pocket the way a small boy caught shooting spitballs in class would a slingshot. 'Anybody who doesn't know Patsy Donahue has missed something,' shouted Stauch. 'Jerry, Judge Parsons, meet Patsy . . . He's the squarest crook in the country.' Patsy made a gesture as if to bring the stamp down on Stauch's head. Stauch backed off with the shaker held like a hand grenade. 'I smiled when I said it,' he whispered, laughing. Patsy's hard blue eyes went from face to face around the room. They all grinned and nodded. 'Gentlemen . . . the pleasure is mine,' he said.

Judge Parsons cleared his throat. 'Well, at home I couldn't exactly accept your notarization, Mr. Donahue, but in this state I guess your record's all right. I gather you've been doing pretty well for yourself, young man.'

'The Judge an' I have met before,' said Patsy. 'He sent me up to the State Penitentiary for five years . . . but no hard feelin's, Judge Parsons. It learned me a lesson. You were doin' your job an' I was doin' mine . . . an' besides the sentence didn't stick. The Superior Court saw to that.' There was a small bland smile on Patsy's face. He sat down coolly at the end of the table and pulled out a pair of hornrimmed glasses and placed them carefully on the mashed bridge of his nose and started to read through the papers . . . 'Mr. Spotswood, do you freely recognize this as your signature?'

'I do,' said Tyler.

Patsy carefully filled out the form in his tiny neat handwriting, stamped the document, got to his feet and handed it over to Lamar Parsons with a halfkidding bow. 'At your service, Judge Parsons . . . If you gentle-

men are plannin' to dine up at the shack let me advise
you to take the broiled live lobster. They are shipped
to me direct from Portland Maine an' I check them over
myself before they go to the kitchen. Tonight I can
especially recommend them.'

'That's a great idea, Patsy,' said Stauch. 'Better save
us a dozen an' tell the cook to put 'em on the fire.'

'Not for me, thanks, Norm,' said Jerry. 'The Judge
and I have to move along.'

'You got to eat somewhere.'

'Sorry, Mr. Stauch,' said Judge Parsons dryly. 'Can't
be done tonight . . . Now I'm taking the signed copy of
both the lease and the assignment.' He folded the
documents and pushed them into his inside pocket.
Meanwhile Jerry was trying to push the black briefcase
into Chuck's hands. 'Better count 'em,' he said.
'There's a thousand of 'em. Down payment as provided
in preliminary agreement.'

'Better turn that over to the treasurer,' said Chuck.
''Rithmetic never was my long suit.'

Tyler found himself with the black briefcase pressed
against his chest. As Evans and Judge Parsons turned
their backs to leave, Tyler, standing stiffly in the center of
the room with the briefcase held awkwardly in his arms,
felt the eyes of the others fasten on him. They were no
sooner out of the house than Chuck, who had gone along
to say goodby, called briskly from the hall. 'Come in
here, Toby . . . Let's look over that stuff . . . My, my,'
he went on as Tyler followed him down the corridor,
'broiled live lobster an' chorus girls that's what they

[162]

used to tell us millionaires' sons were raised on . . . well, it's every man a millionaire for himself.'

'That's the slogan,' said Tyler, without any expression in his voice.

'I'll git the band a-playin' it tonight,' said Chuck, rubbing his hands together.

Tyler half expected to find Eileen McCoy sprawling in her nightgown in the big bedroom at the end of the hall, but the only trace of her was a faint whiff of perfume in the cigarettesmoke that still hung over the twin beds and four cigarette butts with liprouge on them neatly ranged round the copper ashtray on the bedside table. Chuck caught him looking at them.

'I don't like to see a girl smoke, do you? I never did like it.'

Tyler shook his head. Then to do something he took a cigarette out of his case and lit it.

'Cigarettes don't set a man either . . . Coffin nails my daddy used to call 'em an' he was right . . . I'm hungry. Toby, you run along an' play . . . I'll check this stuff off quicker by myself. Where does Patsy keep his safe?'

Tyler laid the black briefcase carefully down on the bed.

'Suppose I ask Norm,' he said vaguely; it was a relief to get the briefcase out of his hands.

'Don't ask nobody . . . Git the boys movin' over towards the restaurant . . . I want to see food on that table when I git there.'

Tyler hadn't taken his hand off the knob of the bedroom door before he heard the key turn with a sharp click in the lock.

In the livingroom Stauch and the boys were knocking off another cocktail before going over to dinner. They said Judge Banning had gone back to the Springs to meet his wife. Herb Jessup came up to Tyler with a brimful cocktail glass. 'Climb on the waterwagon some other night, Toby,' he said, looking him in the face through narrowed eyes. 'This is the night we celebrate station WEMM . . . We're launchin' Number One on the national stage for fair.'

Tyler took the glass in his left hand and felt the cold slippery drink wetting his fingers. His right hand in his trousers pocket clenched into a fist. He pictured himself bringing it up right in the soft cleft of Jessup's chin between the girlish mouth and the flabby curve of the fat neck.

'I'll celebrate the first night we get Number One speaking on a national hookup,' he said and put the glass down on the table. He brushed past Jessup and took Stauch by the arm. 'For chrissake, Norm, let's get going on that lobster. Number One says he's starving.'

As he pushed Stauch towards the door he heard Jackie Hastings hawhawing that if that son of a bitch wouldn't drink it he would. With the feeling of watching somebody else Tyler saw himself turn and stalk back into the room swinging clenched fists.

'Who's a son of a bitch?' he asked, looking them each in the eyes in turn.

'Nobody's a son of a bitch,' said Jackie in a friendly

tone. 'Have a heart, Toby. It's just a manner of speakin'.'

'Nobody's tryin' to pick a fight, Toby.' The words were carefully articulated in Jessup's most greasy voice. 'We just want you to have a good time.' His fat white gills began to shake with laughter. 'We didn't know you were that touchy ... I don't believe we've ever seen the son of a bitch sober before. Have we, Jackie?' He dug his elbow into Jackie Hastings' ribs. 'Take your Uncle Herbert's advice an' go an' get hot.'

'My mistake,' said Tyler sourly and went back to Stauch who stood waiting for him in the doorway rubbing his long nose in a puzzled sort of way. Neither of them said anything as they walked up the loose gravel path through the dense night under the big pines noisy with katydids towards the yellow haze of light pouring out from every window of the long building that seethed inside with the low pulse of the band jazzing 'Loch Lomond' and the rattle of dishes and the smothered hubbub of voices. A smell of frying seeped out from the kitchen into the piney air.

The dining room was crowded. A big round table decorated with dahlias and autumn foliage was being held for them in the corner of the dancefloor. While Herb and Jackie sat down and eagerly drew up their chairs, Stauch went off for the girls. He came back riding herd to Eileen McCoy and three noisy blondes. Eileen turned out to be a tall tough darkhaired girl with very matwhite skin and a figure solid as a marble torso in an art museum under her winecolored draped velvet dress. When Tyler, who had been standing in the door-way, caught sight of them coming past the cloakroom, he suddenly remembered little Francie and dashed into a phone booth.

He put a nickel in the slot before he remembered he didn't know the number. When the operator gave him the Sunnyside Motel he found himself hemming and hawing because he still couldn't remember what name he'd registered under. At last he asked if the parties who had driven in a new light gray Pontiac coupe a couple of days ago had checked out yet. There was a long wait before the attendant came back to the phone saying that he couldn't raise anybody, but that the car was still there. She went away mad, thought Tyler with a certain relief.

After he'd hung up he went on sitting in the phone booth trying to think of other calls he ought to make, anything to keep from going back to that table before he had himself in hand. He called Long Distance and put in a party to party call to Lorna Stockton in Horton. While he waited, actual as nausea the gloom rose in him. Bitter and black it kept welling up, and spread through every nerve like spilt ink spreading on blotting paper. As he looked out through the glass doors of the phone booth at the bustle of dressy people, men in sports-clothes with cigars, frilly stoutish women with skittish hats, pretty girls in long evening dresses, young men out to have themselves a time, he felt an invisible sour smoke swirling between them and him. Just beyond the field of vision of his eyes the nightmare dark was thickening ready to pour in. It was the feeling he knew in his sleep in bad dreams just before the releasing scream. I'll go nuts, he said to himself, if I don't have a drink. Then the thought that he was on the wagon for Sue Ann began to make him feel sweetly soothingly sorry for himself.

When Lorna's voice came over the phone he was already wondering why the hell he'd called her up. She was evidently flattered and puzzled at getting the call. 'I just wanted to thank you, Cousin Lorna, for that little piece you wrote in your column.' 'Why, Cousin Tyler,' her voice answered boisterously, 'I thought you never would speak to me again . . . I just poked fun at the whole business . . . the only way I could get it past that old grouch on the Sunday desk. Anyway . . . I declare I think shootin's too good for the whole bunch of you, stirrin' up all those poor people to vote like that.' Tyler laughed. 'Lorna, your bark is worse than your bite . . . The column wasn't mean and it was real funny . . . it was picked up all over the country . . . ' 'Nobody ever will take me seriously,' she interrupted in a mock exasperated tone. 'Lorna, I was tickled . . . you know the old saying about any publicity being good publicity.' 'Tyler, you're a cynic . . . But it was sweet of you to think of calling me up.' 'Goodby, Lorna.' 'Take care of yourself, Tyler.'

He felt better and even cheerful enough to try to kid the operator a little when she called him for an overtime charge just as he was leaving the booth. As he walked into the noisy chattering jingling throbbing restaurant to take his place at the table he'd almost lost track of his feelings. The gloom still underlay everything like a forgotten toothache but somehow he was walking on the surface of it.

Broiled lobsters were all over the table. The band was playing the 'Big Apple.' Norm had ordered up champagne. Chuck was dancing with Eileen, grinning and shooting out his toes, with his big behind stuck out under his tight blue serge jacket. Herb was already sitting very close to his dinner partner and looking into her eyes. Jackie and his girl were doing some fancy gyving. Stauch and the oldest blonde, who had platinum hair almost white and crowsfeet and bitter thin lips, were talking in a reminiscent drawl about old race meets at Havre de Grace. Everybody was too busy to pay any attention to Tyler, so he sat there, avoiding the glasses, trying to eat a little bread and lobster, relieved on the whole to find that he was the extra man.

After they'd finished their meal Stauch and his girl went in to try their luck in the parlors, and Tyler went on sitting by himself at the table among plates of melting icecream, drinking black coffee and looking out over the dancefloor. Again he had the feeling of bitter gloom thickening around the edges of his eyes. Wherever he looked the sour darkness was just behind.

When the colored spotlights flashed on for the floor show amid a roll of drums from the band, Chuck came back to the table and sat down looking very pleased with himself. The other two came straggling after him. Chuck was pretty high. His cheeks were red and his eyes stuck out, large and bright, from his head. 'My torchsinger, she's fixin' it up with the band . . . Ain't she a looker, though? . . . When they are through with their show I step out an' play 'em a tune on the sweet potater an' the band strikes up "Every Man a Millionaire" an' I lead 'em.'

'Patsy's a great boy,' said Jackie. 'He told 'em to go ahead.'

'Patsy knows which side the butter is on his bread,' said Jessup.

'Sure . . . Ain't we puttin' his shack on the map for him?' shouted Jackie. He let his voice drop to a reverent whisper. 'Number One, there's one thing we didn't take up.'

'What didn't we take up? . . . Looks like we'd taken up every goddam thing in the world in the course of this day includin' that old whited hypocrite Lamar Parsons . . . wait till I tell Sue Ann that old scrooch owl turned up . . . She'll laugh till she cries.'

'Jackie means how are we going to cut the stock in the Every Man a Millionaire Corporation?' The words came from Jessup's cupid's bow lips as smooth as toothpaste squeezed out of a tube.

'Just like an apple . . . a Big Apple pie . . .' roared Chuck, laughing. 'Toby, take dictation.'

Tyler couldn't find his notebook in his pocket, so he used the back of the engraved pricecard for drinks a waiter had just set down in the middle of the table. Obediently he moistened the end of a pencil with his tongue.

'Toby, take a letter . . . First Stauch gits twice the value of his note. Then fifty-five percent goes in the name of Tyler Spotswood . . . you won't be sore, will you, Toby, ole boy, if I ask you to execute an assignment for it to Sue Ann in case you git yourself run over by a truck? We'll need that capital for national politics . . .'

'Why should I be sore? I was going to suggest it.'

'Then Judge Bannin' an' Herb take out seventeen an' a half percent each an' Jackie, because he's the youngest, gits what's left . . . Q.E.D. Anybody want to suggest any amendments?'

They were all silent. Jackie was frowning.

The two younger blonde girls were threading their way back through the tables dressed in identical ruffled pink skirts, ready for their sister act.

'Passed by viva voce vote,' shouted Chuck, and jumped to his feet. 'Now ain't that a sweetlookin' pair of gals? Pretty as a pitchur.'

'Oh, Senator, I hope you'll like the act,' sighed the plump one.

'Ain't no senator here, just poor ole Chuck Crawford off the reservation an' havin' him a time. Sister, if I hadn't gotten messed up in servin' the public I'd a most likely been a nightclub entertainer myself.'

'Senator, I bet you could be a film star right now,' said the skinny one.

'From Capitol Hill to Hollywood in three jumps.' Chuck grinned. 'But I wouldn't care for it. They don't see their audience. I like to see the people an' give 'em a time . . . take 'em out of theirselves . . . it's easy as rollin' off a log . . . All these machine politicians they just think if this organization can deliver a hundred votes . . . Old Snigglefritz in ward ten can deliver fifteen hundred . . . That ain't no way to do. It's so easy to go to the people . . . all the people . . . look in their faces, see what they want, sell 'em your ideas. These are tough times, don't you forget it. They want Moses to lead 'em into the Promised Land.'

A volley of clapping ran round the tables. Automatically Chuck looked around, grinning and nodding. Three softshoe dancers in blackface were finishing up their turn. Before anybody else at the table could laugh he doubled up himself. 'Ain't we all damn fools?' he spluttered. 'Say, Tyler, order up a bottle of whiskey. The drinks is on the Senator.'

The two blondes put on their sister act. An eccentric tumbler team followed. Chuck and the boys were drinking hard. The whiskey got low in the bottle. Eileen McCoy sang 'Night and Day' and then 'My Man' with full orchestra accompaniment, looking straight at Chuck at every refrain. Chuck laughed and bounced up and down in his chair and blew her kisses. Meanwhile the dinner customers were moving along and a different crowd was sifting into the place. There were more men in the room now. The more dressedup people had gone home. There was more noise at the tables, more shoving on the dancefloor. At the next table three lanky red-necked young men in gray business suits who might have been oilfield hands were sprawling over their chairs drinking fast and paying for each round as it came out of big wads of bills. Tyler, who with the feeling of being shut away in a glass case had been sitting in quiet misery watching the others get tight, began to notice that these three were making sarcastic remarks about each act as it came along and about the people in the room. They kept staring at Chuck and snickering out loud. Tyler didn't like the looks of things.

'Say, Chuck,' he whispered quietly when Eileen finished her encore and the lights went on again. 'Suppose we move along.'

Chuck didn't pay any attention. He was sitting there, his throat puffed up like a hoptoad's in the spring, applauding the song with loud slow handclaps. He got to his feet and walked still clapping across the dancefloor. The band executed a flourish. Chuck grabbed an ocarina from a music stand and began to toodle his solo. About half the people in the room laughed and clapped. But nobody seemed to know the song.

Tyler was watching the men at the next table. They had begun to cut up. 'Take him away . . . He stinks,' they hooted. 'Git the hook . . . We ain't payin' for amateur night . . . We want Eileen.' Other voices among the tables took up the cry. 'We want Eileen.' There were whistles and catcalls. Tyler was on his feet. Jackie slipped when he tried to jump up out of his chair, grabbed at the table and upset it with a crash. His face knotted up and white, Chuck was striding across the floor towards the three yelling men shaking the ocarina at them like a baby in a pet shaking a rattle.

It was over in a second. One of them slugged him

twice and he went down. Tyler jumped on the next one from behind and got a hold under his throat with a forearm and pulled him over backwards. As he did so, one of Patsy's bouncers kneeled expertly on his chest.

Tyler let go and scrambled to his feet. The waiters had formed a ring round the upset table. Patsy Donahue, still wearing his quiet little smile, had a grip on Jackie Hastings' right hand that held a bright revolver. The knuckles of Patsy's small hand were white. 'Let's put away that cigarette lighter,' he was saying pleasantly.

Chuck was sitting on the floor with his lip bleeding and a puffing eye and a look of infant astonishment on his face. Tyler pulled him to his feet and out the door. 'Chuck, let's get outa here,' he kept whispering in his ear.

Beyond the row of waiters people were milling about; there was a tittering screech from a woman.

Patsy Donahue followed them slowly out the door, brushing invisible dust off his sharply creased trousers. 'Ain't nothin' happened, Senator . . . Leave everythin' to Patsy . . . Here's a cab . . . Good night, gentlemen . . . If anythin' had happened I'd be the first to apologize for the sake of the good name of Lunt's . . . Good night, gentlemen.'

The cab started off purring smoothly along the dark highway. Tyler didn't look at Chuck, who sat on the seat beside him, but he could feel him shaking.

'Patsy'll handle it, Chuck,' he tried to say in a soothing tone. 'He'll keep it out of the papers. Why, they've had three killings and a suicide at Lunt's in the last five years and never a word got into the papers.'

'I'd a killed 'em,' Chuck was sobbing in a weak voice. 'Since I was elected Sue Ann won't let me tote my sandwiches.'

'Chuck, she's right,' said Tyler, trying to get a little joke into his voice and pronouncing his words carefully as if talking to a child. 'It's not dignified for a United States Senator to carry a gun.'

'All I had in my hand was that goddam sweet po-tater . . . '

Tyler didn't answer. He was staring straight in front of him at the ribbon of road glistening in the headlights ahead.

'I socked that big one. I socked him good. Feel my knuckle where it's almost outa joint.'

He pressed a clammy cold fist into Tyler's hand. Tyler moved his finger along the knuckles. He couldn't feel anything. He kept his eyes on the road ahead. His jaw stiffened so that he couldn't speak. On the seat beside him Chuck huddled shaking and sweating.

'Women's advice . . . ruined many a man . . . I'd oughta had my sandwiches,' he went on in a whining singsong. 'Jesus, you got to git busy to keep this outa the papers . . . That stinkin' lobster made me sick . . . Oh God.' Chuck began to throw up copiously between his knees onto the floor of the cab. Tyler drew away as far as he could on the seat and stared at the road ahead.

At the hotel he left Chuck slumped in the mess until he could get the nightclerk to open the service entrance in the basement. Then he gave the driver a tendollar bill and took Chuck up in the service elevator.

Sue Ann came to the door wearing a pale blue wadded dressinggown. She had forgotten to put her slippers on. Her sandy pigtails made her look very childish. 'Oh my poor sweet boy,' she said in a tiny voice as she pulled open the door. She threw one arm round Chuck's shoulders and led him still trembling with his bowed head waggling on his chest into the bedroom.

'Is there anything I can do?' Tyler called after her in a shaky voice.

'Wait a minute . . . I want to talk to you,' she called back.

Tyler walked up and down smoking cigarette after cigarette trying to decide what to do. He looked at his watch; it was two-thirtyfive. Time after time he went to the phone to make a call, but each time he stopped irresolutely.

He'd just looked at his watch again and found it was five minutes of three when Sue Ann came quietly into the room and plunked down at the desk and began to cry. Tyler hovered over her and gave her heaving shoulders one or two timid pats. She shrank away from him and ran out of the room. Right away she came back rubbing at her face with a damp washrag.

'He's sleepin' like a baby,' she said.

'Was he much hurt?'

'A black eye and a cut lip, looks like a couple of teeth might be loose. Tyler, how can you-all let things like this happen? Oh, you-all make me tired.'

'Horsing around with the band at Lunt's . . . A couple of drunks got ugly and first thing I knew we were in a scrimmage and Chuck got slugged.'

'Many people see it?'

'A whole room full . . . I've been trying to make up my mind whether to try to call up some of the newspaper boys we know to try to keep the press services from handling the story.'

'Do more harm than good,' she said through clenched teeth.

'That's what I thought . . . There was that night club singer Eileen McCoy . . . they can make quite a story of it.'

'We've laughed off worse things than that . . . this is politics after all . . . Oh, but you-all make me tired.'

Tyler had been walking up and down the end of the room smoking desperately. Suddenly he found her quiet white face looking into his out of eyes puffy from lack of sleep. She wasn't crying now. She looked right in his eyes and said quietly, 'Tyler, sometimes I don't hardly see how I can go through with it, I feel so mean.'

He didn't say anything. Her eyes opened very wide and black. 'I'm scared,' she whispered.

'Well, it's all in the day's work,' Tyler heard himself saying lamely. 'Got any amytal, Sue Ann? . . . I find it hard to sleep when I've laid off drinking.'

She shook her head and gave him a bitter resentful look he couldn't understand and went over and sat down at the desk again with her back to him. He stood in the door looking at the neat shape of her head under the hair drawn smooth over her ears by the plaits. Then he said, 'Good night, call me if you think of anything . . . I'll get a room here.' She didn't answer. He lingered a moment with his hand on the doorknob, but she didn't turn her head. Walking to the elevator his head began to ache and his knees began to weaken under him from fatigue.

Number One

WHEN *you try to find the people, in*
the end it comes down to a miner, maybe:

he lives in a row of identical unpainted houses set down
in a gash in the mountain, his landscape is slag, black tip-
ples and railroad tracks, the rainwrinkled clay of a piece of

*the dead moon imitated on the earth by the smoke of the
smelter that's killed the trees and the grass and the weeds;
in this company town nothing can live*

but rats and bedbugs and men:

*he's a whitefaced man, eyes stagily darkened with coal-
dust, no amount of scrubbing will take the grime of the coal
out of his knuckles and fingernails; but he's wearing pointed
shoes and a rayon shirt and a new brown suit too tight for his
workbroadened back; he owns a thirdhand car, the old
woman's got a washingmachine, in the front room of his
home is a highly varnished cabinet radio victrola; the kids
are in highschool headed for college:*

*sure and begod he's a union man; a drill won't work with-
out power, a man can't drill wages out of management without the power of a thousand other miners hooked up in a
union local;*

*his shift is off now, he's walking down the washedout
street to the local;*

*broadshouldered grayskinned men with hard hands dang-
ling sit in a grimy room, smoke and spit in the cuspidor,
and listen*

to the voice with the gift of gab;

*to the chesty voice that jangles loose panes in the windows,
to the platform rant that lashes the ears of the crowded delegates in the convention hall (we pay for their trainfares,
their expenses, their suppers and drinks, their fine hotel*

rooms, *they represent us, we pay for the big mouth's leonine
erudition, for his fine editions of the classics, for his boiled
shirts at banquets, his Hepplewhite and Chippendale, the
fanlight over his door; that's standing and power (that
power represents us); his sentences out of the loudspeaker lash
the air in a summer squall, dictionary words hail on the
ears, Shakespearean ironies, pulpitthumping denunciations,
the slow stinging epithet of scorn*

    direct from the convention hall in Atlantic City,

    the roar of the surf in the peroration,

    the will in the voice a bull charging blind;

    *it takes will to hook up the broad backs and the craft and
the twist of the hands of a hundred thousand miners*

    into power enough

    to drill a livelihood

    *out of the coal and the ruined mountains and the granite
exigence of profits.*

Not a Hillbilly Word

The phone rang. Tyler sat bolt upright in bed. 'Eight o'clock, good morning,' the operator intoned in a singsong voice. After he had put down the receiver he lingered for a minute yawning and stretching on the edge of the bed. He'd only slept four hours and the sockets of his eyes ached. Outside the window opposite he could see inky roofs and a corner of the hotelbuilding thrusting up sharp and stony in the sunlight against a slatecolored

haze. Through the open window came the jangled sound
of an elevated train smashbanging through the roar of
traffic that drifted up from the streets below. A riveter
somewhere was keeping up an endless rat-tat-tat-tat.
The gusty air smelt of dust and coalgas and exhausts of
trucks, with an underlying singed reek from stockyards.
The day was going to be hot. Tyler jumped to his feet
and closed the window. He had to hurry.

He had just begun to soap himself under the shower
over the bathtub when the phone rang again. Trailing
streams of water he ran back to the bed to answer.
'That you, Toby? Ed James speakin'.'

'Hello. Thanks for calling. Did you get my note?
How are you?'

'Sleepy . . . Don't they let anybody get any sleep
in this man's town?'

'Sleep,' said Tyler. 'I haven't had any sleep for a
week.'

'Say, Toby, you are goin' to Gulick's little breakfast
party, aren't you?'

'Sure, so's Number One.'

'What's the number of your room? . . . Okay. Is it
all right if I come around for a second?'

'Of course . . . I'll be dressed in five minutes.'

Tyler put back the receiver. Now he really felt driven.
The minutes seemed to be contracting right as he looked
at his old plainfaced gold watch that stared up at him
from its accustomed place between a crumpled handkerchief and a pile of small change on the night table.
Between now and eleven o'clock there just wasn't time to

get done all the things that had to be done. He finished up his shower in a hurry and started to shave. When he had shaved one side of his face he decided he'd better not wait any longer before calling up Miss Jacoby's room. Miss Jacoby's voice with its particular twang was refreshingly crisp. Of course the mimeographed copies of the speech would be ready in room 1215 at eleven o'clock sharp.

'What do you think of it, Miss Jacoby?'

'Oh, I think it's wonderful, it's so dignified. Oh, I think you did a wonderful job, Mr. Spotswood.'

'Why, Miss Jacoby, you know as well as I do that Number One wrote every word of that speech.'

Miss Jacoby gave one of her little shrieks and said, 'What time do you want it released?'

'The minute Number One starts to speak at the hearing. We are afraid to release it before because there might be a slipup on procedure. I'll see you right after this little breakfast party.'

'Oh Uncle Toby, I'm praying, honestly I'm praying for our delegation to get seated.'

She was still speaking when there was a knock on the door. Ed James walked in, looking very pink and large and sleek in a light gray suit. 'I'm sure glad to see you, Ed,' Tyler said and snatched up the shaving brush and went to work on his chin again.

He could see Ed's round face in the mirror behind his own long haggard hollowcheeked mug. He nodded from time to time as Ed talked: 'You wanted to meet Bruce Slater. Well, his room is just down the corridor from here. I called him up and said we'd drop around before the breakfast. We'll just have time for a couple words.'

'Thanks, Ed . . . Always the old rough and ready.'

Ed was pacing back and forth across the room. 'Say Toby, why in hell don't you cut loose from this stuff and go into politics or any other goddam thing on your own? You've got a lot of friends, boy.'

'Who the hell would vote for me? It's Number One the people go to the polls and vote for.'

'Where would he be without you?'

'Riding high wide and handsome.'

'You could pick yourself off a Washington job at least.'

Tyler was in the bathroom rinsing his cheeks off with cold water. He came out rubbing his face and head with a towel and looked Ed sharply in the eyes. 'How about Washington, Ed?'

'Washington's got its fingers crossed. At least the Administration has . . . that's why I think it's a good idea to get a little crack with Bruce before he sets his lamps on our old palooka here.'

'He must have heard him in the Senate.'

'Bruce don't hang around the Senate much. That's not his beat.'

Tyler was tying his necktie. 'Are you enjoying the convention, Ed?' he asked, still looking in the mirror.

'Give me the World's Series any day. They are both in the bag, but at least a ballgame is good clean fun.'

Tyler was dabbing nervously at a drop of blood on his chin with a piece of toilet paper. 'Ed, do you have days when you can't even give yourself a decent shave?'

Ed went right on: 'Toby, I meant what I said. In my line of duty I run into plenty people who think the world of you and they wonder why the hell you run with this Every Man a . . . shoot, I can't even say it . . . Chuck'll go pop like the weasel one of these days.'

'You put in some time on him yourself, don't forget that, Ed.'

'You win . . . But I'd like to see you on your own . . . Honestly, Toby, you're as bad as your kid brother, only he wore himself out to save the world for the reds . . . What ever happened to him?'

Tyler reddened. 'Let's get a move on,' he said sharply. 'I've got more goddam people to see this morning,' he added between gritted teeth. He pulled the door to behind them harder than he had intended to, so that the key shot out of the lock. He began to feel foolish leaning over groping for it on the dark carpet of the hall. A pencil dropped out of his pocket. His hand struck both the pencil and the key between Ed's neatly shined tan and white sport shoes.

Ed beamed down on him. 'Conventions are a jumpy business,' he was saying, cheerfully changing the subject. 'I ought to know . . . I take 'em all in, includin' the Prohibition Party . . . That's my job with this dope sheet . . . We tell the tremblin' business man what trends to deplore.' He led the way down the corridor with the slow walk of a man who had made his mind up to keep himself cool all day.

'Sent out any dope about Chuck?' asked Tyler in a tone he tried to keep casual.

Ed had stopped to knock on a door at the end of the hall. 'I got to wait to see if you get his delegation seated,' he whispered.

'Come in,' called a deep voice from inside. A very tall man in yellow suspenders was standing in front of the long mirror in his bathroom door tying his necktie. He gave it a last yank as he turned towards them apologetically. He had long feet encased in black shoes and long hairy hands and a long dark face with a fold of skin each side of the chin that gave him a little of the serious mournful look of a bird dog.

'Bruce, this is Tyler Spotswood.'

Bruce Slater shook hands silently.

'Weren't you tellin' me, Bruce, that you took a course or something at Columbia under Tyler's old man?'

Bruce Slater nodded his head sadly as he shambled with his long awkward gait over to the other side of the room to take his coat off the back of a chair. He put it on slowly with puckered forehead as if he found getting his long arms into the sleeves a difficult problem. When Ed reached out to straighten his collar in the back he ducked away embarrassed, stammering, 'Thanks, thanks . . . Let's sit down, gentlemen,' he added and folded his long legs into the seat of the armchair. 'I wanted to ask Mr. Spotswood something.' Abruptly he turned his mournful stare on Tyler's face. 'You don't have to answer . . . Has Senator Crawford given up drinking?'

'He hasn't had a drink in six months.'

'So I had been told . . . Very much the happy family man, I believe?' Tyler felt his face getting red. 'Mrs.

[187]

Crawford's one of the smartest little women in Washington,' he replied glibly.

'Of course ole Chuck's story is,' said Ed, 'that it's only by sugarcoatin' them with a certain amount of tomfoolery that he can get over the wholesome truths to Mr. and Mrs. John Citizen ... Isn't that about the size of it, Toby?'

Tyler nodded. 'After all somebody's got to explain the possibilities of the modern setup to the people in words of one syllable. Abe Lincoln did the same thing in his day,' he rattled on, feeling his words empty as a parrot's.

Bruce Slater gave a sort of umph. He sat there looking solemnly from one to the other, as if some unspoken secret lay heavy between them. At last Tyler broke in on the uncomfortable silence. 'I'm afraid I must hurry along ... I'll be looking forward to seeing you both at Mike Gulick's breakfast,' he said.

With some difficulty Bruce Slater unfolded his legs out of the deep seat of the armchair. 'Ah ... Lincoln,' he sighed and stood looking straight before him. As Tyler went out the door he gave him a slow wave of a long hairy hand. Looking at his watch, Tyler hurried to the elevator.

There was no answer when he knocked on the door of Chuck's reception room. He knocked again, waited a moment, his pulse throbbing with the feeling of time lost, and then walked down to the next door. After he'd knocked for some time the bedroom door opened suddenly a hand's breadth and he saw Saunders' tall dirty

face, set askew on his lean neck, frowning at him. He
had his knee back of the door to keep it from opening
further. He had his hand in the pocket of his tight pants.
Below it against his leg bulged the outline of a gun.
'Okay, Saunders,' said Tyler. 'This isn't a holdup. I
want to see Number One.' Saunders let the door swing
open and pointed down the hall with the thumb of his
free hand. 'Go in the other way. I'll send Jackie to
open up . . . I ain't lettin' nobody in this-away.'

'But hell, I've got to talk to Number One before this
breakfast . . . ' Tyler was talking to himself. The door
had already closed in his face. Cursing quietly he went
back to the reception room door and waited. After a
while Jackie Hastings opened up, his face with its turned-
up nose looking more like putty than usual. 'This is
orders,' he said in a heavy whisper blowing sour breath
in Tyler's face. 'There's somebody in this hotel tryin'
to get a shot at Number One.'

'You boys have been reading detective stories,' Tyler
said.

'No, we ain't,' said Jackie. 'Saunders can't read and
I ain't got time.'

'Sue Ann here?'

Jackie shook his head. 'The missus took a room on the
top floor, to git away from the cigarsmoke an' cursin', I
guess.'

Tyler's eyes moved around the reception room.
Newspapers were piled on the seat of every chair. In
the corners upset wastebaskets had spilled out crumpled
wads of yellow flimsy over the floor. Handbills, each

[189]

featuring a curlyheaded portrait of Number One, littered everything. In the center of the green carpet stood a cuspidor crowned with tornup papers and surrounded by cigarbutts and not a few spat-out plugs of chewing tobacco. Against the wall facing the entrance was propped a sixfoot enlargement of a photograph of Number One in the middle of a speech, mouth open, eyes rolling, curly hair tossing. Tyler looked at it for a moment. Then he turned to Jackie: 'Say, Jackie, how about getting Saunders and Crummit to clean up some of this mess? Looks like a pigpen in here.'

Jackie didn't answer. Saunders had slouched into the passageway from the bedroom and was beckoning to Toby to come on with a jerk of the head. He didn't move his lanky carcass out of the way. As he squeezed past him to get through the passage Tyler found the back of his hand brushing against the hard shape of the automatic in Saunders' pants pocket. Something started at the pit of his stomach and ran all through his body contracting every muscle in a spasm of irritation. He shoved his clenched fists deep into his trousers pockets as he walked on into the bedroom.

In the middle of the baywindow Chuck, wearing white silk pajamas with purple trimming and with red morocco slippers on his feet, sat in a high straight chair facing the light with a towel under his chin and his face covered with lather. A very small Italian barber, smiling continually out of a small cherubic oliveskinned face, was moving deferentially round the chair as he shaved him. On the bed that hadn't been made up, Herb Jessup, his head propped by two pillows, lay stretched out in a cream-colored summer suit, smoking a cigarette and blowing smokerings at the ceiling. In the middle of the floor a large elderly man in white was walking up and down and talking at the back of Chuck's head. Pressed down over a mass of silky white hair cut bowlshape below the ears the man wore a dusty black ten-gallon hat. He punctuated the end of each phrase by bringing his fist down into his open hand with a resounding whack.

'Commodore Pendleton, meet Toby Spotswood,' said Herb sleepily without moving. 'Your servant, sir,' the elderly man said and went on with what he was saying. Jackie, who was standing beside Tyler, knocked with his knuckles against his skull. 'You know . . . the Commodore of Bayou Honda,' he hissed in his ear and let himself drop in a chair at the desk and started poring over the morning papers. Tyler brought out his cigarettecase and leaned fidgeting with it against the wall waiting for the man to finish. Out of the corner of his eye he noticed Crummit stockily blocking one entrance to the room while Saunders' lanky shape sprawled across the other.

'It ain't hardly necessary for me to reiterate to your ears, Senator, the importance of the Bayou Honda region with its myriad untapped natural resources in oil and gas and timber and turpentine so strangely neglected both by private enterprise and by the federal government until we are led to the unworthy suspicion that we, who dwell in that smilin' region upon which the hand of the Creator has lavished every gift, are the victims of some dark conspiracy that don't want the competition of the Bayou

Honda region with its deepwater creeks, its marine ship channel, which, once a few triflin' bars and shallows are eliminated at very slight expense, can rival the majestic Ambrose Channel that brings the seaborne commerce of the world into the port of New York . . . It is not necessary for me to tabulate for you the incredibly short distances by rail between Bayou Honda and Chicago, Kansas City, Dallas, Los Angeles . . . It is not necessary for me to bring to the attention of your enlightened and progressive mind the fact that no dark conspiracy of Eastern interests can keep the light of truth from hurlin' itself in bright indestructible letters against the dark canopy of the sky. All I ask you, Senator Crawford, is to remember in the halls of Congress to keep the light of Bayou Honda burnin' before the nation for the initiation of that development as inevitable as the risin' of the sun tomorrow and tomorrow and tomorrow of a series of harbors inestimable in time of war, invaluable for the proper balance of commerce and trade of the mighty industrial empires of our nation in time of peace . . .'

Tyler looked at his watch. It was nine-thirtyfive. He had a sharp hungry gone feeling in the pit of his stomach. He pulled out a cigarette. The doctor had told him not to smoke. He stuck it in his mouth without lighting it.

A smell of quinine water floated through the thick air of the room. The barber had finished his work and was disentangling the towels from round Chuck's neck. Suddenly as if released by a spring Chuck jumped to his feet. 'Beat it, Tony,' he said to the barber. Then he cleared his throat noisily and spat into a cuspidor at the foot of the bed. 'Commodore,' he intoned, 'there's no man livin' more sensible to the importance of what you've been sayin' . . . I thank you . . .' He shook him warmly by the hand. 'You kin rely on me.' He yawned. 'Now you must excuse me . . . Herb, you come in here while I pour some water over this pore ole wornout carcass.'

While Herb Jessup was getting his flabby bulk off the bed, Tyler spoke up. 'Chuck, I just saw Bruce Slater.'

'What does he want? He can go slapdamn to hell.' Pulling off the upper of his pajamas Chuck trotted into the bathroom. 'I got to git my bath an' git a move on.'

Tyler followed him talking after him in a tired voice. 'We're going to have breakfast with him and Gulick. I hope you haven't forgotten. Gulick's one of those professors. He throws his weight around Washington a good deal . . . I don't know how much it means . . . Bruce Slater is something else again. He goes in the White House whenever he feels like it and they bring him his lunch on a tray.'

'He better not try to mess with me.' Chuck had stepped out of his pajama pants and was standing up in the tub of warm water. The air was steamy with lavender bath-salts. He slapped himself several times on the belly happily as a baby. 'What do you think of that, boys? Three months off the booze and I've lost my pot.' He slid down into the water and started soaping his neck. 'Go on, I'm listenin'.'

Herb had crowded after Tyler into the narrow door of the bathroom. Tyler could feel him breathing down the back of his neck. He choked down a wave of ill temper, and went on slowly. 'I figure he's about half sold. If he says the word down at the Credentials Committee we'll get seated. If he says thumbs down . . .'

'Like hell he will. He ain't heard me talk to 'em yet. He don't know what I'm goin' to say to 'em, does he, Herb? These highfalutin' liberals, they think I'm jess white trash born in the dark of the moon.' He started splashing the water over his chest and shoulders. 'If it's book learnin' they want I'll throw it into 'em . . . Who says I don't know good form?'

Tyler had kept his eyes on the bathmat. 'Well, we'd better not be late,' he said slowly. 'It's pretty near ten.' As he turned to go he glanced at the wet curly head, the thick pink neck, the rounded white back and shoulders, and the fat knees under the soapy water that had something womanish about them. In an instant's flash inside his head he saw himself pointing a gun at that wet womanish back, squeezing the trigger. 'Allright, granma,' Chuck was jeering. 'You'd oughta know by this time Number One's never late except on purpose.'

Tyler turned his back and walked into the bedroom. Herb Jessup, slouching over so that he filled up the bathroom door, was shaking with silent laughter.

The Commodore had gone leaving a stack of leaflets behind him. Tyler grabbed up a morning paper and leaned against the wall between the windows reading the account of the arrival of the delegates. The feeling in his stomach had become a sharp jagged pain. As he ran his eye down the column on an inside page without reading it, he was telling himself in a peevish sorry-for-himself voice: It isn't good for my stomach ulcer waiting for my breakfast this way.

The Reverend Chester Bigelow bustled into the room. 'Well, men,' he was saying in a deep elastic voice. 'This is the great day. We either get seated or we go home to hide our heads.' He rubbed his hands as if he enjoyed the prospect. 'In any case I have been asked to proffer a prayer.' Tyler went on reading the paper.

At last Chuck was dressed in a doublebreasted brown suit with a pale blue shirt and with two triangles of a bluebordered silk handkerchief sticking out of his breast pocket. 'Well, what are we waitin' for?' Chuck called back suddenly from the door. Tyler folded his paper and followed. Jackie had started off first down the hotel corridor with Chuck a step behind him and Saunders and Crummit on either side each a step behind Chuck again, all walking with the usual short fast steps. Tyler straggled a few steps after so that the elevator doors almost slid together in his face. When they got off at the mezzanine he led the way to one of the private dining rooms. The door was open. Chuck brushed past him and walked right in, leaving the others slouching around in the passage outside. Tyler straightened his shoulders and followed.

The room was bright and in the light reflected by the polished knives and forks and the white crisp tablecloth the men all looked fresh shaved and well washed. There was still a little whiff of toothpaste and shaving lotion about them. Professor Gulick, tall, with a long head plastered thinly with silvery hair, came forward to the door to meet Chuck. He shook hands effusively, asked a number of questions in a soothing tone with his head thrown back at an angle so that his adamsapple stuck out, and didn't listen to the answers. Back of the round table Steve Baskette stood talking in drowsy monosyllables with Bruce Slater. In a corner Ed James was beaming and giggling to himself softly like a kettle about to come to a boil. After a certain amount of shunting about Professor Gulick got everybody seated.

Tyler absentmindedly spooned a piece of too cold and too sour grapefruit into his mouth. He swallowed it with difficulty and reached into his pocket for the typewritten diet list Dr. Edgell had given him. Bland foods, he whispered to himself. He leaned back and beckoned to a waiter and ordered cream of wheat.

Chuck had pushed away his grapefruit, grabbed a cup of coffee and started to talk: 'Now everybody knows I entered politics down home as a reformer. Don't anybody kid themselves about this one point . . . if it was money I'd been aimin' for I wouldn'ta chose this way of makin' it, not by a jugful. I coulda made me an' my family a perfectly good livin' at the law an' if I'da put in some time monkeyin' around with oil leases instead of losin' my shirt on a radio station I'd be in the gravy . . . I intended something different. I set out to serve the people back home an' now I intend to serve the Democratic Party an' the people on a national scale.'

'That is . . . Chuck,' said Steve Baskette drowsily looking across the table from under his big drooping lids, 'if Galbraith and his boys don't manage to pry your delegation loose.'

Professor Gulick let out a shrill short laugh. 'It's mighty hard to pry loose a United States Senator ... from anything.' His voice broke.

Ed James was the only one that laughed. Chuck brought his fist up to his chin and stared out of the window for a moment. Then he shook loose the curly bunches of brown hair over each temple. 'That highbinder bunch don't mean a thing,' he said, pronouncing his words carefully ... 'You watch me pin Galbraith's ears back an' show him what a smart man he ain't ... But what I was tryin' to explain, gentlemen ...' Tyler could see that Chuck was talking directly at Bruce Slater ... 'is that one reason why reformers in politics lose out ... It's easy enough for 'em to tear things down; Henry George criticised the moneymad society of his day beautifully ... Marx's strictures on the industrial system of England were profoundly just ... Men with brains an' plenty of spare time kin always show us what's wrong with the system, but where they always fail is on the constructive side ... I've laid awake nights thinkin' about this thing time an' again an' I've come to the conclusion that one reason they turn out such small potaters an' few in a hill is that they bend their erudite gaze on society from the outside ... they are never on the inside where the plain or'nary run of the mill citizen is strugglin' with the day to day business of livin', doin' his fall plowin' or sellin' some product from door to door, payin' his family's doctor's bill, gettin' his children

[197]

schoolin' or maybe just scrapin' up a lil fatback an' hominy grits to keep his belly from hurtin' so bad . . . Well, by the time they've thought up all their high intellectual theories about society . . . society's a plant like a cornstalk or an oak tree. It grows an' bears fruit an' flower . . . it's changin' all the time . . . by the time they've got their theories ready out of a lot of fivedollar words all tacked together, the plant's grown into somethin' quite different. Society's got to be reformed by practical politicians who keep track of it from day to day. If you want to raise a crop of corn you go out an' hire you a good tenant farmer, you don't engage a cryptogamic botanist.'

There was something irresistibly funny about Chuck's face when he said it. Ed and Tyler started to laugh. Silent mirth knotted up Bruce Slater's long countenance.

'We agree with you there, Senator Crawford,' he blurted out and then stopped suddenly as if afraid he'd already said too much.

'Suppose we ain't lookin' to reform society?' drawled Steve Baskette. 'Maybe I just don't understand these things, but it looks to me like this convention was gathered together to nominate us a set of good honest able Democrats that'll bring home the bacon in November.'

'We've got to go further than that,' muttered Bruce Slater, looking down into his plate of scrambled eggs as if he were reading something there. Everybody waited for him to say more but no more words came.

'We've either got to reform American society or to see

it go to the dogs,' said Chuck in a loud confident voice. 'Any man who stands up before the American people an' tells them that things can still go on in the old way is either a fool or a knave . . . ' His voice filled the room.

Tyler pulled out his watch and glanced down at it held in his lap. He drank off the rest of his glass of buttermilk. 'Professor Gulick, if you'll excuse me,' he whispered across the table, 'I have to run along.' Professor Gulick got up and put an arm round his shoulder and escorted him cosily to the door. 'I particularly wanted you to come today, Mr. Spotswood, because of my affection for your brother Glenn who was an old pupil of mine . . . ' he said in a low voice under the rising boom of Chuck's speech . . . 'a most courageous and straightforward young man . . . Have you had any news of him recently?'

Tyler knitted his brows together and shook his head. 'Poor Glenn, he sure has wasted his life,' he said.

'I'm not so sure, I'm not so sure,' whispered Professor Gulick, lifting an index finger and waving it in front of him in a classroom gesture.

'Well, thank you very much . . . It was a pleasure to meet you and Mr. Slater,' Tyler said. As the door to the private dining room closed behind him he could hear Chuck's confident even voice carefully enunciating his words as he capped his period with the couplet:

> Ill fares the land to hastening ills a prey
> Where wealth accumulates and men decay.

Crummit and Saunders were standing stiffly on either

side of the door of the private dining room. Crummit gave Tyler a leering grin when he came out, but Tyler turned his face away and walked hurriedly down the hall towards the elevators.

The mezzanine in a queasy mixture of daylight and electric light was already stuffy with cigarsmoke. The halls were packed with stoutish men with goldlettered badges dangling from their lapels standing around talking in knots in low voices. Here and there as he walked through, Tyler picked out the face of one of the Galbraith crowd. They weren't letting any grass grow under their feet, not they.

Bulky men were seated round all the tables in the reading room and leaning busily over the desks in the writing room. Round the entrance of each committeeroom there was a densepacked crowd. A sound of typewriters clicking came from every open door. Bellboys and Western Union messengers threaded their way among the mumbling groups. When Tyler was standing packed tight into a bunch of men waiting for the elevator, a bluejowled young fellow in a soft felt hat slid up to him and grabbed him by the arm from behind. 'Say, Toby,' he whispered, 'what's your story about Chuck's bodyguards? . . . There are two guys standing outside the private dining room right now . . . all the boys say they are bodyguards and that Chuck won't move without 'em since that guy blacked his eye down at the Springs . . . there's a guy from New Orleans claims to know one of 'em for a notorious local gunman, Squinch Eye something . . .'

'Joe,' said Tyler turning with his quietest smile, 'I'm

glad you asked me . . . Well, you know that down through the canebreaks and out across the plains where the buffalo don't roam no more, Number One's got some pretty fanatical supporters . . . He can't help it if they turn up and follow him around from time to time, now, can he?'

'All right, Toby,' said Joe, grinning. 'I just wanted to know what your line was . . . I'll do the best I can to get you a break on it.'

'Sure, Joe, I know you're okay.' Tyler was carried by a sudden surge of men into the elevator.

Going up in the elevator he tried to run through the pages of his little black notebook, ticking off the items, but the man in front of him kept backing up against him and blocking off his view of it. At last towards the tenth floor the crowd thinned. As he stepped out at the twelfth the name of Marcellus P. Bond scrawled in the corner of a page caught his eye bringing vaguely to mind a fat retiring softfaced man who was a smalltown banker in Southern Ohio. He was still on the fence. He had to be talked to. Tyler had clean forgotten to get hold of him.

Looking up from the notebook he suddenly saw against the windows on the landing a plume of white hair that could belong to no one but Senator Johns. He walked over and stood beside him, looking out for a second between oblongs of buildings at a segment of blue lake that glistened pale and clear as an aquamarine beyond railroad tracks and a smudgy wharfbuilding. 'Goodmorning, Senator Johns,' he said smiling boyishly into the old man's face. There was a trace of blue in Senator Johns' gray eyes. 'Tyler, how are you making out?'

'Just about ridden ragged . . . You look at home in the world this morning, Senator.'

'This is my tenth or eleventh Democratic Convention, to say nothing a few Republican and Bull Moose gatherings. I ought to be used to this sort of thing by this time . . . This is a fortunate encounter for me . . . You can tell me the truth about this story that's going around about young Crawford's bodyguard and somebody trying to shoot him. Sounds like balderdash and piffle to me. Or is this his calfish idea of publicity?'

'Senator, you know that Galbraith gang's got some pretty tall liars among them . . . there isn't anything they wouldn't stoop to to keep from losing control of the party patronage . . . It's a surprise to me that they aren't circulating anything worse . . . In my opinion Chuck Crawford's friends have to be ready for anything.'

'Well, I hope what you say is true . . . That young man can have one of the greatest careers this country ever offered a man of genius, if only he'd grow up and come out of the foothills. You know what I mean . . . Instead of trying to ram all this nonsense about Every Man a Millionaire down our throats he ought to settle down to study and think . . . The United States Senate has been many a man's university.'

'Senator, you wait till you hear him present his case before the Credentials Committee.'

The Senator pulled a large gold huntingcase watch out of his pocket, clicked it open and looked down at it thoughtfully.

'Well, goodby, sir,' said Tyler. 'I've got work to do.'

He rushed off to room 1215. There seated with an air of soothing calm Miss Jacoby was quietly typing a letter at the desk. Frank Goodday, still wearing ranchers' high leather boots under the trousers of a palm beach suit, was sprawled in an armchair reading a mimeographed sheet. He looked up at Tyler with a happy grin. 'I'm stealin' a march on you-all,' he said. 'This, sir, is a very remarkable speech. What surprises me is that lil ole Chuck Crawford from Texarkola found time to get all this schoolin' and real legal ground work. There's not a hillbilly word.'

'It's a good speech,' said Tyler hurriedly. 'I hope it has the desired effect . . . Miss Jacoby, would you see if you could get Mr. M. P. Bond in his room, and then Joe Hazard of Royal Features. I'll take the handouts down to the press myself.'

With her ear to the phone Miss Jacoby turned her face up: 'Tell me honestly what you think, Mr. Spotswood. Oh I'm so nervous . . . Mr. Bond doesn't answer . . . nor does Mr. Hazard.'

'Well, I'm off.' Tyler was fumbling with a batch of the sheets as he tried to shove them into a manila envelope. Miss Jacoby took them from him with a cool smile and deftly poked them in.

'Do you want me to page Mr. Bond?'

'No, it's too late. I'll catch him going into the committee room.'

'By gum,' Frank Goodday was saying. 'Half those U-nited States Senators ain't got the brains to understand a speech like this, much less to make it.'

Leaving the door open behind him Tyler was hurrying down the corridor to the elevator again. On the mezzanine, he could feel a definite movement in the crowd towards the large committee room in the end of the wide central corridor. It was five minutes to eleven. With the nightmare feeling of being about to miss a train he had to catch, he started roaming from room to room. Now and then he gave a quick vague grin in the direction of a face he knew. At last he caught sight of a large quietlooking man he thought he recognized as Marcellus P. Bond.

The man was hurrying in the wrong direction. Tyler caught up to him just as he was turning into the men's room.

'Hello, hello,' he said.

The man turned and shook hands with him warmly as if he were a longlost brother. 'How do you do?' he said. 'How have you been? How's the wife and kiddies?'

'I've been hoping all morning we could get together and have a little talk . . . There's some dirty rumors going around this hotel I want to nail down.' The man's benign gaze was getting blanker every moment, his eyes were losing their focus.

'Well, well,' he said vaguely. 'It all brings back the good old times.'

'I bet you don't remember me . . . sometimes it's hard to fit the name to the face . . . to make the punishment fit the crime.' They stood facing each other laughing heartily. 'Mr. Bond, you remember Toby Spotswood?'

The man's eyes all at once grew small and black with suspicion.

'That may be your name but Bond isn't mine . . .'

'Aren't you Marcellus P. Bond?'

'Last time I heard it my name was MacAvoy . . . Spotswood, Spotswood . . . You're the boy that's trying to put that rattlesnake Crawford over on us . . . Well, I'll be damned.'

'You're the MacAvoy on the Galbraith delegation?'

'I sure am, brother, and I don't wish you fellows anythin' worse than bad luck.'

They both laughed. Tyler held out his hand. 'The drinks are on me this time . . . I beg your pardon, Mr. MacAvoy.' They shook hands again a little stiffly. 'Comes from not wearin' our badges,' said Mr. MacAvoy to help smooth things over. As he hurried off Tyler couldn't help calling back, 'Too bad you boys had that long trip for nothing.' Mr. MacAvoy turned with a snort and stalked into the men's room.

Tyler dragged his badge out of his pocket and pinned it onto his lapel. He had to hustle. In the room at the end of the corridor, the Credentials Committee was being called to order. It was a large room, but the fumed oak panels and the brass chandeliers of the ceiling seemed to press down on people's heads. The seats were all taken.

Just as Tyler slid in the door a bellboy handed him a note. Absentmindedly he felt in his pocket for a dime. He opened the note and read it as he worked his way along the back wall of the room to a place from which he could get a view of Chuck's face. It was Sue Ann's hurried scrawl in blue ink. The letters danced before his eyes. He held the paper away from him to read them, feeling his heart begin to clang like an enginebell in his chest: *Tyler, meet me for lunch at twelve at the Lakeside Cafeteria down the street. I want to know what's going on. Your poor old friend Sue Ann.*

Tyler hadn't felt like this since he'd been a boy in his teens. The room with its four windows curtained in red and the long oak tables and the intent faces packed into rows like peas in a pod spun dizzily around. He closed his eyes and leaned back against the wall, trying desperately hard to pay attention to the proceedings.

The question of the rival delegations had reached the floor. Lamar Parsons, speaking for the Galbraith crowd, was talking endlessly and dryly. There wasn't enough air in the room. Tyler felt that he was going to pass out. Instead of listening to what Lamar Parsons in his dusty rude lawyer's voice was saying, he was making up in his head what he was going to say to Sue Ann. He was telling her that he was through and that she was through after the way Chuck had treated her. A man or a woman had to have selfrespect. You had a right to put up with a certain amount from a friend or a husband but no more. They had come to the sticking point. They were pulling out on Chuck at the moment of his greatest success. Good luck to him. They'd both of them slaved their lives away to put him over, now to hell with him. They had their own lives to live. Sure, he knew he'd been a soak ever since he got out of the army, but he was through with that now. He was a sick man,

but he'd go to the Mayo Clinic and get fixed up. He'd
go back to business. He was barely forty. There were
all kinds of opportunities ahead of him. He wasn't a
dead bunny yet. Plenty of men started their careers
after forty. Look at the experience he'd had . . . But I
have turned over an entire new leaf . . . Sue Ann, there's
nothing in the world I want except to make you happy . . .

Lamar Parsons had finished speaking. Tyler hadn't
heard a word he'd said. One of the committeemen
mumbled something. There was a laugh along the tables
where the committee members sat. When the heads
between moved Tyler caught sight of Bruce Slater's long
jowls, solemn as an undertaker's, in the front row, and
his long tangled together legs out in front of him. Chuck
was on his feet.

Tyler began edging around the room slowly towards
the presstable as Chuck began to speak. He leaned over
Joe Hazard's shoulder, grinned at the boys he knew and
distributed the copies of the speech. Then he tiptoed
sideways towards the door. At the door he stopped a
moment to listen. Chuck was talking copybook English,
modestly and quietly: 'The problem before us today is
not one of personalities,' he was saying. 'The question
we have to decide is which of these delegations really
represents the Democratic voters of the state, an' in our
state that means all the voters . . . '

Like a tightened string on a guitar Tyler could feel the
crowd grow taut with attention. As gently as if there
were somebody asleep in there he didn't want to wake he

[207]

closed the door behind him and ran down the nearest stairway into the hotel lobby.

Above people's heads a clockface signalled him with friendly arms. It was only eleven-thirty. He had to have some air. He pushed his way through the throng in the lobby out into the street.

On the sidewalk, in the rattle and roar of traffic and the scuttle and hurry of people back and forth in front of storewindows, walking fast through the gritty wind under the colorless sunlight, he suddenly felt more like himself than he'd felt for years. He turned his face away when an unshaven man in a brokenvisored cap pushed under his nose an afternoon paper topheavy with convention headlines. With his chest out and his head thrown back he began walking fast. Today the knowledge, often painful to him, that to half of the people he brushed past on the street these headlines were only headlines and that most of the other half didn't even read the papers, made all the cobwebby strains and tensions of the morning break away from his temples. It was like having a headache suddenly leave him. The last frail strands of anxiety faded away in the wind and the sunlight.

At the bridge over the river he stopped, while trucks clanged past behind him, to look at the towboats and the tiedup excursion steamers and the barges and the gastanks and the wharves and the dark water. A husky young man in a torn undershirt, his hair bleached yellow and his shoulders blackened by the sun, passed under him headed out into the lake at the wheel of a stubby twocylinder powerboat. Tyler thought to himself that if he could change his life for that man's life he'd do it sight unseen. Why not a column of ads in the evening paper for swapping lives? He started to itemize his own: political hack, aging reformed soak with small stomach ulcer . . . but he winced. It hurt too much. Trying to think of nothing he walked on. He ought to go to some bathing beach and take a swim in the lake.

He cut down a side street and came out on the broken granite blocks of the breakwater. Everything was suddenly quiet and relaxing. The wind was offshore. There was a scattering of young men and boys sunning themselves in their trunks, an elderly man reading a book, a tanned young couple in bathingsuits huddled together leg to leg on the same warm rock. Out in the paleblue water the bobbing heads of swimmers, a red canoe, a couple of small sailboats, a towboat with a string of barges leaving a smudge along the horizon. He stood looking dreamily out over the lake until with a swoop like the drop of a fast elevator he remembered the time. He looked at his watch. It was ten past twelve.

In a crazy sweat of anxiety for fear she'd be gone he hurried back towards the main streets. Breathlessly at the corner of an avenue full of hustling cars he hailed a cruising taxi. The driver didn't see him. The next one stopped. The drawbridge was up, so that he had to sit there bolt upright on the front of the seat painfully ticking off the minutes trying to get himself used to the idea that she might be gone. He saw himself stepping out of the cab in front of the restaurant, looking through the plateglass window at other women waiting in chairs for other men, threading his way hopelessly among tables where single women sat who weren't her. Sooner than he expected the cab drew up in front of the cafeteria. His knees were weak as he stood with his back to the broad plateglass window fishing change out of his pocket. He hadn't dared look yet.

The moment he walked in the door past the cashier's desk he saw her. She seemed pale and tired. She was wearing a floppy wide green hat that hid her face and a print dress with green flowers on it. Her green gloves were not quite the same color as the dress or the hat.

'Oh, Tyler,' she said, 'weren't you mean to make me wait?'

'Sue Ann, I'm so sorry. I've been so rushed this morning.'

'Of course you were . . . Did Homer speak at the hearin'?'

'What hearing? . . . Gosh, I'd almost forgotten. I've been roaming around the lake front looking for a place to swim.'

'And me sittin' here thinkin' you'd stood me up.'

They had each gotten a tray and were moving slowly in the line of men and women along the counter where the foods were on show. Tyler couldn't see anything but baked apples and pink jello. He had lost all appetite. 'Sue Ann,' he asked dreamily, 'did you ever want to change your life for someone else's?' Sue Ann stopped in her tracks and stared in his face with wide eyes. 'Tyler, you don't think you're havin' a nervous breakdown?'

'It's a breakdown all right . . . Sure, I went to the hearing. He was just right . . . there might be a slipup of course, but it looks to me like his delegation would get seated in spite of all the moneybags behind Galbraith.'

'My, I hope so . . . I've been hopin' and prayin'.'

'So has Miss Jacoby,' said Tyler in a teasing tone. He was trying to keep the bitter peevishness out of his voice.

'Isn't she sweet?' Sue Ann said innocently.

'Sue Ann, I don't believe I give a single good goddam any more.'

She gave a dry little laugh. 'I thought I was the one that was feelin' mean . . . but let's get a move on. We are blockin' traffic. My, don't they push and shove in this town?'

'Help me pick out some bland foods . . . I don't feel hungry, but Doc says I've got to feed my ulcer.'

She gave a little shriek. 'Get some hominy grits . . . Oh, Tyler, you-all are goin' to drive me to drink one of these days.'

They balanced their loaded trays in front of the sharp suspicious eyes of the longnosed girl who made out the slips at the end of the counter. Then they walked to an empty corner of the cafeteria and sat down at a small red enamel table. Tyler sat staring out through the window at the crowds moving along the pavement outside while Sue Ann deftly took the plates of food off the trays and set their table for them. 'Tyler, be a good boy and take these ole greasy trays away from here.' He got up and took the trays back to the counter. He was trying to think how to say it. It was too soon. How would he ever say it? When he came back he let himself slump in his chair. 'Sue Ann, I'm through.'

She gave him a scared look from under her hat. 'What do you mean, Tyler?'

'I'm going to pull out of all this. First I'm going some place like the Mayo Clinic and get all fixed up.'

'But Homer needs you so bad . . . you've always been a team.'

'I'm full up.' He drew his hand across his neck. 'I can't take any more.'

'Lemme tell you, Tyler, sometimes I feel so mean I don't know what to do.' All at once she started to cry. She groped for a handkerchief in her white bag with green stars on it.

'Don't, Sue Ann. He isn't worth it . . .'

She blew her nose and smiled. 'I must be losin' my mind . . . You know I'm not the cryin' kind, but now whenever we start to talk I bawl like a baby.'

'I love it, Sue Ann.'

She looked at him sharply and shook her head. 'Of all the silly ways of eatin' lunch . . . Tyler, you're a sweet old thing, but I think you're crazy.'

He started to talk very fast without any expression in his voice: 'Maybe I am . . . Of course I am . . . I'm absolutely crazy about you, Sue Ann, and I can't go on like this . . .' She interrupted as if she were talking to one of her little boys. 'Tyler, don't be silly . . . You always said you were like Barnacle Bill the Sailor . . . love 'em and leave 'em . . . a girl in every port.'

'I thought I was, but I'm not . . . the only girl I care about in the world is right here at this table.'

'I have to think of the boys first anyway.'

'Wouldn't it be much better for them to be brought up by plain decent ordinary citizens? He hasn't a thought in the world except for himself. You know that.'

Sue Ann had slumped down in her chair. 'I don't want to talk like this . . . I wanted us to have a pleasant little lunch an' get the giggles over stories about the hearin' . . . We all used to have such fun.'

'Sue Ann, I just had to come out with it . . . I'd like never to go back . . . just to drive down to the station and take a train and be gone.'

'You aren't the only one who's thought things like that . . . Don't think I don't feel mean sometimes . . . most all the time . . .' Suddenly she sat up straight in her chair and put her two little hands on the edge of the table. 'I won't talk this way. Look, our lunch is all cold . . . Tyler, have you seen any baseball games lately?'

A band was tightening around his temples. He couldn't answer.

'Oh, this is terrible,' she said and pushed her chair back a little from the table. 'When I was a little girl I thought life was goin' to be so wonderful. I was so happy as long as Dad was alive . . . When I first married Homer he was the cutest thing . . . You oughta seen the socks he wore . . . I used to wake up at night sometimes laughin' fit to kill about how funny he was. Do you suppose people are like Jerseys? A young Jersey bull's the cutest thing, we had one once who'd play like a kitten, an' then suddenly he grows up an' tries to kill you.'

Tyler began to feel full of warm sweet sorryforhimself sadness. It was melting the tension in his temples. 'It's no use,' he said. His eyes were full of tears. 'I'm sorry . . . I had to have you know . . .' He felt dizzy and sick. He wished he'd never started to talk about how he felt. 'It doesn't matter.' He took hold of the edge of the table. Her small square hand shot across the table and gave his knuckles a timid pat. Quick as a chipmunk it had gone. 'Poor ole Tyler,' she said. She tried to grin. 'Ain't we a pair of gloomy Guses? People must think we've lost our last friend on earth.'

'I have. I know that . . . I don't know about you.'

'No, you haven't,' she said, her voice coming out loud and sharp. 'But let's talk sense . . . What I wanted to talk about was Every Man a Millionaire. I had a long sentimental tête-à-tête with ole Senator Johns . . . I just love Senator Johns. There's somethin' about him a little like Dad . . . You know, when I was a little girl an' things used to start to go wrong, I'd just go runnin' to Dad an' he'd pick me up in his big strong arms an' I'd feel he was standin' on the rock . . . The Senator isn't the man Dad was, not by a jugful, but he's got real good sense.'

Tyler couldn't seem to listen. 'Funny how much you sounded like Chuck then,' he drawled vaguely in a sulky whisper. She pulled off her hat and put it on her lap. 'I hate this hat.' She shook her head so that the end of one of her long braids came out of place and spilt a comical little wisp of hair out over one ear. Tyler's fingers itched to push it back into place. He sat staring at her feeling his eyes growing wet with tenderness like a dog's.

'Well, the Senator says it's time for Homer to fold up all that sort of thing and put it away in mothballs. He says Homer has a great national career open to him with his drive an' his brains an' his knack for gettin' out the vote, but that people around the country don't understand all this big talk about dividin' everythin' up right away like we do down home. Folks down home know Homer's speakin' kinda metaphorically ... You know what I mean ... They don't understand that up North.'

Tyler cleared his throat. 'The Galbraith crowd don't understand it either,' he said huskily. He cleared his throat again.

'That's exactly the point ... The Senator says now's the time to bury the hatchet an' bring out the peacepipe ... You know Steve Baskette spent a weekend at the White House this spring ... Steve bears watchin'.'

'I know this bodyguard story is doing Chuck a lot of harm. If only I could get to talk to him like I always used to without any of that bunch around ... They stick to him like flies.'

'Oh, my,' she said suddenly. 'It's nearly two o'clock. The convention was called to order at noon ... Hadn't you better get goin', Tyler?'

'They won't do anything but hear prayers for a while.'

'After all it wasn't me started you on this job, Tyler.' She picked up her bag and gloves and got to her feet and

[215]

flopped her hat back on her head any which way. 'I've got to go an' do some shoppin' for the boys.'

Tyler rose slowly and stiffly. 'Do you suppose I'm going to turn out to be one of those starryeyed idealists like my kid brother after all these years?'

'Homer is, underneath . . . Honest, he is.'

Tyler gathered up the two checks and followed her to the door. In a second she'd stepped into a cab and was gone and all he could remember was the sound of her voice and the tired tender look round her eyes. He tried to imagine that he'd just come, that none of it had happened yet. I must be going nuts for fair, he said to himself and set out on foot down the street.

It was only a couple of blocks, but he began to feel fagged before he reached the great stone pile of the hotel. Under the shade of the canopy over the main entrance he stopped to catch his breath. His stomach was knotted up with pain.

Several men in panama hats and white suits with badges fluttering in the wind were piling into a shiny black limousine. 'Come on, Toby, we got room.' Chuck's voice pulled him out of his daze. Tyler walked shakily over to the long shiny black car. Hands grabbed him and pulled him in. The car started before he had time to settle himself on the creamcolored upholstery of the folding seat. 'Ain't this somethin'?' shouted Chuck . . . 'Every inch of it's bulletproof . . . Jackie hired it from one of the local guineas . . . How do you think I did?'

Chuck was sprawled at full length on the back seat with a cigar tilted up out of his face and his feet stuck across

Herb Jessup's knees and propped against the window. 'Ain't I the gangster's moll?' Herb said in a falsetto voice pulling back his puffy lips to show his small yellow teeth in a grin.

Jackie Hastings was driving. Crummit and Saunders were squeezed into the seat beside him.

'Ain't this style? These gangsters they live high . . . An' Clyde Galbraith says I don't know good form . . . Well, Toby, old cock, how do you think I did?'

Tyler's mouth was dry. 'You did allright, Chuck.'

'Allright,' drawled Herb mockingly. 'It was the greatest piece of pleadin' since James G. Blaine.'

'We got 'em on the run . . . It didn't even give me a light workout . . . It was too easy."

'Of course,' said Tyler. He couldn't get the stiffness out of his face. 'We don't know for sure till the committee reports its findings.'

'Findin's, shit . . . they found . . . That pal of yours, Bruce Slater, the one looks like he's swallowed a pickle eight feet long, he came up to me an' said: Senator Crawford, that's the greatest little piece of pleadin' that's been heard in any political convention since the days of James G. Blaine.'

'Senator Johns threw his arms around him. I thought he was goin' to kiss him,' said Herb, dragging his words out.

Chuck began to laugh. 'Don't mind him . . . Herb's got a dirty mind.'

'Did you get a chance to have a talk with old Billy Johns?' Tyler started in a businesslike tone. 'He's got some ideas about things in general.'

'I ain't goin' to talk to nobody till this delegation is sat.'

'Sue Ann did.'

'Sue Ann . . . Jeez, I'd almost forgotten I was a family man.'

'We had lunch together . . . we ought to do something nice for old Billy Johns.'

Chuck roared: 'What do you think of that for service, Herb? . . . Your secretary takes your wife out to lunch while you're busy. Ain't that somethin'?' Tyler felt his face getting red. Herb and Chuck were poking each other in the ribs and laughing. 'So long as it's only to lunch, but I wouldn't want no secretary takin' my wife out to dinner in the evenin',' Herb squealed.

'Toby's safe. He's housebroken, ain't you, Toby? Cathouse broken . . .' The three men on the front seat let out a whoop. Herb was shaking with silent laughter. Saunders turned his head around on his neck and winked his off eye. 'Damn if that ain't a good 'un, Chuck.'

The car stopped with a jerk in front of the convention hall. Chuck disentangled his feet from Herb Jessup's fat lap and plunged out of the car with Saunders and Jackie close on his heels. Herb had his handkerchief out and was standing on the curb trying to brush off a print that Chuck's rubbersoled shoe had left on his white trousers.

Tyler couldn't help the look of contempt he felt coming over his face. Their eyes met for a second. Tyler felt the hair bristle on the back of his neck. He turned suddenly and walked with long strides into the crowded lobby of the hall.

Once inside he found he'd forgotten what he intended to

do there. He roamed vaguely around through the corridors among the delegates trooping back and forth. The hall was an immense cave of red, white, and blue bunting hung against bluish empty space where the seats in the galleries hadn't filled up yet, crisscrossed with spotlights picking out enormous faces on transparencies, resounding hollowly with amplified voices. After Tyler had looked around the corridors a little, he climbed up to the gallery to get a view of the auditorium. Panting he looked down into a crater of pinkish fog full of voices gushing out from everywhere except from the tiny black shape gesticulating on the platform.

There was nothing he could do till the delegation was seated. He was dead tired. The gnawing pain in his stomach kept coming back. If he could only have a drink. He started down the steep cement stairs. The thought of taking a drink put him into a sort of panic. The thing for him to do was to go home and get hold of his doctor. Funny word home. Home was a hotel room, any goddam hotel room. The last flight of stairs that led into the lobby was carpeted in red. The pain was so sharp he had to sit down. He burst out in cold sweat all over and sat there shakily hunched up on the redcarpeted stair. He felt dizzy, sick at his stomach. Men with badges looked at him curiously as they brushed past him moving up and down the stairs. The halls resounded with 'The Old Gray Mare,' played jerkily on the organ. The roar deafened him.

At last he was strong enough to walk carefully down hugging the rail and out through the lobby into the garish afternoon sunlight. He was able to stumble into a cab. Back at his room at the hotel (home is where the stomach ulcer is, he said to himself halfwittedly), he took off his clothes and got into a bathrobe and stretched out on his bed.

He turned on the radio on the nighttable. A convention voice blared out. As far as the speeches went he could hear them better here than on the floor of the hall, he told himself. God knows he didn't want to hear them. He lay on his back with his eyes closed. The pain was relaxing a little. The big rounded words rolled into his ears without making any impression. He didn't want anything in the world except just to lie there. He fell asleep.

The phone ringing woke him. Outside his window the light was tawny with evening. 'Hello, hello . . .' It was Sue Ann. He couldn't hear what she was saying. 'Just a minute, Sue Ann, please.' He turned off his radio. His head was full of confused thoughts scampering to cover.

'Why, Tyler, you were asleep.'

'I had to have a little rest . . . I'm not a well man.'

'Tyler, you get yourself a doctor, do you hear? You need a general overhaulin' . . . Isn't it wonderful?'

'What?'

'That our delegation was seated . . . you dummy . . . I met Lamar Parsons in the lobby of the hotel. He was fit to be tied.'

'Well, wasn't that a foregone conclusion, Sue Ann?'

'You didn't talk that way at lunch.'

'I guess I'm superstitious . . . I guess I make things out worse than they are.'

'Tyler, I just wanted you to know . . . I'm at the railroad station. I've got a compartment on the B. and O. train this evenin'. I'm goin' to pick up the boys in Washington an' take 'em home for the summer. I don't want 'em hangin' around the East too much. The East'll ruin 'em.'

Tyler's heart was thumping again. The cold sweat was breaking out at his temples. All he could think of to say was: 'Oh, you're wonderful, Sue Ann.'

'Now, Tyler, you listen to me.' Her voice was quite sharp the way he'd heard it in court when she was trying cases in the old days . . . 'You go out to that clinic an' get a complete rest an' overhaulin' . . . An' do what the doctors tell you . . . I'll be down home this summer . . . See you-all in the fall.'

'But, Sue Ann . . . couldn't I see you . . . once more?' he started to stammer. He was talking to himself. She had already cut off.

Number One

CHAPTER

V

W<small>HEN</small> *you try to find the people,*
always in the end it comes down to somebody: to a man in
a business suit driving to the office in a closedup coupe, his
briefcase on the seat beside him, the dashboard radio hur-
riedly whispering news, breakfastfoods, custommade clothes,
credit, busy hillbillies, blues moaning low;

his briefcase is full of typewritten reports, multigraphed directives;

his head, while the taste of the breakfast bacon lingers still on his tongue, while his eyes are attentive to weave through car-jammed streets, and his fingers nimbly shift gears at the traffic lights, and the ball of his foot coddles the throttle, is already intent on the office:

his desk, the wire basket piled high with correspondence, the brown and blue folders, the interoffice communications, the telephones, the dictaphone linking the voice of the man higher up at the end of the hall to the ears and the voice that says yes;

on the fluffyhaired stenographer who'll take his letters, on the smoothhaired secretary who delves in the files, on the cardcatalogues that fill the end of the room where past policies are stored, where names are listed alphabetically, reports, diagrams, statistics, directives for future action:

keyboard of a myriad combinations

where at his desk he can play (off notes okayed by the man higher up),

distant instruments in the field;

the office is names in alphabetical order, figures, graphs, voices on the telephone, letters pounded on typewriters, the man with the appointment taking off his overcoat and sitting in the chair to the right of the desk, the offered cigarette, the refused cigar, the interview cunningly broken off just at the right time, the pad of engagements, the talk over lunch, the conference with the heads of departments to hear a report, to study trends pictured on a map on the wall, to see a reel of a film, maybe to discuss a directive;

every day in the changeless climate of an airconditioned millionwindowed Olympus they press the buttons, adjust the typewritten levers: in the field the instruments respond but the climate is changeable: it rains, it hails, it's muddy, subject to sudden frosts and heats, people get chickenpox, divorce their wives, fall downstairs, chance on bonanzas, hang their cars up on hydrants;

events occur; they filter back through agents, telegrams, phone calls, letters, are muffled in the millions of words of reports;

systole and diastole,

the arterial blood flows back through the veins; the directive returns as reports;

but the man with the briefcase sees smells hears feels only the morning streets driving down to the office, the evening streets driving home, the vestibule where men button up raincoats, the jampacked elevator, the corridor where the steps of latecomers resound so loud, the empty sky that stares through the shined office windows, and

a rose perhaps in a thinstemmed glass

which his secretary has placed on his desk.

The State Park
Bottoms

The plane purred quietly northward through the night. Muffled from the world by the even roar of motors at eight thousand feet the neat cabin gave Tyler the feeling of a hospital ward after the patients have been put to bed. The hostess just like a nightnurse sat under a shaded light in the rear quietly intent on a magazine open across her knees. One by one the other passengers had turned off their readinglamps and gone to sleep. The big man just behind Tyler was snoring regularly and smoothly. Tyler had been lying back in his seat with his eyes closed, now and then drifting into a glary halfsleep ... The chair was an invalid chair. In a hospital being treated for fraudulent delirium. Strapped in a chair in a narrow operating theatre with gray walls. Newsprint unrolling column after column on a screen in front of him. Squinted up his eyes to read it, but it was too small, too sharp. Can't dope it out, could hear his voice saying to himself. Roaring the letters began to swell and bloat, shapes under a microscope, until they'd grown into unrecognizable scared blockhigh headlines and a hard lawyer's voice read out: Defendant did maliciously and intentionally and conspicuously and deliriously and with malice and fore-thought ... No, please not. They had him in the hospital because he had d.t.'s. He was in a straitjacket. It was a nightmare. He woke up with a jolt.

Moistening his pasty lips with his tongue he looked from side to side in the dimlit cabin. The regular roar of the motors was cosy in his ears. The cabin was too hot. His shoes felt tight on his feet and pressed painfully on the corns on his toes. His eyelids were gritty from so many sleepless nights. His drawers had pulled up round his thighs and were cutting into his flesh.

He halfrose to his feet to hitch up his trousers and shake down his drawers, and tucked his bagging shirt in under his belt. When he settled into the springy seat again he switched on the readinglight in the trembling curved metal flank of the plane beside him. No use trying to sleep. He took his glasses out of his breastpocket and adjusted them on his nose. Then he reached down to pull the backrest up straight and yanked his heavy briefcase up onto his knees. No use letting himself go to pieces. He might as well use the time to sort out these damned papers. He hauled out of the briefcase onto his lap a wad of typewritten material, some bluejacketed legal documents tangled in columns of print clipped out of newspapers, carboncopies of letters fastened together with clips and a yellow pad scrawled over with notes. Might as well pull himself together.

First he started straightening out the clippings and fastening them one on top of the other in chronological order. He couldn't help reading snatches here and there. His teeth grated together a little as headlines, chance phrases, fragments of paragraphs fell under his eye:

CRAWFORD'S SECRETARY TAKES STAND ... Prosecution rests in Income Tax Case ... Affairs of Struck Oil Corporation Ventilated at Last ... POLITICS, CHARGES 'CHUCK' ... 'NUMBER ONE' CLAIMS ADMINISTRATION HITTING BELOW THE BELT ... STATE PARK BOTTOMS SCANDAL LOOMS ... it is impossible for an impartial commentator not to see the fine Italian hand of the Administration in the tempest that has been unloosed upon the heads of Senator 'Chuck' Crawford and his close-linked organization in his home state since his open break with the White House some months ago ... That his one man filibuster which so neatly upset one of the majority's most cherished applecarts has so angered Administration stalwarts that they are willing to go the limit ... is an inescapable conclusion ... On the other hand it is very doubtful if the investigation will ever get very far in his home state . . . where he has organized a machine that makes Tammany Hall in its palmy days look like a sewing circle . . . in the clearings and the foothills and, we may add, in cotton brokers' offices and among some wealthy independents in the oil business . . . the redoubtable 'Chuck' is alleged to have swarms of fanatical adherents . . . who against all common sense . . . really believe in the Every Man a Millionaire program.

CRAWFORD'S THUGS CAUSE REIGN OF TERROR . . . allegations of the chairman of the Good Government League interviewed today in a downtown hotel . . . STATE PARK BOTTOMS REEK TO HIGH HEAVEN says reform candidate . . .

'That's a hot one,' said Tyler halfaloud, and found himself almost chuckling as if he weren't involved in this business himself.

His mind turned suddenly back to the way, when he was in hot water as a kid, he used to makebelieve that he wasn't really the Tyler who lived in a yellowbrick walkup apartmenthouse off a stagnant treechoked street, with a preachy bookish father who was always broke and a sweet mother with trailing sleeves and a goodygoody kid brother who was a hopeless sap; but another Tyler of the wealthy branch of the family. Lulled by the regular throb of the motors and the low hiss of the warmed thin air of the high altitude that came in through the little socket of the ventilator over his head, his thoughts drifted off into a hazy region of schoolboy memories.

It was wonderfully cosy and serene up here in the plane. He caught himself wishing childishly he were headed for the Coast instead of . . . or to come down unexpectedly in a forgotten valley like in the movies . . . God, he was sick of this life.

CHUCK CRAWFORD LAMBASTES DEMAGOGUES IN HIGH OFFICE

In what his supporters claim to be the most successful rally ever held by the Every Man a Millionaire forces outside of their home state, 'Chuck' Crawford, 'Number One' as they call him around the organization headquarters, flayed the Administration for letting loose on him what he stigmatized in picturesque language as the bloodhounds of the Treasury. 'Let 'em take somebody their size,' roared Chuck, scoring the belated interest of revenue sleuths in the income tax returns of several of the higherups in his smooth rolling machine, as he concluded his speech amid the vociferous applause of his motley adherents who packed the hall to suffocation and milled about the adjoining streets, giving the rally something of the earmarks of an oldfashioned campmeeting.

'Damn tootin' that was a good rally,' said Tyler to himself, remembering the amens and the singing and the big sale of the mimeographed sheet, *The Broadcaster*, that advertised the radiostation. 'Damn tootin' that was a good rally.' He couldn't help wincing when he read the next one:

. . . it is impossible to read through the testimony of Senator 'Chuck' Crawford's confidential secretary and Man Friday, Tyler Spotswood, without realizing that, though the redoubtable 'Number One' himself seems to have come out unscathed, there is something rotten in the state of Denmark. Even if 'Number One' has managed to exonerate himself, the suspicion still remains that,

[230]

though no newspaper in his home state has dared print the facts, many of the 'Number Two' and 'Number Three' men of his organization have been filling their pockets at the public till . . .

'God damn the soul of the man who wrote that.' Tyler sat bolt upright in his seat while the papers cascaded off his knees. 'You damned idiot, you've been in this game long enough to have a thicker skin,' he told himself. Oh hell, what was the use of reading 'em over. He'd read 'em all before. The beagles were in full cry. Didn't matter a tinker's damn so long as everybody kept together and kept their mouths buttoned up. 'We'll git tarred up high wide an' handsome'; Tyler had still in his ears Chuck's confident voice the day before the trial of Horton had been adjourned . . . 'A little mud don't do nobody no harm.' Tyler started collecting the clippings off the floor around his feet. One had stuck in the cuff of his trousers. He started to read it without intending to:

Whether it was the result of accident or intention, the fact that the searchlight of the Federal Grand Jury investigating the sources of the funds of certain inflammatory radio stations has been turned on 'Chuck' Crawford's notorious WEMM could not be more opportune . . . It coincides with some very interesting testimony by several of his closest lieutenants given in defending themselves against the prying eyes of the revenue sleuths investigating their income tax returns. The inference is that the funds that have paid for these nightly broadcasts in which the ineffable Senator and his loudmouthed coadjutor the Reverend Chester Bigelow have lambasted the Administration . . . have been mulcted from the public . . .

Somebody had underscored the last phrase and written 'libelous,' followed by a question mark in red pencil in the margin. Libelous. The word was soothing. Sure it was libelous. With his lap and his hands full of papers he let his head drop back on the little pillow.... 'We'll git tarred up high wide and handsome,' Chuck's voice was roaring joyfully in his ears. 'A little libelous question mark don't do nobody no harm, now do it . . . question mark.' He was driving the soundtruck down a straight street packed with faces, delegations of faces, and bands were playing 'Every Man a Millionaire' and Chuck was shouting into the mike, 'High wise and handy is the watchword of the plain people . . . The development of the State Park Bottoms flows right into the pockets of the plain people. We'll all git tarred up with every man a millionaire, folks . . . We'll git tarred up with oil. We'll git tarred up with money.' The truck was a mardi gras float. This isn't a nightmare, a friendly voice was saying inside Tyler's skull. This is a funny deliriums tremum. This dream's a funny dream. They were all wearing silk hats and cutaways and striped trousers. The delegations of plain people all wore silk hats and cutaways over their overalls. Chuck had been nominated president. 'Tyler Spotswood, I indict you Secretary of State,' he roared down from his golden throne on top of the float. People threw streamers, red, white, and blue confetti. The confetti was jamming the gears. Tyler kept trying to step on the gas, but the motor was missing. This isn't a nightmare, this is a funny dream, he kept calling out to pretty blonde girls dressed as drummajors that lined the curbs with their bare legs. Yow, they shouted. Bump, bump, bump. He was getting a flat tire. He woke up.

The motors sounded different. The bundle of clippings had dropped to the floor. Listening carefully to the motors, he tried to make out whether the plane were climbing or losing altitude. He was collecting the clippings into a manila envelope. He put the envelope back into his briefcase, thinking, 'Let Miss Jacoby worry about these,' and began to look through his letters. On top of the packet was a letter in Sue Ann's blue ink and scrawly handwriting. He'd read it before that same night. It was on pale blue notepaper with Bar-Z Ranch engraved in large white script across the top. He started to read it again with stinging eyes. He couldn't help his breath catching in his throat as he read:

Dear Tyler

Homer spent the weekend here and we talked about this little mess. Poor old Tyler. It made us feel real bad talking about it although the weather was delicious and we had a high time all the while he was here. We went deerhunting and Andy shot a buck. At least he pulled the trigger while his daddy held the gun. Ted Wheatley shot right after and shot him right through the head which was just as well because Andy's bullet just grazed his back. Still it's pretty good for a twelveyearold. We all wished you could have come. The boys are all the time asking for Uncle Toby. You can't imagine how they've grown and how this life agrees with them. I don't see how I ever lived without the Ranch. You remember how mean I used to feel all the time? Well, out here I feel like a schoolgirl. I wouldn't care if I never saw Washington and those awful social functions again. Of course Homer can't think of anything but his career and his work.

I'll never forget what you said about bringing up the boys as plain ordinary citizens, but honestly, Tyler, the Ranch is wonderful for them. They ride like regular cowpunchers already . . . Poor Homer, he says he's a natural hillbilly and can't abide horses. You ought to see how cute the boys look on their ponies.

One thing that made me real happy was that Chuck told me your health was better. I do hope you'll take good care of yourself and not do anything foolish. You know what I mean.

Now, Tyler, don't you worry. This smear game is all just politics and don't forget that you have one of the smartest politicians in the world and a mighty good lawyer behind you. Homer says all we need do is take it easy and ride out the storm.

The pain went through him like sweet on a hollow tooth. 'Oh hell, I'd like a drink right now.' His lips formed the words as he pressed his head back into the pillow again. God, he was pooped. As he tried to will himself back to sleep, a cloud of thoughts of what might have been rose and settled stinging like mosquitoes in his head.

Again his ears caught an uneven thump in the sound of the motors. Suppose it was engine trouble. Suppose they crashed. No more threat of indictments. No more hearings. No more lawyers' exceptions. He tried carefully and meticulously to imagine absolute blackness, like passing out but deeper, darker, forever. This bundle of querulous nervetissue blown out like a match into blackness inevitable and always. He shook his head. He didn't want to die yet. He opened his eyes.

In the groundglass slot above the door in front of him the 'NO SMOKING . . . ADJUST SAFETY BELTS' sign had flashed on. Suddenly feeling quite cheerful he cupped his eyes with his hands against the window to see if he could look out. Three frail strings of light swept in tremulous diagonals across the darkness of his field of vision; streetlights; then he caught sight of the reassuring glare flooding the runways of an airport blurred in the mist. He let out his breath. A chance to walk around. Stretching his legs a little might make him feel better. As he got his papers together to put them back in the briefcase he caught sight of that postal card that had been forwarded from Washington and that had puzzled him so. Written across it in a small neat hand was:

Dear Sir,
For several months I have been most anxious to contact you in connection with a communication from a near relative. At last through the newspapers I am in possession of your esteemed address. Please call me before ten A.M. at Cap 9799. Later I am not in. Accept the sincere consideration of
BENJAMIN BATTISTA, JR.

The plane had landed so smoothly Tyler couldn't tell when the wheels had touched the ground. The cabin shook a little as they taxied in across the grass. The attendant opened the door the moment the plane came to a dead stop. A rush of raw night air poured in.

Tyler shivered as he sat staring at the writing on the postcard. Could it be some detective's bright idea, or some nut who wanted only a few dollars to get him a fortune out of the French Spoliation Claims? If it was a

Treasury dick he'd better see him, maybe he'd be able to smell out what the guy was up to. Tyler shoved the card back in with the rest of his papers, took the precaution of locking the briefcase with the little key that hung on his watchchain, and climbed stumbling a little out of the cabin. The raw air cut his wind. Shivering so that his teeth chattered he ran with yanked up coatcollar across the wet cement to the waitingroom. The faces of the other passengers had a bleary look as they stood around, men and women staring sleepily at each other out of their furs and buttonedup overcoats. There was nobody he knew. Their faces had a ghastly haunted look under the reddish halo the mist had given the unshaded light.

When he came out of the toilet he got himself a paper cup of water from the cooler. He'd found in the upper pocket of his vest two of the sedative tablets that doctor at the clinic had given him to take when he felt a craving for a drink. He put them in his mouth and swallowed them. He had to get some sleep. The tablets gave him confidence. As soon as he'd climbed back on the plane he fluffed up his pillow carefully and settled comfortably into his seat. As the vibration from the climb smoothed out and the plane settled into the easy roar of its northward course again, he found himself drifting amid humming fragments of halfremembered phrases out of the lawyers' briefs, demurrer, plea in abatement, bill of exceptions, helplessly off to sleep.

'Washington, sir, Washington,' an attendant was shaking him by the shoulder. He opened his heavy eyes.

Faint indigo light was filtering through the cabin window beside him. 'Washington, sir,' shouted the attendant. 'Of course. Thank you,' Tyler said in a thick voice. He got shakily to his feet, grabbed his hat and briefcase and stumbled out into the cold gloaming of a drizzly sleety dawn.

The lights of the airport were blurred in his eyes. The man in the big coat was Chuck. 'No overcoat . . . you'll catch your death of cold.' Chuck's voice rasped harshly. 'Say, Toby, you're sober, ain't you? . . . We need to have our dukes up this day, if it's the last thing we do on this earth.' Tyler was staring dazedly into Chuck's round gray face that blobbed out of the fur collar of the big overcoat, as full of little wrinkles as a stale apple. His large eyes bulged anxiously into Tyler's out of rings of bruisedlooking violet flesh. Tyler's teeth started to chatter. 'I'm all right,' he stammered. 'A cup of coffee'll wake me up.'

'My God, Toby, you're lookin' awful. Here's the car an' the . . .'

A white light flashed in Tyler's eyes. He blinked and drowsily brought his hand up in front of his face.

'Git 'em,' Chuck's voice ripped out. 'Git those men, Crummit . . . Saunders, smash that camera.'

A group of raincoats had rushed out at them from behind the airport building. Flashlight bulbs bloomed against the rainy sky above white faces forming words.

'Use your knee, you sonofabitch . . . Come on. We're gittin' outa here.' Before Tyler could see what was happening he was shoved, with Chuck's grip tight on the muscle of his arm, into a long towncar that moved off smoothly with old Sam in uniform at the wheel, and they were speeding across the empty bridge above the shimmer of the old Potomac towards the city. Tyler hardly knew whether he'd really seen Saunders' long arms flailing above a struggling pile of men on the wet pavement or had heard the thud of slugging blows and the light brittle smash of metal and glass on cement.

'Toby, we're in a fight.' Chuck spat the words out through panting breaths into his ear. 'Ain't no time for lilypads . . . That there tinhorn lawyer who's investigatin' radio stations before the Grand Jury, he's out for blood . . . I ain't fixin' to have my pichur taken with no jailbird . . .' He let loose a kind of grim cackle and leaned forward to speak to old Sam. 'Sam, why are you pokin' along like we was mourners at a funeral? You drive, boy . . . You ought to know where the Senate Office Building is by this time . . . Been there every day for the last three years.'

Tyler shook his head to get the dense numb cottonwool feeling out of it. 'Chuck, you came out of the business down in Horton all right . . . It's Norm Stauch and me got the dirty end of the stick down there.'

'If you-all do what I tell you you'll be all right everywhere, every goddam one of you. I ain't never let nobody go to jail yet . . . This here lil chinchbug from the Middle West, this here Mackenzie Turner, a little ignoramus who wants to be Attorney General, he's agoin' to put you on the stand this mornin' an' you're agoin' to sweat . . . Watch out for one thing . . . Like as not he's got a transcript of your testimony down in Horton. Him an' Steve Baskette, that ole snappin' turtle, they've had their heads together, both of 'em plannin' to be nabobs of the reignin' empire of St. Vitus' dance. My organization kin buck the gang of 'em, but damn they jumped me before I was ready . . .'

Tyler was looking out at the topheavy manycolumned façades, reduplicated as if in a mirror, late additions still gleaming vaguely through scaffolding, along the edge of Constitution Avenue. The glisten of the wet asphalt on the wide empty streets gave him the feeling the car was a boat skimming across dark ponds and broad canals. He found himself remembering the ominous dark red the bricks used to have on the building of the old Friends' School rainy days and the clopclop of the big white horses of brewery trucks over wet woodblock pavements. Everything he saw brought up recollections. He couldn't seem to bring himself up to date.

'Now, Mister Chuck, you caint say I didn't git you here quick,' said old Sam in a voice like thick chocolate, turning his black face back into the car and showing all his teeth in an indulgent smile as he slowed the car gently to a stop at the inside entrance of the great palegray office building.

'Sam, it was masterly,' said Tyler with a vague tinny giggle. 'The old hand hasn't lost its cunning.'

Sam began to grumble: 'This time o' mornin' I ought be in bed or in church, Mister Toby.'

Chuck had shot out of the car without a word. Tyler had to run to keep up with him as he crossed the vestibule, skirting a pool of soapy water where two colored men were washing the marble pavements with mops and buckets. They had to ring several times for the elevator. Chuck kept up a low whine of cursing while they waited. 'Excuse it, gentlemen,' said the elderly night watchman, touching his visored cap as the bronze doors finally slid open. 'Good mornin', Senator. Up early this mornin'.' Chuck scowled at him as if he were going to haul off and hit him. To smooth over, Tyler rattled off in a chatty tone that sounded silly in his ears, 'Early? I haven't been to bed myself. For me it's late.'

Chuck hurried on ahead down the corridor and opened the receptionroom door with his own key. Tyler strode after him through the little vestibule into the great office with its big polished desk and its red morocco furniture, with brasstacked bindings and its familiar smell of papers and furniturepolish and stale cigarsmoke. The row of big windows along the wall let in a skyful of steely morning light. Chuck dropped his furlined coat on a chair. His black felt hat dropped off his head as he stretched out on his back on the couch across from the desk. 'Damned if I been up so early sence I been in Washington,' he gasped. 'Toby, you're causin' me a whole lot of trouble . . . ' 'Me?' started Tyler. Chuck interrupted: 'For crissake call up that guard downstairs an' see if the boys is come in yet.'

Tyler walked sullenly over to the telephone on the desk. When he put the receiver down he looked at Chuck and shook his head. 'Don't you make mean eyes at me, you sonofabitch,' said Chuck. He took his eyes off Tyler's face and stared at the ceiling. ' . . . There's nothin' in my career, sence I was a little shaver totin' those tiedup newspapers too heavy for me down State Line Avenue . . . there's nothin' in my career that can't bear the scrutiny of the most holierthanthouest sugarsuckin' reformer in this whole mess of crackpots an' visionaries they've got a-cloggin' up the wheels of gover'ment in this town with all this Jew peddler's ragbag of theories and pretenses' . . . Chuck lay on his back talking in a singsong voice. 'I'm goin' to say that tonight,' he said in a matter-of-fact tone. Then he looked sharply at Tyler. 'But no man's reputation is better than the company he keeps.'

'Hold your horses, Chuck.' Tyler was trying to get a smile out of him. 'I thought we were the crackpots.'

Chuck didn't answer. Tyler started walking up and down in front of the windows. Across broad stretches of wet asphalt shining in the morning light he could see beyond russet trees the square bulk of the Senate wing with the dome of the Capitol rising against the tinsellined clouds behind it. A flight of starlings was blackly circling the cluster of columns that held up the small topmost dome. His mind still kept skidding off into odd backtracks. He was remembering the peculiar awe he'd felt as a small boy seeing the Capitol dome rise high and rosy into the evening sky at the end of a long tree-bordered avenue while he was trotting along with a stitch in his side keeping up with his grandfather's fast limping walk, when the old man used to take him out to lecture him on the historic sites of the city. He shook his head to get the fog out of it. But his mind would go slipping off the track like the needle on a wornout phonograph record. To be saying something he muttered vaguely: 'This thing's got me worried.'

'You better be,' Chuck roared scornfully from the couch. 'They've got you hoppin' on the griddle, boy . . . I don't know if I kin git you off or not.'

The phone rang. Automatically Tyler went over to answer it. 'Yes, send 'em right up . . . It's the watchman asking if it's all right for Crummit and Saunders to come up . . . He must be a rookie.'

'Thank the Lord . . . If they mixed it up with the cops I'll can the sonso'bitches.'

There was a stamping of feet in the vestibule. Looking pleased with themselves Crummit and Saunders came shambling in. 'Well, we're back,' they were shouting. 'I was jess sayin',' Chuck went on without lifting his head, 'that if you two punks had messed with the po-lice I'd let you go back where you came from.'

'No, sir,' said Saunders, who was patting at a cut on his lip with a handkerchief gray with dirt and covered with little spatters of blood. 'Number One, we didn't mess with no po-lice. A patrol car did give us a little chase, but we lost 'em back of the railroad station in Alexandria.'

'They got our number all right,' Crummit piped up; 'but it won't do 'em no good 'cause I had my extry plates.'

'We come back in a taxicab . . . Did you see me paste that cameraman, Number One? He won't take no pichurs for some time, no, sir, he won't . . . I had a little bit of sompin' under my glove.' His long calf face glowing with workmanlike pride, he brought a set of brass knuckles out of his pocket.

'You git them things out of this office,' shouted Chuck, half sitting up. 'I didn't tell you to kill the pore fellers.'

'No harm in makin' sure they don't take no pichurs.'

'That boy was tough,' said Crummit. 'I had to close in an' give him my lil ole rabbit punch . . . did you see him fold up, Number One?'

'Now one of you grunt and groan artists git the hell outa here an' go to a lunchroom an' git us some breakfast . . . Be sure the coffee's scaldin' . . . Too early to git it here, ain't it, Toby?'

Tyler nodded. 'Better send out for it, Number One.'

'These here solemn Solons in Congress assembled, they don't see the light o' day till ten o'clock in the mornin' . . . Lemme tell you boys somethin' . . . When you see a man in this world git up early every mornin', that's the man's a-goin' to git what he's after . . . Allright, what are you standin' around for? Crummit, you go git the breakfast. Let Saunders wash his face . . . I declare,' he said to Tyler when they'd left, sitting up in the middle of the couch looking down at the red silk clock on his blue sock as he waggled one foot in an ornate tan oxford over the edge '. . . the way you boys all depend on me it's a wonder I don't have to take down your pants an' set you on the potty.'

He lay back again laughing and stretching out his arms over his head. 'Chester Bigelow's comin' in a minute an' then the Judge, an' if you-all stop runnin' around like a chicken with its head cut off, we'll decide how we're goin' to handle this thing . . . I'll git tarred up some, like I said down home . . . we'll all git tarred up some . . . but they can't do me no harm . . . I got the people behind me, don't forgit that.'

'Won't do you any good if they break up the organization . . . I don't need to tell you that, Chuck.'

'You don't need to tell me nuthin'.'

'I'll go an' see what I've got on my desk . . . Call me when you want me,' said Tyler huffily.

He went through the communicating door into his own office and sat down at his desk. With a soothing sense of routine he began to look through a mess of papers and clipped-together letters. If only everything would just go on as usual. When he ran his eyes down his appointment pad, Miss Jacoby's little notes swam before his eyes. His swivel chair made a familiar cosy creak as he leaned back in it. He found himself studying the duplicate of the penny postal card he'd found in his briefcase. The same neat laborious handwriting: Dear Sir, for several months I have been most anxious . . . the same phone number. He got up and walked into the outer office to leave a note for Miss Glendinning. *Please call Cap 9799 tell Mr. Battista I can see him here after twelve this noon. T.S.* Tyler found the performance of pencilling out the note on a small blue scratch pad habitual and soothing. He settled back at his desk again and started to draw spirals on a piece of legal cap with his fountainpen.

Suddenly Chuck was there standing over his desk. 'Toby,' he said quietly. 'You've always been a drinkin' man, we mustn't suppress that . . . It's too bad . . . but it's true.' His voice grew loud and dramatic. 'You ain't got no more head for figures than that birdbrain Saunders. The hookworm ate up that boy's brains so's he kin only count up to the number of his fingers an' toes . . . that is, if you don't hurry him . . . It's notorious that any soak's memory's weak . . . I used to be a drinkin' man myself, so I ought to know . . . I shouldn't wonder if you couldn't remember a goddam thing. The trouble down in Horton was that Sue Ann had the bright idea of keepin' you sobered up. Ain't that like a woman? . . . Now Norm Stauch . . . He's a gambler an' a brothel keeper an' a lowlife, you know that. What he did was to throw a lot of wild parties an' had you signin' documents you wasn't fit to read . . . You don't remember a goddam thing. You signed 'em by the yard. Tell 'em to ask Stauch why he tried to debauch my private secretary . . . Wouldn't be surprised if the interests put him up to it.'

'Norm Stauch's on the level . . .' said Tyler, without lifting his eyes from the spirals he was drawing on the pad.

'He better watch hisself before he messes with me.'

'He's a friend of mine.' Tyler started slowly getting to his feet. There was a knocking on a door outside somewhere. Tyler saw the corners of Chuck's mouth twitch. 'Saunders, see what that is,' he shouted in a startled voice.

From the other office came Chester Bigelow's booming 'Top of the mornin' to you, my boy . . . Number One in yet? . . . Well, well.' He strode in the door with his arms outstretched. 'Tyler, I hear Number One got you past the reporters safely . . . We sure were worried for fear you'd get off the plane, having a drop taken . . . and you

[245]

know . . . let the old tongue rattle.' The Reverend Bigelow looked as if he had been up all night too. His aging too boyish face with its broad lips and high cheekbones had a battered unbathed gray look.

'I bet you ain't slept a wink, Reverend,' said Chuck teasingly.

'Quit the Reverend when we're among friends; I'm no different from any other man. Whose business is it if I spent the night in watching and . . .?'

'Watchin' some floosie shake her shimmy off, eh Chet?'

'Skip it, Homer . . . This situation has forced me to come to a decision . . . '

'Say, Saunders, has that dope come back yet?'

'Yessir,' came two voices in chorus from the other room. Crummit appeared in the door with his arms stiff at his sides; 'Number One I set it out for you on a tray on your desk.'

'Come an' git it, boys.'

As he followed Chuck into the private office, Chester Bigelow went on talking, opening his mouth wide so that his voice rattled the glasses together that stood grouped round a pitcher of icewater on the sidetable. 'It is with the greatest pain that I have been forced to repudiate the political doctrines I learned at my mother's knee . . . No thinking man can face the situation in this country today without coming to the conclusion that our democracy is rotten beyond repair. No honest man can forbear to say that force is the only remedy. We are faced with a plot against the supremacy of all the ideals we hold most dear, against our deep faith in our fathers' God, against the sanctity of our beautiful American womanhood, against the existence of the white race itself. . . . That vile conspiracy, that has subverted and degraded that great Christian civilized continent from which our forefathers sprang, has established itself in this country. Its slimy tentacles are twined about the executive and judiciary branches of the government . . .'

Chuck had settled at his desk and drunk off a glass of orange juice. He poured himself out a cup of coffee from a tall carton and snapped his fingers and cursed under his breath at the heat when he put it down. 'Better have a cup of coffee, Chet,' he said, breaking off a piece of toast to dunk in his cup and stuffing it into his mouth.

'Fortunately, the legislative branch has remained more or less untainted by this plague of isms that darkens the skies of our beloved nation . . . but of what avail is it when they depend for their votes upon an electorate already devitalized and poisoned by the taint of the dark bloods? The great white Anglo-Saxon race was born to empire, Homer Crawford. The time has come for patriotic men to take the law into their own hands. The conspiracy . . .'

'Have a cup of coffee, Chet,' Chuck interrupted, talking with his mouth full of toast. 'This ain't no time for Lexington and Concord . . . You wait till I'm President sittin' up at my desk down there at 1600 Pennsylvania Avenue . . . We'll start to fix things so's an American kin be proud of his flag . . . You wait.'

'Wait? . . . Wait till they murder us in our beds . . . No, Homer, the day has come for the white people of this country to rise in their wrath.'

Chuck stopped with a piece of dunked toast halfway to his mouth, letting it drop back into his cup. 'What I'm worryin' about is one little federal district attorney that's risen in his wrath an' his wrath ain't worth a pipsqueak ... All this big colored shirt talk of yours, Chet, might come in handy in a presidential campaign, but now it's the cart before the horse. What we need is to work on that card catalogue.' He put the toast in his mouth and pointed to the row of yellow pine cases with ranks of little lettered drawers in them along the wall. 'I keep it in here so that nobody won't mess with it. Every man an' woman in that catalogue gits litrachur regular, most of 'em tune in on our programs, an' they'll go to the polls an' vote when I tell 'em to an' they'll stay away when I tell 'em to. An' if I tell 'em to give their chillen castoroil, they'll give 'em castoroil. If I told 'em to go jump in the crick I bet a whole lot of 'em would jump in the crick ... If the day should come when I was forced to tell 'em to come to Washington an' drive the moneychangers out of the temple, by God, they'd come ... Wouldn't they, Toby?'

Tyler didn't answer. The oldfashioned mahogany clock on the mantel chimed nine. He wished its sweet tinkle would never stop.

Saunders leaned inquiringly into the room from the vestibule: 'Number One ... hit's Judge Bannin' an' Herb Jessup.'

'Bring 'em in ... I didn't tell you to leave 'em out in the rain.'

Judge Banning came in first. His face looked almost as

white as his hair. The lower lids hung loose and red from his eyes. His whole face had a smudged look. His back was bent and he felt his way carefully with his small shiny pointed feet as if he expected to find the floor uneven before him. His shoes creaked with each step. Right on his heels slouched Herb Jessup's big looselyhung paunchy figure. The pouches of skin under his small eyes were all crumpled up. Under his pouted fish's mouth the flabby chins bulged smoothly over the wing collar. As the two of them came into the room their eyes lit first on Tyler's face. Tyler could feel them apprehensively searching out the lines and contours of his face. He didn't want to catch their glance. He tried to sit still. With one hand he fished out his cigarettecase and started to fidget with it. He took out a cigarette and put it in his mouth without lighting it. In spite of himself he started to snap his cigarettecase open and shut.

'Hello, Herb.' Chuck let out a shout of laughter. 'If ever I saw a man with his ass in a sling . . . Ain't nutten to be ascared of, boy . . . Judge, what time did you tell Grossman to pick up Toby?'

'Nine-thirty, Number One.'

'That's your lil Jew lawyer, Toby. You didn't think I was goin' to send you down there without a lawyer, did you? What time is he subpoenaed for?'

'Ten o'clock.'

Tyler got to his feet to set his empty coffeecup on the corner of the desk. Chuck had started to study some typewritten sheets he had picked up from the wire basket in front of him. Tyler lit a cigarette and stood

[249]

with his back to the window. Judge Banning, Herb Jessup, and Chester Bigelow had settled themselves in a row along the couch. Herb still had his rubbers on. They all had their faces twisted towards him and their eyes screwed up against the light to look in his face.

Miss Jacoby poked her head round the door that led in from the outer office. 'Good morning, Senator . . . Good morning, gentlemen. Aren't we all early birds?' she said in her cheerful shriek.

'Any danger of that plane bein' grounded? Weather don't look any too good.'

'I'll call right up,' said Miss Jacoby. 'I've got all the reservations.'

'We're goin' to need four seats: Saunders, Crummit, Herb, an' me. It's too late already to make Atlanta by train.' Miss Jacoby's head disappeared.

'I hope you lay it on the line, Homer,' began the Reverend Bigelow. 'We must arouse the people of this country to the dangers . . .'

Chuck had switched on the interoffice dictaphone on his desk. 'Miss Jacoby,' he called. 'Suppose you order us up some more rolls and coffee . . . plenty coffee . . . Some of us are goin' down for the third time.' He jumped to his feet and walked to where Tyler stood in front of the window. 'Well, Toby . . .?'

Tyler avoided looking straight in Chuck's face.

'I don't see why I can't say the same thing I said in Horton . . . the profits, at least my share of them . . . were merely placed in my name through loose bookkeeping. Your good friends who had made a killing on a little gamble in leases turned them over to the radio station to promote our political ideas . . . The money was never part of my personal income. That Treasury agent finally admitted we'd paid our corporation taxes all right.'

'Son,' said Judge Banning smoothly. 'It won't do. Too many other names involved. These people are out for blood.'

'Stauch got away with saying his was in repayment for a loan . . . which was the truth.'

'If they pin him down he can't prove nothin' unless he finds that cancelled note,' said Chuck.

Herb laughed. 'He won't find that.'

'Hell, you've got the transcript of my testimony . . .' said Tyler. 'My head's in a whirl . . . I don't remember what I said.'

'That's more like it, Toby,' said Chuck in a wheedling tone. '. . . You might have been drinkin' right through the trial.' The three men on the couch seemed hardly to breathe. The room was so quiet noises of streetcars began to seep in from the street. Sparrows were chirping on the window ledges.

Tyler rammed his clenched fists into his pockets. 'You know as well as I do that I haven't had a drink in six months.'

Chuck dropped down into the chair back of his desk again and started running his fingers through his curly hair. 'Folks kin say I oughtn't to a been associatin' with a hopeless soak, but after all ain't no harm in bein' a little softhearted. I ain't let down an old friend yet.'

Tyler backed up against the windowsill. He could hear his own breathing in the intense quiet of the room.

'You sure were hittin' it up last time I saw you,' drawled Herb. 'Don't you remember the Club Nautilus? That can't have been more'n a couple of months ago.'

The buzzer sounded on Chuck's desk. He switched on the dictaphone. It was Miss Glendinning's voice. 'Senator, I have a longdistance call for Mr. Spotswood. Will he take it in there?'

Tyler started towards the door. 'I'll take it at my desk,' he said.

'He'll take it at his own desk,' echoed Chuck.

As Tyler walked to the door he felt all their eyes focus on the small of his back. 'When are you leaving town?' he turned and asked stiffly.

'Don't you worry, Toby, I'll see you before I go, you and your lil Jew lawyer.'

As Tyler pulled the door to behind him, they all began talking at once. He heard the words ... 'Too bad ... unfortunate ... misplaced confidence ...' He settled into his swivel chair and picked up the receiver.

'Hello.' The voice was Sue Ann's. It sounded so faint.

It was all he could do to keep his voice quiet. 'Where are you, Sue Ann?'

'At the ranch ... Tyler, I wanted to talk to you. I couldn't get a thing out of Homer when I called him last night ...You don't think they can hang anything on you? ... Have you got a firstrate lawyer? Everybody says Mackenzie Turner is a holy terror ... I wish I could get hold of him an' talk to him ...'

'Sue Ann, let me get another connection. I can hardly hear you.'

Her laugh fluttered so sweetly on the humming wire. 'Tyler, it's that my voice is kinda weak. You see I'm kinda weak too . . . I'm in bed . . . had a little accident . . . too much horseback ridin', I guess . . . no, an internal accident . . . I've got Dr. Hildreth out here stayin' at the ranch for a coupla days . . . Don't tell Homer. I don't want him to know until after he's made his speech tonight . . . Might throw him off. I'll be allright, but Dr. Hildreth says I may have to be in bed a coupla months . . . No, it's not really dangerous . . . I just don't want to worry Homer while he's so busy an' I wouldn't do a thing in the world to interfere with his speech tonight . . . It's goin' to be the greatest speech he ever made . . . Honestly, it is. He read me some of it over the phone. Tyler, I think this little scare is all for the best . . . I think it'll make him revise some of his ways of doin' things. You an' me always felt alike about that . . . Tyler, are you allright? You sound worried . . . No, I'm goin' to be perfectly fine . . . I don't want to talk about it over the phone. Homer can tell you all about it when he comes back to Washington . . . I guess we're none of us as young as we used to be . . . It's silly, but the more worried I got . . . I been worried about all kindsa things since the convention . . . the more I worried the more I rode an' it wasn't quite so good for my insides as I thought it was. I might have to have an operation. Do you know what I've been thinkin' layin' up here? I've been worryin' because I don't seem to have any girl friends any more . . . I guess it's that Washington atmosphere, but I always used to have so many girl friends . . . Do you remember Ella McCoy? My, she was cute . . . Say, Tyler, why don't you go an' marry some sweet wonderful girl like you deserve? . . . I want to meet her. I don't have any nice women to talk to any more . . . Don't be silly, Tyler, you're a cute faithful old thing an' you know it . . . Here I am lyin' in bed rattlin' along like a sorority sister . . . Well, take care of yourself an' don't worry. I don't want you to start you know what. What's Homer doin'? Oh, if he's in conference don't bother him . . . just tell him I'm expectin' him some time tomorrow. If he wires me I'll have the car meet him at the airport. I wish you-all were comin' down. It's just lovely out here . . . The loveliest fall weather . . .' The voice had faded out and was gone.

Tyler couldn't just sit there at his desk staring at the silent telephone. He went out into the corridor and started walking up and down smoking a cigarette. The corridor was already full of men and women hurrying back and forth. People glanced in his face curiously as they brushed past. Their faces all looked blank to him. He couldn't tell one from another.

Mousy serious little Miss Glendinning pulled at his sleeve to get his attention. 'Why, Mr. Spotswood . . . We've been looking for you everywhere . . . Mr. Grossman's here,' she said in her mournful voice. She looked so intent and innocent he had an impulse to run at her and pick her up in his arms. Instead he followed her into his office.

Mr. Grossman was sitting in the cane armchair beside

Tyler's desk. He was a bald squat cheerful little man shaped rather like a frog. He got to his feet and said, 'Mr. Spotswood, the pleasure is mine . . . My old friend Judge Banning has assigned to me the pleasant duty of assisting you in your tilt with the Terrible Turk . . . That's what we used to call Mac Turner in lawschool . . . Oh yes, I know him well . . . I've known him for years . . . in fact I know him better than he knows me . . .' Laughing silently he settled down into his chair and stuck his short fat legs out towards Tyler. Tyler had started drawing spirals on the pad again.

'My difficulty comes from the fact that I've always been pretty harumscarum about my records,' he said slowly in a low voice, almost as if he were talking to himself.

'There's no harm in it . . . Now is there? . . . Harumscarum . . . let's call it the artistic temperament . . . an artist in politics . . . an artist is not expected to have a very good memory for detail . . . Particularly . . .'

'If he's drunk half the time,' said Tyler flatly.

Mr. Grossman nodded his head and rolled pallid eyes towards the ceiling. 'Spirituous influences . . . sidereal influences . . . ladies . . . whose bright eyes . . . rain influence . . . money, large sums of money gone before you know it . . . As the poet says: If ignorance is bliss . . . 'twere folly to be wise.' When he'd spouted that out, Mr. Grossman leaned back in his chair and beamed at Tyler across his fat cheeks. Tyler reached for his watch.

'We'd better go,' he said.

As he raised his eyes from his desk, he found himself looking full in Chuck's face. Chuck stood behind his desk with his hands on his hips. His eyes bored into Tyler's with a bluish porcelain stare as if he didn't recognize him at all. He talked as if he were talking to a child. 'Well, ole cock, I wish I could stay over to see you an' Max Grossman here have yourselves a time with the D.A. Hell, I've seen you handle worse'n him with one hand . . . His bark's worse'n his bite, ain't that so, Max?'

Tyler drew himself up straight and sat there looking at him without saying anything.

Chuck had a yellow telegraph blank in his hand. He waved it under Tyler's nose. 'Just had a wire from the missus. I thought you might want to look at it.'

Looking forward to your coming to Ranch for a rest Boys fine Tell Tyler we both have every confidence in him.

Tyler got to his feet to read it with his lips moving like a small boy reading out a theme in class.

'Confidence, that's the word I wanted you to read . . . You know Sue Ann always did have a long head for a woman.'

'She called me up on the phone . . .' stammered Tyler, 'said you ought to have a rest.'

'You know what she meant, Toby . . . You're the boy that never let a friend down yet . . . and neither did I, don't forget that.' Tyler found that Chuck's arm was hugging tight around his shoulders as he pressed him gently towards the door. Mr. Grossman trotted ahead. 'You made me what I am today,' Chuck hummed in his ear. 'I hope you're satisfied . . . Say, you're forgettin' your hat and coat . . . you're forgettin' everythin' . . . amnesia, ole cock.'

[256]

Chuck walked over to the rack and picked off Tyler's hat and raincoat. Tyler stuck his arms out behind him helplessly. Chuck helped him on with his raincoat, reached his hand under from behind to pull down the tail of his jacket underneath. Then he gave him a little slap on the back. Tyler obediently took his hat and walked out the door. He walked out without looking back.

Tyler couldn't find much to say to Mr. Grossman in the taxicab. The sky showed signs of clearing. Traffic was heavy in front of the Union Station.

'I never pass that building,' sighed Mr. Grossman, 'without wanting to hop a train for New York.'

'I'd hop a train for hell,' said Tyler, 'if anybody handed me a ticket.'

Mr. Grossman made a clucking noise with his lips. 'My dear Mr. Spotswood,' he said in a hurt tone. 'Things aren't so bad as that . . . Our only difficulty is that we are faced by a very ambitious young man.'

The car drew up with a jerk in front of the District Court. The old building so spaciously designed in the style of the early republic looked disarmingly familiar.

Tyler suddenly began to feel confidential. 'I don't believe I've been into this building since my grandfather brought me down to see it when I was kneehigh to a grasshopper,' he said. 'He wore muttonchop whiskers and carried a silverheaded cane . . . We used to call him Old Soul.'

'You are a Washingtonian, Mr. Spotswood?' said Mr. Grossman in a deferential tone.

'A cavedweller . . . Born here . . . God, how I hate the

place. My dad was a Y.M.C.A. director, a kind of Unitarian minister without a congregation . . . He didn't do so badly at it in the end . . . the League of Nations racket. He's got a job at Geneva. I'm just as glad he's out of the country. I was the black sheep . . . By the time I was fourteen I was hanging round the poolrooms on Four and a Half Street . . . Anywhere to get away from all that brotherly love.'

Mr. Grossman was steering him through the crowd in the vestibule. 'You don't say,' he was murmuring vaguely. They were shoving their way between fat men and thin men, bodies hot under raincoats, puffing faces under felt hats.

Among the blur of faces a face Tyler knew stood out sharp. 'Hi, Toby,' said Joe Hazard. 'Wait till you see the afternoon papers . . . Whew.'

'We are late, Mr. Spotswood,' Mr. Grossman hissed in Tyler's ear as he hurried him to the foot of the stairway.

Tyler waved with his hand. 'I'll be seein' you, Joe.'

Mr. Grossman's breath was beginning to whistle a little in his thick neck by the time he got to the head of the stairs. On the landing he put his hand on Tyler's sleeve. 'As you know, Mr. Spotswood,' he panted, 'a Grand Jury . . . is a Star Chamber proceeding . . . Let's sit down . . . in the library . . . for a moment . . . before I deliver you to the witnesses' room.' He led the way into a long room cluttered with stands of reference books between walls lined to the ceiling with calfbound volumes. The place smelt of dust and old bindings. Two stubby men whispering together at a corner of a table looked up at them for an instant as they passed and immediately lowered their eyes. 'Now if in your opinion, Mr. Spotswood, any question is too . . . er . . . difficult, you can stand on your constitutional rights . . . I shall wait here . . . if the question raises points of law in relation to constitutional rights you can ask Mr. Turner, the Special Assistant District Attorney, to allow you to go out to consult counsel . . . answer nothing that may incriminate or degrade you.' Mr. Grossman stretched his wide mouth in a smile.

Tyler didn't answer. He sat hunched up in his chair looking down at his tan shoes. A splatter of mud had dried on them. He was wishing he'd had a chance to get them shined.

Mr. Grossman was rummaging among the folders in his briefcase. 'Judge Banning,' he was saying, 'turned over to me some certified copies of the minutes of meetings of the board of directors of the Every Man a Millionaire Corporation . . . When did your resignation become effective, Mr. Spotswood?'

Tyler looked sharply in Mr. Grossman's placid eyes. A feeling of panic began to get hold of him. He bit the air a couple of times before he could speak.

'I never did,' he stammered '. . . unless I'm crazy.'

'Weren't you at the meeting of the board of directors on August 5 last at the Alcazar Hotel?' Mr. Grossman was talking with his eyes on the papers before him. 'No, I gather not.'

'No . . .' At once Tyler remembered. 'Of course, when the . . . at the time of the incorporation we all of us wrote out our resignations and gave them to . . .' He stopped suddenly. He felt himself getting red.

'Humph,' said Mr. Grossman whose shortness of breath seemed suddenly to have come back. 'Would you like to look over the minutes?' Tyler shook his head and got to his feet. Mr. Grossman looked up at him with an expression of pain on his face and let himself settle back into his chair. 'I shall be here,' he panted. 'I shall be here, Mr. Spotswood, delving into a few points of law.' A shade of unction came into his voice as if the prospect gave him great pleasure. 'The Grand Jury room is in the hall to the left, almost at the end. You'll see the deputy marshal standing there . . . There's a waitingroom for witnesses across the hall.'

Tyler felt strangely unlike himself as he walked with long strides down the dingy courthouse corridor. It was as if the wish he had sometimes entertained half in fun to change lives with some other man had all at once come true. He wasn't himself. He was the man who was asking an old fellow in a dark blue uniform at which door witnesses before the Federal Grand Jury should present themselves. He was the man who was being ushered into a little room with benches that reminded him of the waitingroom of a country railroad station. The other travellers turned lacklustre eyes on him when he came in but none of them spoke or smiled. There was a young man in a light tweed suit he'd seen some place before, but he didn't look up, and Tyler couldn't remember his name. He was wondering if he could remember his own. He was a man who'd lost his job sitting there staring at nothing on the hard bench with his raincoat folded into the crook of his arm and his felt hat on his knees.

When the elderly man came to the door and called his name, it was like the stationmaster announcing a train: Tylerspot's Wood. He hardly recognized the name as his, but automatically his leg muscles tightened and got him to his feet and his feet walked him to the door. Crossing the hall he caught a glimpse of Joe Hazard's thin back and Ed James' fat one. They were talking to a tall man he didn't know. They didn't see him. They looked inaccessibly far away like people seen through the wrong end of the telescope.

The door of the Grand Jury room closed behind him. Inside it was a like a schoolroom during an examination. Gray north light came in through the long windows and lit up the intent profiles of two rows of faces. The pink-faced man in black at the table must be the foreman. Tyler wondered if he mightn't be an undertaker or a head waiter by profession. As he was shown his chair nobody paid much attention. There were coughs and rustlings of papers, whispers back and forth, feet scraped on the floor. The pinkfaced man was unctuously pushing a black book at him. It was the Bible he had his hand on. 'Do you trulyandsolemnlyswear to tellthetruththe wholetruth andnothingbutthetruth?' The mumble stopped. The room was silent. The man was looking at Tyler. It was his cue. His voice sounded unexpectedly loud in his ears when he said, 'I do.'

It was like turning a switch. The rustling and whispering stopped. Throats were cleared. As the faces turned toward him all the eyes from the twentythree faces in the back of the room focussed on his face like searchlights. They made him feel frail and transparent. He caught himself wishing he'd eaten a good breakfast. Again he wished he'd had time to get his shoes shined.

'Your name?' snarled from very close to him a voice that had a middlewestern rasp to it. For the first time he saw Mackenzie Turner's white face across the table. It looked surprisingly like the face of a plaster bust of Napoleon as a young man except that the chin was square and that the raven's wing of black hair over the forehead ended in a little corny wisp of a ducktail. Tyler couldn't help smiling.

'Tyler Spotswood,' he said.

The Special Assistant District Attorney was a small man in a doublebreasted dark blue suit. He had broad shoulders but spindly legs and small feet. The big pale face and squarish head of hair looked too large for his body. He sat at the end of the table blocking off Tyler's view of some of the jurors. He was looking him up and down with his severe black stare.

'Home? . . . Where's your home?'

'I was born right here in Washington.'

'What's your home now? Where's your present legal residence?'

'Since I got out of the army it's been down in Horton . . . I still vote from 1827 Sunrise Avenue, in that city . . .'

'Your job is in Washington, isn't it?'

'I spend a good deal of time in Washington, at least when Congress is in session.'

Turner started rummaging among sheafs of papers on the table in front of him. His voice muffled by the papers sounded less unfriendly. He spoke without raising his head.

'Tell us a little about your present occupation, Mr. Spotswood.'

Tyler found himself answering in an almost whining tone: 'I work in Senator Crawford's office on the Hill.'

'You are his confidential secretary, are you not?'

'I am one of his secretaries.'

'Therefore you are thoroughly cognizant with all his affairs, are you not?'

'No . . . I can honestly answer that I am not.'

Turner suddenly held up a single typewritten sheet of paper and glared across it into Tyler's face.

Tyler screwed up his eyes to see if he could read whatever was on the paper, but Turner began to wave it back and forth. 'What's your salary?' he suddenly shouted.

'Thirtyfive hundred . . . the usual thing.'

'And what salary do you receive from the Every Man a Millionaire Corporation?'

'None.'

'And from the Senator's other . . . propagandistic enterprises?'

'Most of my work has been political,' Tyler started in a confidential tone, trying to get Mackenzie Turner to look him full in the face . . . 'I have occasionally . . .'

'Answer my question, please.'

'At present, nothing.'

'As the Senator's representative you are cognizant of the affairs of Station WEMM?'

'To a certain extent.'

'Answer yes or no.'

'Yes.'

'You are a member of the board of directors of Station WEMM?'

'The station is run by a manager.'

'Is the station owned and operated by the Every Man a Millionaire Corporation?'

'Part of its financing may have come from there.'

Turner drew down the corners of his mouth and threw his head back so that the raven's wing flopped on his square bleached forehead. 'Are you or are you not a member of the board of directors of WEMM?'

'No.'

'Of the Every Man a Millionaire Corporation?'

'No.'

At last Turner's black eyes were looking straight into his. He stared back. In spite of himself he felt a redness starting at his neck and creeping up his cheeks.

'Have you ever been in the past?'

Tyler tried to smile disarmingly. 'I don't remember very well . . . I might have been a kind of dummy director when it was first gotten up. It was gotten up on a shoe-string by a few friends who felt the Senator was being unfairly discriminated against on the air . . . It was gotten up as kind of a joke . . . almost . . . I am not much of a businessman, I'm afraid.'

Turner spun around on his chair and looked down the room in the direction of the intent faces of the jurymen. When he turned back he was smiling. 'The Treasury Department has been somewhat interested in that little joke, has it not?'

'Yes, sir. Our bookkeeping wasn't of the best . . . But the matter is being straightened out.'

'The Treasury has recovered its sense of humor, eh?' He almost looked as if he were going to laugh. 'Then the records of that jocose piece of bookkeeping are accessible to you?'

'To a certain extent.'

'Roughly, what has your income been during the last five years . . . your complete annual income . . . upon which you based your income tax.'

'I am afraid . . . without refreshing my memory . . .'

'We are quite willing to have you go home and refresh your memory . . . I'll adjourn the rest of your examination until two o'clock this afternoon.'

'Thank you, sir.' Tyler couldn't help letting his breath out with relief.

Mackenzie Turner slumped drowsily in his chair with the air of a schoolmaster about to dismiss the class. 'Before I adjourn your examination,' he said offhand, 'perhaps you can tell us how you kept your accounts when you handled sums of money for Homer T. Crawford.'

'I've handled plenty campaign funds,' said Tyler quickly. 'But in that case I was responsible to the various committees.'

Mackenzie Turner wasn't looking at him. He was lost

in contemplation of some sheets of scribbled notes he'd taken out of a brown folder. 'Did you,' he asked in a low voice without looking up, 'on January 31, 1935, as Secretary-Treasurer of the Every Man a Millionaire Corporation, cash a check for eighteen thousand, five hundred and six dollars drawn upon the funds of the corporation in the East Coast National Bank of Horton?'

'I'd have to refresh my memory.'

'After you had removed this sum from the bank, what did you do with it?'

'I'd have to refresh my memory.'

'Did you hand it to Mr. Crawford?'

'Not that I remember.'

'Answer yes or no.'

Tyler sat straight upright in his chair. He couldn't help moistening his lips. A chair creaked. 'On that question,' he answered slowly, 'I stand on my constitutional rights . . .'

'Then you took the money yourself?'

'I did not . . . If such a sum was drawn out it was used for other purposes.'

'What purposes?'

'Political purposes . . . It would probably have been accounted for among campaign funds.'

'It was not.' Turner's voice cracked. 'On January 31, 1935, did you as Secretary-Treasurer draw out of the funds of the Every Man a Millionaire Corporation the sum of eighteen thousand, five hundred and six dollars?'

'It is possible.'

'Are you withdrawing your appeal to your constitutional rights?'

Tyler did not answer.

'What do you know about the State Park Bottoms oil
leases?'

'What I have read in the papers.'

'Have you ever been in the oil business?'

Tyler tried to smile. He leaned back in his chair and
crossed his legs. 'Down in our part of the world everybody's in the oil business . . .'

'You know nothing about the negotiation of the oil
leases referred to in the press as the State Park Bottoms?'

'I know what I've read in the papers . . . That's all
politics.'

'Answer yes or no.'

Tyler cleared his throat. He answered carefully and
slowly as if the words were heavy and had to be raised
from a great depth: 'On this question I am afraid I shall
have to stand on my constitutional rights, at least until I
have consulted my attorney.'

'And you've come before this Grand Jury to tell me
under oath you are not an officer of the Every Man a
Millionaire Corporation?' Turner leaned towards him
across the table with his hands clenched into fists on top
of the mass of papers in front of him. He was speaking
slowly and mournfully looking at something on the wall
over Tyler's head.

'No, sir, I'm not,' said Tyler.

'Examination adjourned,' whispered Turner in a sigh-
ing tired kind of tone. 'Please be here at two o'clock

with what records you can get together in the meantime. It will save us the trouble of issuing a duces tecum . . . David C. Galloway, please.'

When Tyler got out in the corridor he found he was sweating. His shirt stuck cold and wet to the small of his back. Mr. Grossman was standing in front of the door to the Grand Jury room with his legs planted wide apart telling a story about a Scotchman and a Jew to a small haggard bottlenosed man in a tweed overcoat. Tyler strode across the corridor towards them just as the laugh came. 'Pretty good,' squeaked the bottlenosed man.

'Mr. Grossman,' Tyler interrupted. 'The D.A. wants me back at two with records . . . What time is it?'

They both brought out their watches simultaneously. 'I make it twentytwo minutes to twelve,' said Mr. Grossman ponderously.

'Gosh, I thought I'd been in there all day . . . I've got to go to the office.'

'But we should confer,' said Mr. Grossman.

'Come along.' Tyler took his arm and hurried him down the corridor. 'I've got to get to the office and catch the Sen . . . well, I have an appointment . . . Let's duck these newspaper boys.' He plunged down the stairs. Mr. Grossman was puffing by the time they reached the back entrance to the courthouse downstairs. 'I left my hat and briefcase in the library,' he panted. 'It'll only take a minute . . . I'll go back and get them.'

'Mr. Grossman, suppose you meet me for lunch at the Burleigh at twelve-fortyfive . . . I must go.' Already Tyler was running across the sopping grass under trees red and yellow with fall, fluttering the pigeons as he went. At the curb he flagged a taxi.

'Take me to the Senate Office Building quick . . . God, I feel like a dishrag,' he said half aloud as he lay back in the seat with his eyes closed. The taxi was not moving. He sat up suddenly. 'For God's sake, make it speedy there, brother. I've got to catch a man who's leaving on a plane.'

'You don't mean the airport?'

'No, I said the Senate Office Building.'

'If you don't want us both to go to the hospital you'd better calm down, mister,' grumbled the driver as he drove without changing his speed through the dense noontime traffic. 'I'm goin' the fastest I can. I don't want to end up in court or in the hospital either. Now, do you?' The taximan laughed as if he'd made a joke. 'More haste less speed, that's my motto.'

'Okay, okay, have it your own way.' Tyler was mopping his forehead with an already damp handkerchief. 'It wouldn't make me mad to land in the hospital,' he shouted at the back of the taxidriver's head. 'I'd get a rest.'

When Tyler hopped out of the elevator the corridor that led to the office seemed strangely quiet. He'd expected for some reason to find a howling mob of newspaper men milling around outside. He let himself in with his key. There was nobody in the Senator's office, nobody in Miss Jacoby's office. From her desk in the reception room Miss Glendinning gave him her quiet vague smile. 'Oh, Mr. Spotswood, there's that young man . . .'

'Where's the Senator? Is the Senator on the floor?'

'Oh, no, he had to run off to his plane. Miss Jacoby drove down to the airport with them to take some dictation. Some kind of a statement he promised the press . . . But that young man . . .'

'What time does the plane leave? I might catch them. I've got to see him.'

'I think I heard them say the plane left at twelve-fiftyfive.'

Tyler pulled out his watch. He had the feeling of having run blocks and blocks for a train and then getting to the station winded and weak in the knees just in time to see the gate slam in his face. It was eleven minutes to one.

'Maybe you could phone.' He shook his head. The sweat was standing out on his forehead again. 'Mr. Spotswood, there's that young man.'

'What young man?'

'You told me to tell him to come at noon. He's been waiting quite some time . . . You remember, Mr. Spotswood . . .' she began to rummage among the notes on her desk. 'It was a Capitol number.'

'Oh, the one that wrote the postal card . . . What did he say he wanted?'

'It's some foreign name,' whispered Miss Glendinning. 'He doesn't look as if he ate very regular, poor kid . . . kinda seedily dressed.'

'I don't think I've got time . . . I've got to meet Mr. Grossman at lunch before one. I'll be at the Burleigh if you need to get hold of me.'

Miss Glendinning made a motion with her head towards the door behind her. 'I asked him what he wanted,' she said mysteriously. 'He said he had to see you in private, that he had a message for you . . .'

'He probably just wants a handout.'

'Shall I get my lunch or shall I wait for Miss Jacoby to come back?'

Suddenly he lashed out at her in a burst of temper. 'How should I know? Do what you usually do.' Her face drew up in a little knot. Her lips winced as if he'd hit her. As he charged through into the next room, he had half a mind to go back and say he was sorry, but he hadn't time. He jammed his hat back on his head as he went through the door. 'You wanted to see me, Mr . . . Mr. . . .'

'Battista's my name.' A slight young man with rusty black hair and greenish olive skin got to his feet. He didn't hold out his hand. 'Meester Tyler Spotswood?'

'Yes. What can I do for you?'

'Ever since I been back in dis lousy capitalist country I been tryin' to git aholt of you. I knew your kid brudder.' His voice was very hoarse. The intonation was Brooklyn waterfront, but every now and then a trace of a Spanish accent broke through.

'Well?' Tyler looked him over carefully. He did look as if he didn't eat regular. His face was thin with thin clearly marked blue lips and arched black eyebrows. His blue serge suit, worn almost white at the elbows and knees, looked as if it had shrunk on him. There was a line of dirt round the frayed collar of his pink shirt.

'I see by de papers you're havin' a little trouble widde capitalist system yourself, Mr. Spotswood. Well, Sandy

[271]

an' me we had pleny. We palled around for a while over on de udder side in de International Brigade. I guess he never wrote about me. If he did you didn't ever git 'em. Your kid brudder an' me we seen pleny trouble togedder, an' I don't mean maybe.'

'I know all about that,' said Tyler, impatiently pulling out his watch.

'What you don't know, Meester Spotswood, is that Sandy gave me a letter . . . Dey had him in jail an' he was killed by de Fascistas . . . dey had me in jail too . . . too much hell widde señoritas. How much would it be wort' to you if I gave you de last letter he ever wrote in his life addressed to his big brudder?'

'No, I'm not interested.'

'You don't like because I use capitalist met'ods, eh? . . .' The young man showed his small neat teeth in a smile. 'What can I do? I do my best to overt'row de capitalist system an' I git de livin' Jesus kicked out of me. De Fascistas didn't shoot me, I run too quick. Now what's de use? I got to use de capitalist system to eat.'

'Allright, you win. How much do you want? . . . Here. I'd better see it first.'

The young man pulled a tattered billfold of Mexican stamped leather out of his pocket and produced from out of a mess of soiled papers a stained envelope. The writing on the envelope looked like Glenn's.

'Twentyfi',' said the young man, holding it out to Tyler.

Tyler took the letter out of the stumpy brown hand with black fingernails. He drew the letter half out and shoved it back as if he were scared to look at it. It was the kid's handwriting allright. He reached for his wallet. His heart had started to pound. It was hard to keep his fingers from trembling as he counted out five fives. He put the letter carefully in the wallet beside the remaining bills and slipped it back into his inside pocket. The young man had snatched at the bills and stood looking down at them with glistening eyes.

'Ain't you goin' to read it now?' he asked anxiously. 'If you wan' I wait while you read it in case dere's sumpen you wan' I should explain. If you wan' you an' me'll go to some ginmill an' chew de fat.'

Tyler shook his head. 'No time today . . .' He opened the door out into the hall. 'Buddy, you run along now,' he said in a more friendly tone. 'Good luck.'

'Okay, boss. No hard feelin', eh?'

When he'd gone Tyler wished he'd told him to wait. Miss Glendinning had gone too. He stood there for a moment in the middle of the empty reception room, with his hat on the back of his head and his cold hands rammed down into his trousers pockets, trying to decide what to do. His feet were cold and the palms of his hands were wet. He had to have some air. He'd walk down to the Burleigh and decide what to do as he walked. What the hell if he was late!

The sky had cleared. Ruddy sunlight was drying the pavement out in patches and bringing out the shine on the plump breasts of the starlings hopping about the grassplots. Crossing in front of the glinting radiators of ranked cars waiting with grumbling motors for a green light, he noticed the wet rising in light wisps of steam off the edges of the dry spots on the asphalt. On the sidewalk he caught himself kicking out his feet like a small boy playing hooky. He could hardly remember when last he'd strolled idly down the street like that. He made a point of not looking at his watch or at the headlines of afternoon papers laid out at the street corners. No spikka de Engleesh, a voice was talking idiot gibberish inside his head.

He stopped on the uneven brick pavement of one corner and carefully read the menu spelt out with chipped enamel letters in a metal frame in the window of a small lunchroom for colored people. The top line read 'FRIED CHIKEN 35 cents.' As he stood there with the warm sun on his cheek teetering on the balls of his feet he began to wish he was a young buck nigger with just thirtyfive cents in his pocket. Through the unwashed window he caught a suspicious glance in his direction from a pair of beady eyes in a dark face and walked on. Further on he found himself studying beersigns, cigarette ads of gleaming girls on cardboard cutouts. In the window of a poolroom there was a flyspecked copy of the oleo of Custer's last stand he remembered from his boyhood. Custer with his yellow hair flying shooting the last cartridge out of his revolver, among dead horses and the tumbled bodies of dead men in blue that the Sioux were working on with their scalpingknives and tomahawks. 'Poor old Custer,' he whispered as he walked on.

At the next corner he found himself quite casually ordering a glass of beer. It was so long since he'd had a drink in the District he'd forgotten you couldn't stand up at the bar. Sitting at the oilcloth table he began to fidget and to worry about the time. The cold beer tingled on his tongue. He drank it off so fast he got some of it down his windpipe and went hurrying off down the street choking and coughing.

The clock in the hotel lobby read eight minutes past one. Through a forest of women's dresses and well-pressed trouserlegs he caught sight of Mr. Grossman's bald head bent over a book. For a moment Tyler stood over him looking down at the pages: *Collected Poems of Alfred Lord Tennyson.* Mr. Grossman looked more frog-like than ever as he sat with his legs apart hunched in the deep easychair reading with a broad placid smile on his face.

Tyler cleared his throat, but Mr. Grossman didn't look up. Then he raised his voice. 'Mr. Grossman . . . I'm terribly sorry to be so late.' Mr. Grossman gave him a flustered look out of his pallid eyes. 'Quite allright, quite allright,' he said, getting to his feet with a series of spasmodic jerks and shoving the book into his pocket. 'When I read poetry I forget . . . It calms my nerves . . . People think it odd . . .'

'I'm only sorry I kept you waiting . . . but for me, Mr. Grossman, this is a rather peculiar day.'

'Ha ha,' said Mr. Grossman. 'We all have those days, don't we, now?'

'I suppose we do,' said Tyler as they squeezed into the last small table left in the diningroom. 'I wonder if you'd like a drink.'

Mr. Grossman gave him a frightened look. 'No, thanks. I never drink.'

'I do, Mr. Grossman . . . Waiter, four Martinis. We're in a hurry . . . What would you like to eat? The food's terrible here, but we can't help it.'

'I never eat much lunch,' said Mr. Grossman. 'What do you think of ham and eggs?'

'I think very highly of ham and eggs, Mr. Grossman. I'd like to see them on every breakfast table in the land.' Mr. Grossman rolled his eyes up towards the ceiling as the waiter put two Martini cocktails down in front of each of them. 'Forgive me, I'm not a drinking man.' His eyes timidly searched Tyler's face. 'Don't you think, if you will excuse the observation, that we should keep our heads clear for this afternoon?'

'They are tiny things . . . I'll drink them,' said Tyler, laughing heartily. 'I don't know much about the law, Mr. Grossman, but I do know how to get goddam stinkin' drunk . . . Well, here's how.'

With a look of patient suffering on his face, Mr. Grossman watched Tyler drink down first one, then two, and then the third and fourth Martinis. Tyler started to laugh again. 'The olives were excruciating,' he said. He felt that this time he'd said something really terribly funny. When Mr. Grossman managed to raise a little embarrassed titter, a surge of warm feeling went through Tyler. 'Mr. Grossman, did anybody ever tell you you were a prince?'

Mr. Grossman, who was carefully spearing little pieces of ham and egg and toast with his fork, looked across the table at Tyler with hurt wrinkles round his eyes. 'Mr. Spotswood,' he said, a little tartly, 'hadn't we better get down to cases?'

'First would you oblige me by eating my eggs?'

Mr. Grossman made a gesture of pushing something away from him with the palms of two fat hands. 'Thank you, thank you. I really couldn't. I'm a small eater, almost a vegetarian.'

'Waiter,' Tyler shouted in a louder voice than he intended. 'These eggs are looking at me crosseyed . . . Please take them away . . . They don't like my face.'

'Aren't they quite fresh, sir? Would you like something else, sir?'

'Don't worry, George, they are delicious . . . But I'm on a diet . . . Bring me one little Martini without any olive in it and take the eggs back to the cook with my compliments. Tell him to give them to an old beggarman.'

Mr. Grossman was clucking with his tongue against his teeth. 'Oh, I wish you'd eat something . . . er . . . er . . . what sort of questions did young Mackenzie Turner put to you?'

'I can't remember.'

'But then how can I help you?' said Mr. Grossman testily.

'You can't, Mr. Grossman. Jesus Christ himself couldn't help me . . . as you know He only helps those who help themselves.'

'Come, come, you must remember something.'

'My mind, Mr. Grossman, is a blank . . . Except for those damned olives . . . Did you know that an extremely dangerous kind of poisoning comes from bad olives? Now, what's the name of it? No, it's not botulism.'

Mr. Grossman had begun to frown and to tap with one forefinger on the table, but he couldn't help smiling a little greedy child's smile when the waiter brought him a big piece of devil's food cake for his dessert. At the same time another cocktail appeared on the empty tablecloth in front of Tyler. Tyler smiled across the table. 'Now have a nice lunch, Mr. Grossman. Let's not worry about botulism.' He drank the cocktail off and called for the check. When he looked at his watch it was two on the dot. He got to his feet and leant over and put his hand on Mr. Grossman's. 'Now you finish your lunch quietly, and remember what kind of poisoning comes from bad olives while I follow your excellent advice . . . you know . . . By the waters of Lethe they sat down and wept . . . I've read some poetry myself from time to time.' He shoved the waiter a dollar tip and before Mr. Grossman had time to answer was out of the restaurant and in the back seat of a taxi.

It seemed only the batting of an eyelash before he was out of the cab at the courthouse and running up the steep stairs. Newspaper men were still bunched on the landing. He caught sight of Ed's moonface and Joe's skinny black jaw. Leaving various greetings and expressions of surprise behind him like garbage in the wake of a fast steamer, he tore through the group without saying a word and settled down at his old place in his little waiting-room again.

He was glad to be there. He grinned at the elderly

deputy marshal, who sat beside the door with the look of a man who was digesting his lunch with difficulty, and got a nickel'sworth of sour smile in return. Where were the witnesses? Mowed down by botulism? He had the place to himself. Maybe he was the only surviving witness. Now he had a chance to think. The Martinis churned entertainingly in his head, but he wasn't so drunk as he'd expected. It couldn't be that he'd forgotten how to get drunk. If he wasn't drunk he'd have to think. In the first place ... Then he remembered the greenfaced hoarse young man in the threadbare suit. Where had he put the kid's letter?

He took his glasses out of his breastpocket and placed them carefully on his nose. Getting old. Not quite used to his reading glasses yet, but they were the first sign. When he got old would he get so that he couldn't get drunk when he drank? He unfolded the letter. There was no date. No name of a place. It was the kid's handwriting allright. A smell of tobacco and stale clothing came from the paper. There were wavy brown stains around the edges as if it had been wet and dried out again. The words were blurred and hard to make out.

Looking down at the letter he sat wondering how Dad felt. As it turned out it was just as well that Mother died when she did. Poor Mother. He remembered the smell of lavender in the linen closet and her long trailing leg-of-mutton sleeves with lace on the edges that used to get into things at the breakfast table and make Dad so sore. He never used to get along with Dad, or with Glenn either, the little sap ... He was shopping downtown with

Mother, carrying all the soft tissuepaper packages and holding open the swinging glass doors of the department-store for another lady to come out too, and outside it was snowing so quietly and Mother had ordered a Herdic cab, and when he opened the door to help her up the little step he brushed the snow off, and when he got inside, holding all the packages carefully tight to his chest and holding the top one down with his chin, Mother leaned over with that frail sweet proud look and said, 'My little boy's grow-ing up to be a regular little man, isn't he?' And the cab-driver had clucked from the box and the horse had started his cloppetyclop muffled by the snow, and he'd sat there pressing her hand in the creaky rumbling cab that smelt sharply of mould in old upholstery and stables and horse-blankets.

He squinted his eyes to focus on the squirming letters.

The letters would jog a little, but he could read remark-ably well. Gosh, why had all these damn fool things had to happen? Right from the beginning, right from the day Mother died, so many damn fool things.

It was a long letter closely written on both sides of the thin sheets of paper. It was Glenn's writing allright.

Dear Tyler,

Do you remember how you and Dad and I used to get into arguments and blow up and lose our tempers and fly off in six different directions? I wonder if we'd still do that if we got together. Sitting down after my evening bowl of weak bean soup to write you a letter from this forsaken little place I mayn't tell you the name of is a poor substitute, let me tell you, for saying hello and settling down to a good old family wrangle.

[280]

Well, in the long run it turned out I wasn't cut out to be a labor leader. It was only by getting into a kind of youthful sulk that I could avoid seeing the other fellow's point of view. Then I began to find I couldn't get myself into that special kind of sulk any more. One thing I can say is that I feel a whole lot better since I've been working as a mechanic in a repairshop on this strange road to the Fortress, replacing stripped gears on republican trucks, and relining brakes and cleaning carburetors and grinding valves.

Sometimes we work to all hours and sometimes we have damn little to do and time hangs heavy on my hands and I get lonely, but I know that the Fortress has got to be held and if I do a halfway decent job it means just one truckload of munitions more towards holding it. You'll laugh at the idea of me turning out a mechanic, but compared to the local mule-drivers who are doing the work of this war, guys I admire enormously for their deportment — you know the kind of dignity Old Soul had in spite of all his fluff and feathers — well, compared to these boys I'm Henry Ford. They think a monkey wrench is something to crack nuts with.

Times like these, especially when you're doing purely mechanical work, your mind sometimes runs away with you, not thinking, but mulling over old times. I find myself chewing the cud of all the rows I ever had with you and Dad. Tyler, I don't think you and I have exchanged a civil word since we left the Friends' School.

And now I find myself wishing we'd been able to talk things over more reasonably. It takes so much experience to get any sense into your head, and these days a man stands a pretty good chance of losing his head while he's picking up the experience. Why, every time I haul myself up out of the cellar after an airraid I find I've lost a few more party labels. Getting the liver and lights scared out of me regularly once a day fills me with respect and tenderness for every man woman and child I see, for anything that is alive.

I keep remembering one day years ago back in New York when I felt particularly down and out and took a girl I used to go around with for a walk in the zoo. I was talking her ear off about how this man was a rotten Stalinist and that man a Fascist and this group a menace — you know the 'ism' talk — when I found myself looking straight in the face of a badger. He was in a little round cage. A badger's a mighty comical looking animal. Well that badger listened attentively for a while and then he looked up at me out of his little suspicious hick eyes and turned up his nose and yawned. My, what a yawn! I got to laughing and, honestly, I think that badger saved me from losing my mind because I sure was slipping off the deep end. Too many things had gone wrong all at once. You probably think I'm going off the deep end right now, but remember how difficult it is for a man to put what he truly means into words.

After all it's what you do that counts, not what you say. One thing I've learned in my life is that everything every one of us does counts.

Running the kind of medicine show you seem to be so good at, you must see even more than I have of the seamy side of government of the people, for the people, and by the people. I keep wondering how you feel about it. Days I feel out of my depth over here, I get to brooding about it.

Tyler, what I'd started to write you about was not letting them sell out too much of the for the people and by the people part of the oldtime United States way. It has given us freedom to grow. Growing great people is what the country's for, isn't it? So long as the growth of people to greater stature all around is what we want more than anything, it will keep on. But we've got to make more and more of the promises come true. If we let too few kinds of people find space to grow in our system, nobody will believe in it any longer. If not enough people believe in a way of life, it comes to an end and is gone.

[282]

But here I am getting preachy on you again. I guess it's in the blood. Take care of yourself, boy, and best of luck. When and if I get out of this particular situation I'll try to get to see Dad in Geneva before coming home.

Affectionately yr. bro.

GLENN

Tyler read the letter with puckered brows. It hurt his eyes to focus on the letters. The smudged pages were all a blur now. It was quiet in the waitingroom. The elderly man in blue sitting near the door had gone to sleep and let his newspaper drop to the floor. Occasionally he emitted a gentle wheezing snore. Tyler cleared his throat and shook his head to get the blur out of his eyes.

He didn't feel drunk any more. His mind seemed full of bright clear sorrowful light. He felt like the last time, before their home was broken up, he'd gone on a walk with Dad and Glenn and they had walked crunching through the fallen leaves in that cemetery in Georgetown and stood for a minute without saying a word beside Mother's grave. Glenn was in that grave now. He folded the letter carefully and put it back in his wallet. Better send it to Dad. Then he took his glasses off and wiped them and put them back in their case.

Behind his eyes he could see sharply Glenn's white intent face, the reddish brows drawn together in a frown above the slightly lopsided nose, the childish mouth, the long rusty head tilted over his shoulder like when he used to try to lay down the law. In his ears he felt the clear ring of Glenn's voice, even the little squeak that came into it when he began to lose his temper. 'Anyway,' he

[283]

heard his own voice rumbling inanely inside his head, 'the kid had what it takes.' Already the swirl of thoughts was smudging his memory. He couldn't remember what the kid looked like any more. When had he seen him last? What did Dad look like? Sue Ann? He couldn't remember. Funny the way you could go on and on and then suddenly . . .

Well, Glenn would never know whether his big brother had turned out just another bigmouthed doublecrossing bastard or not. Sue Ann would know.

In the first place it was up to him to make up his mind. In the second place he ought to have put his foot down. 'Good old Toby's always kept his trap shut.' That's what they thought. 'One thing I've learned in my life is that everything every one of us does counts. . . . I'd look pretty, wouldn't I, sobbing out the story on the D.A.'s shoulder.' And there's Sue Ann and the ranch and the kids. It wouldn't stop Chuck, not by a jugful. In the first place a lot of people ought to have started a long time back to tell the truth, the whole truth and nothing but the truth. Now it was take the rap or turn state's evidence and save your shivering skin. The People against Spotswood. Spotswood against Crawford. Crawford against the People. The sentences began to whirl around faster and faster in his head like the painted horses on a merrygoround until his mind was a resounding blank. In the first place. In the second place. In the third place. Every so often 'in the first place' came back and the whole thing started off again.

Hell, he didn't have to make up his mind yet. He'd

make up his mind when they got him back on the stand.

After he'd sat there so long in the same position that he found his legs were going to sleep, he got up and started walking up and down. He had to stamp his feet to get the circulation back. His stamping woke up the deputy.

'Say, isn't it getting kinda late?' Tyler said. 'Suppose you ask 'em when my act's coming on.'

'What? What? What time is it?'

Tyler looked at his watch. 'It's after four . . . I'm pretty near gone. I didn't have any sleep last night.'

The elderly man went out and closed the door carefully after him. When he came back he gave Tyler a kind of sidelong glance. 'They ain't hearin' testimony,' he said. 'They're votin' a true bill. Witnesses are excused.'

'Do I have to come back or is Mr. Turner tired of my conversation?'

'You won't be recalled as a witness,' said the elderly man, standing aside to let Tyler walk out of the room.

With his raincoat on his arm and his hat jauntily on the side of his head he walked down the corridor to the head of the stairs. In the vestibule on the ground floor he caught sight of Ed James. What the devil was he hanging around here for all day?

'Hey, Ed, what gives? What's going on around here?'

'I'm askin' you, Toby . . . All I know is that Mac Turner is preparin' a statement for the press. This business is stirrin' up considerable interest . . . Didn't you like Mac? He's a great fellow.'

'A prince among men,' said Tyler tartly. 'But for crissake what's cooking?'

Mr. Grossman was standing beside them. His face was all shadows under the eyes. His fat cheeks seemed to have fallen in. 'Hi, Grossman, what's the trouble?' said Tyler. 'Mr. Grossman, meet Mr. James.' All the curves and smiles returned to Mr. Grossman's face. 'Mr. Ed James?' he asked coyly. 'Delighted, sir, delighted . . . I'm a reader of your column, a constant reader.'

Tyler groaned. 'Oh, I'd forgotten about that column, Ed . . . for crissake give us a break . . . you know . . . old lang syne.'

'Mr. Spotswood,' Mr. Grossman was saying in a hollow voice. 'May I confer with you for a moment?' He reached up and took Tyler by the lapel and led him out the front door under the Ionic portico. 'Mr. Spotswood, I have rather bad news . . . The Grand Jury has indicted you for perjury committed . . . er . . . allegedly committed in your examination this morning. Mr. Perry, deputy for the United States Marshal for this district, has the warrant and would like to serve it on you . . .' Tyler noticed a skinny man in an illfitting dark blue uniform who was leaning against a column looking intently in his direction.

'Why, that's a damned silly thing to do . . . Every word I said was true.'

'Let's hope so . . . let's hope we can prove it . . . As I told you Mackenzie Turner is a very ambitious young man.'

Tyler found himself shaking hands with Mr. Perry, the man in the blue uniform, who stared into his face with a yellow apologetic smile. 'You see, Mr. Spotswood, Mr. Grossman an' me we agreed it would be more convenient for you to be brought in now than later in the day . . . Easier to arrange bail etcetera . . . Now if you wouldn't mind stepping out of the precincts of the court . . .'

Mr. Perry and Tyler and Mr. Grossman walked in single file down the steps and out onto the sidewalk. A bunch of children romping home from school, led by a little girl with red hair and freckles who was lurching desperately along the pavement on roller skates, made a racket round them for a moment and plunged out of sight among the legs of homebound officeworkers thronging the sidewalk. 'Would you like to see the warrant, Mr. Spots-wood?' Mr. Perry was fumbling in his inside pocket.

'I don't want to see a goddam thing . . . Let's get this over.' Tyler struck off back towards the courthouse. Mr. Grossman and Mr. Perry, on either side of him, had to trot to keep pace with his long strides. As he walked up the steps he found a camera poked in his face. Photographers were scuttling about between the columns. Joe Hazard waved at him from out of the crowd. 'Sorry, old man, but it was too good to miss.' Tyler felt suddenly as if he were the center of a sort of parade proceeding through the vestibule and around the darkening corridor to the courtroom.

The judge was a tiredlooking man with pouches under his eyes. The clerk of the court sat at a desk under a bright light with a green glass shade. His small face with pointed nose and pointed chin stuck yellow out of the shadow. Nobody seemed to pay any further attention to Tyler. They talked about him over his head as if he were a bale of goods. He gave up trying to follow the pro-

ceedings and let the words buzz about his ears like a man
in a swarm of gnats who has decided it's no use trying to
fight them off. Luckily it was getting late, he told himself. They all wanted to go home. At length he made
out in the middle of one of the judge's long purring weary
sentences the words, 'Two thousand dollars bail.'

'Golly, I don't know where I can raise it tonight,' he
muttered, looking down at his shoes that he still hadn't
had time to get shined. Mr. Grossman looked up at him
reproachfully and hissed in his ears in a hurried whisper:
'We have made some arrangements. We have already
contacted a representative of a bonding company.' Tyler
opened his mouth to answer. Mr. Grossman shushed him
sharply as if he were a noisy child.

The judge had gotten to his feet. The clerk halfraised
himself from his seat with a jerk like an oldfashioned
jackinthebox and rattled off some words. The judge
hurried out the back door of the courtroom. The moment
court was adjourned, everybody began to behave more
naturally.

'Excuse me, Mr. Spotswood,' said Mr. Grossman in his
usual loud deferential tone. 'Allow me to introduce
Mr. McIlhenny, who represents the surety and bonding
company.' Mr. McIlhenny was a rolypoly man in tweeds
who had a sympathetic confidential way with him that
made Tyler feel as if he were buying insurance or betting
on a horserace. Ed James' moon face had loomed over
Mr. Grossman's broad back as he leaned over the clerk's
desk studying the printed form. 'I put up some securi-
ties,' Ed said.

Tyler's head was whirling. 'Ed, I don't want you to do that. Suppose I just go to jail?' Then he added peevishly, 'Everbody seems to know all about this business except me.'

'Keep your shirt on, Toby. You an' me'll have a talk,' Ed whispered in his ear. Tyler couldn't get himself to listen. All he could think of was getting out of there.

When the last signature had been scrawled above the last dotted line, Tyler, who had been feeling as if his lungs would cave in if he didn't get any fresh air, hurried out, with Ed a step behind him, through groups of newspaper men who tried to stop him. 'Boys, I can't say anything tonight . . . I don't know a goddam thing,' he called back at them as he ran.

Then he was out in the street again standing at the curb beside a taxi, breathing the cold northwest wind in the claret twilight. Down the street the lights were coming on. Ed was standing beside him saying over and over again, 'Now, for gosh sake, don't forget, Toby, you and me have got to have a talk . . . We'll eat an oyster at Dudley's at seven.'

'Allright allright . . . Thanks, Ed . . . for everything . . . I'll be at the office till then.'

At last he was alone in the cab. To be on the safe side he had the driver stop at a drugstore where he bought himself a quart of whiskey. When he stepped out of the elevator he was so tired he could hardly force his legs to carry him down the corridor. The office door was locked. He had to fumble in all the pockets of his vest before he found his passkey. The string of offices was empty, thank God. The first thing he did was to draw a paper cup of icewater from the cooler, which he rimmed with whiskey and plunked down on the corner of his desk. He sat there sipping it, leaning back in the swivel chair.

Now what? He sat there a long time sipping the whiskey and water out of the paper cup and staring up at the ceiling. When the whiskey began to taste weak, he got to his feet and reached for two more paper cups. He filled one with whiskey and another with water. A good slug of the straight whiskey set him up a little. Now he'd pull himself together. First . . .

He crossed the room to the typewriter desk, taking his two paper cups with him and settling them on the edge. Then he turned the big typewriter up and slipped in a fresh sheet of the office's best grade of official stationery.

> *Honorable Homer T. Crawford*
> *Senate Office Building*
> *Washington, D.C.*
> *Dear Chuck*
> *You God damned lousy yellow doublecrossing bastard.*

He gritted his teeth as he tapped the words out. Then he wrinkled up his nose. Oh hell, what was the use? He ripped the sheet out of the typewriter and tore it into small pieces and dropped it in the wastebasket.

He got to his feet again and carried his two little paper cups back over to his own desk. The whiskey one was empty. He filled it up again. He felt sober and buoyant now. His sleepiness was gone. He took out his fountain-pen, got a plain sheet of paper from the drawer and, forming the letters carefully, wrote out his formal resignation as secretary, effective immediately, dated it, signed it, folded it and put it in an envelope which he marked in his careful slanting hand:

Immediate attention Senator Crawford. T. S.

He tossed it into the wire basket on his desk.

Then he started staring at the ceiling again. The phone rang in the next office. He picked up his receiver. The line was dead. He went out and stumbled around in the reception room until he found the little switchboard at Miss Glendinning's desk. It seemed hours before he could get the plugs right. Full of unexpected patience he stood there at the desk pulling the plugs out and pushing them in until he got a connection. It was Ed. 'Say, Toby, it's half past seven . . . I'm awful hungry . . . I'm sittin' here in the restaurant eatin' oyster crackers and drinkin' cocktails.'

'Allright, Ed, you go on and start eating . . . I've got one more phone call to make, then I'll come along.'

'Now, Toby, you won't stand me up, will you? I have something very important in connection with this indictment I want to talk to you about . . . I've got to see you tonight . . . I'll come by the office if you don't want to come here.'

'No, Ed, I'll be along . . . I want to get out of this goddam place . . . Order me some Chincoteagues . . . I'll be right along.' Tyler rang off.

'Give me Long Distance, please, operator . . . Hello, I want to put in a party to party call to Mrs. Senator Crawford, Bar Z Ranch . . . Chincapin, New Mexico . . . all right, call me, please.' He sat waiting at Miss Glendinning's desk in the dark. He wanted to smoke. He got out his cigarettecase. It was empty. After searching through his pockets, he started walking from desk to desk through the office, looking in drawers to see if he could find a cigarette.

He was in Chuck's office when the key turned in the lock. The door from the corridor opened and there was Miss Jacoby staring at him with black pinpoint eyes. He stood there looking at her with his hand on the edge of the little drawer. For some reason all at once he felt like a sneakthief.

Miss Jacoby looked him in the face for a moment with her head cocked on one side. Then she burst into loud crying and threw herself in one of the leather chairs. 'Uncle Toby,' she sobbed, 'how could you? how could you?'

'Now, now . . . Miss Jacoby,' he was saying. 'Shall I turn on the light?'

'No, no, go away,' she only sobbed the louder. Tyler backed into the lighted doorway and stood here talking into the dark. 'Now, now, Miss Jacoby, don't take on so . . . This is a difficult situation, but we are all doing our best,' he was murmuring in a singsong tone.

'You can talk like that, but the harm's done,' she screeched.

'Now, now,' he murmured again.

She didn't answer. Gradually the sobs subsided into sniffles. He turned away and walked back into the reception room and picked up the phone: 'Long Distance, please

. . . Long Distance, please cancel that call . . . yes, that's it. I don't want it. No . . . absolutely not . . . That's right . . . cancel it.'

Then he sat there in the dark reception room listening to his own breathing until the phone ringing loud as if inside his head brought him to with a start. It was Ed. '. . . Say, Toby, gosh almighty, man, what's the trouble? I've gourmandized slowly through my dinner from soup to nuts an' I'm gettin' drunk an' blue sittin' here drinkin' and waitin' . . . Man, don't you ever get hungry?'

'Honest, I'll be right there, Ed . . . I just finished up all the unfinished business.'

'Lemme tell you what I ate. Maybe that'll hurry you along. I ate your oysters an' an elegant broiled seabass an' . . .'

Tyler interrupted. 'I'll be right there . . . don't worry, Ed.'

He hung up and looked around his office for his hat and coat. He noticed the bottle of whiskey and took another drink with plenty of water this time. Then he noticed that he'd had his hat and coat on all along.

Miss Jacoby hadn't put the lights on in the Senator's office. She must still be there because the crooning of 'Oh Johnny, Oh Johnny, Oh' came softly from the radio. Standing with his hat and coat on and a paper cup of whiskey in each hand, Tyler began to laugh quietly to himself. She was searching for another station now, she was turning up snatches of dinner music and snags of static. Then it was the hollow sound of a hall and Chuck's voice, loud and clear:

'Folks, I stand before you tonight the target of the slings and arrows of outrageous fortune. But not for long. I tell you folks my innin's is a-goin' to come. Because I've stood up on my hind legs an' said my say . . . Because I have shown myself to be one of the few who reachin' high office does not forget the people from which he came, because I have spent my good money an' given my good time on station WEMM to instruct an' develop the political eddication of the plain people an' to learn 'em what's what in this country an' explained to 'em a few plain rough truths about how this country is run today an' how much better, so help me God, it's a-goin' to be run in the future . . . Because I've shouted myself hoarse sayin' to the free people of this country, government is your job, you do it, I find myself assailed on every hand by the slimy forces of privilege an' monopoly that lurk in the night, by the alien band that is chokin' Washington like an octopus, that united with the nabobs of the empire of St. Vitus' dance that reigns on Pennsylvania Avenue an' in the halls of the Capitol, of this mess of crackpot professors an' visionary social workers we've got here a-cloggin' up the wheels of government with their Jew peddler's ragbag of panaceas an' snake tonics an' horse liniments . . .

'Lemme tell you fine honest citizens gathered together tonight in this great city of the reborn South that . . . although it's always possible that once in a while I have been deceived by the fair faces an' false smiles of some of those I trusted as Caesar did Brutus . . . ah, there was the unkindest cut of all, the stab in the back from a friend . . .

[294]

I tell you-all here in this hall tonight that I have looked into the bottom of my heart an' I have found no guilt . . . Sence I was a little shaver toting those bundles of news-papers too heavy for me down State Line Avenoo down home, tryin' to help out my poor weary mother with the wherewithal to buy a few groceries, there is not a thing in my career that cannot bear the scrutiny of any investi-gation, any grand jury, any court in the land. Among that gallant band of friends an' associates who have fought with me up the slippery slick trail to victory they may find a couple who've gotten themselves tarred up through no fault of mine, or mebbe through no fault of their'n . . . but I defy the holier-than-thouest sugarsuckin'est reformer of all that doleful crew that are sickin' their dawgs on me right now to find one smut or smirch on my career. Come on, I cry in their faces as they circle around for the kill, bayin' like the lowdown hounddawgs they are every one of them . . . I say to them in the words of the poet:

'Out of the night that covers me,
　　Black as the pit from pole to pole,
　　I thank whatever gods may be
　　For my unconquerable soul.

'In the fell clutch of circumstance
　　I have not winced nor cried aloud.
　　Under the bludgeonings of chance
　　My head is bloody but unbowed. . . .'

Tyler had stood bolt upright in the middle of the floor listening, sipping first from one then from another crushed and leaky paper cup. 'He's going to recite the whole god-dam thing,' he said to himself aloud all of a sudden in a normal voice as if he were really talking to somebody else. He crumpled the empty paper cups into the wastebasket and strode out the door and slammed it behind him.

On the way to the elevator he found he was lurching a little. He had to stand a second leaning with the flat of his hand against the wall while he was waiting for the elevator. He managed to stand straight and solemn in the elevator as he went down and to walk sedately through the vestibule across the marble pavement out onto the street to find himself a cab.

Driving over to Dudley's he began to feel sleepy again. Lights seemed to be going by awful fast. When he lurched out of the cab, a gust of cold wind blowing down the avenue gave him a sudden brace. He walked stiffly into the restaurant. Most of the tables were empty. The man reading *Barron's Weekly* must be Ed. The paper was lowered and there was Ed, his face pink from eating, looking up at him out of rounded eyes.

'Well,' Ed said. 'Well, well, well!'

'Ed, I'm drunk,' said Tyler, dropping heavily into the opposite chair.

'Don't you want to take your hat off an' stay awhile?'

'Doan' need take my hat off . . . I'm Quaker.'

'How about some hot soup, Toby? We've absolutely got to have a sensible talk.'

'Hot coffee's better . . . scalding hot . . . I'm drunk, Ed, boy, but I'm congenial drunk . . . Talk all you want . . . Talk till Christmas. Talk through my hat and coat just for an old friend.' The waiter was bending over him and Tyler allowed his hat and coat to be taken away.

'Now here's what we got to talk about, Toby. I spent an hour with Mackenzie Turner before comin' over here. Old Mac means business, but he's got nothin' against you . . . not a thing in the world . . . He had to put you on the spot like he did to make you produce your records . . . not another way in the world to do it.'

'Haven't got any records.'

Ed leaned across the table towards him. 'He's not after you . . . He hates to bother you, Toby . . . He thinks you're okay, but he thinks the time has come to stop our old friend Chuck dead in his tracks, and I do too.'

'Just heard him in A'lanta . . . I heard him . . . on the radio. He's been betrayed by false friends . . . Well, he's a goddam liar . . . Anyway, it don't matter . . . All last night on that airliner, all day in that little waitingroom for witnesses I've been thinking . . . We can't sell out on the people, but the trouble is that me, I'm just as much the people as you are or any other son of a bitch. If we want to straighten the people out we've got to start with number one, not that big wind . . . You know what I mean. I got to straighten myself out first, see . . . Thinking hurts, Ed.' He looked down at the cup of coffee that suddenly yawned black and steaming under his chin. The smell of the coffee opened a door in his mind . . . the kitchen door at home and little Glenn in there with an apron on helping Mother get breakfast. 'Girlboy,' he'd yelled and slammed the door. . . . 'I've got to lay off this drinking, Ed,' he was saying in a slow reasonable voice into the coffeecup. 'It mixes up your head. . . .' Now it was a roulette swinging past triangles, redblack redblack,

slower, slower; red; black. He had to shout to get rid of
the roulette in his head: 'Well, there's that picture you
know used to be in every barroom . . . my, I used to like
barrooms and poolrooms and the little hustlers on Four
and a Half Street on a rainy night, poor little bitches,
made up for things being so preachy at home . . . but
what I'm trying to talk about is Custer's Last Stand.
That's the picture used to be in all the barrooms.'

'Toby, old man, why don't you drink your coffee?'

'I doan like it . . . might catch botulism . . . Well,
Custer made his last stand and the redskins scalped him,
and I used to feel like that walking around Washington
when I was a kid . . . My old man's old man was a funny
old geezer, used to call him Old Soul. Liked nothing
better than to take us kids to the Smithsonian Institution
to see Langley's plane. They called it Langley's folly . . .
or up to the Hill to visit the Halls of Congress . . . that's
what Old Soul called 'em . . . and trotting after him I
used to see the dome of the Capitol at the end of an avenue
of trees in the fall . . . high among the clouds . . . Sometimes I feel that way. This mornin' I felt that way.
That way and Custer's Last Stand . . . order me up a
drink, for crissake.'

Sometimes Ed's face was big and round and near and
sometimes it was tiny, way way off. 'That's just what I
meant, Toby.' Ed was preaching like Dad used to. 'It's
your duty to go down to that Grand Jury and tell everything you know. All Mac Turner needs is your assurance
that you'll cooperate to the best of your ability and he'll
quash the indictment.'

Tyler reached for the drink and swallowed it down. He pushed a strand of wet hair off his forehead. The restaurant was full of empty roaring. 'No, you don't,' he yelled. 'Indicted we stand, indicted we fall . . . like Custer.'

'Let's talk quietly, Toby . . . It's your duty as an American citizen, Toby . . . besides I've got a magazine contract all laid out. A nice fat one. You an' me, Toby, we built up Chuck Crawford. He turned out a lemon . . . Now we lay him to rest.'

'No, that's not like Custer . . . Lemme explain.' He made a great effort to stop the roaring. He had to have quiet in the restaurant to explain. He waved his forefinger across the table for quiet, but it upset the cup of coffee. Waiters were buzzing around. A waiter was bringing his hat and coat. He got to his feet with dignity. 'Lez gerrout ahere . . . too drunk in here.'

Going out the revolving door he leaned heavily on Ed's arm. Outside under the streetlamp the wind braced him up again. He backed away from Ed, feeling his mouth creasing into a little wise smile. 'What I want to explain . . . they doan like me in there . . . Mackenzie Turner doan like me . . . Custer was profoundly wrong, he'd made a profound tactical mistake. Like me. You remember poor lil old Glenn?'

'Sure, sure, it was through him we first met back in Horton, Toby. Don't you remember? I was still with the East Coast.'

Tyler planted his feet firmly apart on the swaying pavement: 'Anyway, Custer was profoundly wrong, see?

But he didn't run out. He made his last stand and he got his . . . that's what makes me feel like that kid's letter and the little dome above the big dome and the clouds around and Old Glory nailed to the top of the mast . . . Shit, I can't explain.'

Ed had flagged a cab.

'Toby,' he shouted in his ear. 'Suppose we go to my place an' sober up a bit an' I'll get old Mac to come over.'

Tyler felt the bitter anger getting hold of him. His fists were clenching. 'No, you don't.'

The driver of the cab had leaned out from his seat and was saying in a soothing tone: 'Easy does it, gents . . . easy does it.'

Ed tried to grab him by the arm to pull him into the cab. 'Toby, for gosh sakes, act your age, act like a reasonable being. You don't want to go to jail.'

'No, you don't.' Tyler pulled his arm away.

'It's your duty as a citizen.'

Ed reached out to grab his arm again. Before he knew what he was doing, Tyler had hauled off and hit him in the face with his fist. His fist glanced along the jaw. Ed backed off and stood there under the streetlight staring at him. Ed's head had jerked back and he'd staggered a little. Now he had raised his hand and was rubbing his jaw in a puzzled sort of way. Tyler opened his mouth to speak, but he couldn't. Before Ed could say anything, Tyler walked right past him lurching as he walked with fast strides up the windy avenue.

Number One

When you try to find the people,
always in the end it comes down to
the old man with chalk in his knuckles selling pencils on a
windy streetcorner, the sweaty small boy with grime behind

his ears who runs lugging the heavy pack of evening papers, the girl in a scurry to get home after ten hours in a department store raising her patent leather handbag to signal the streetcar, the foxyfaced young man with a lunchbox under his arm hurrying to his job on the night shift, the ruddy man who's just been commissioned a major sitting bolt upright in the back of the taxi looking joyfully forward to the cocktail lounge where at five-fifteen he's going to meet the girl he's going to marry before Christmas, the stoopshouldered convict on parole dragging his feet with his eyes on the curb, the stout mother of many children who's waiting for the bus; she's been shopping; her legs are heavy; one heel's run down; her arms are full of bundles; she has two smeary brats in tow:

when you try to find the people, myriadfigured pyramid precariously balanced on every one

alone:

lathe operator, welder, bench hand, mechanic, filing clerk, brakeman, lawyer, cook, girl in a beauty parlor, doctor, barber, radio repairman, truckdriver, rigger, watchmaker, seaman, babbiter, farm hand, tester, surveyor,

or the portly man in brown Harris tweed with silver hair in ducktails over his ears portentously eating an omelet in the Senate restaurant; or the lanky politico from the cowcountry thrusting out his hand to shake as he barges through the swinging doors off the floor of the House; or the jowly *lobbyist with loose eyes ordering up drinks at the dinner dance; or the slowspoken cudchewing dairyman out to trade a heifer, who's milling in the crowd at the county seat Saturday night that swirls round brightlit drugcounters, dimestores, chain groceries, dammed on the pavement by ranked trucks, muleteams, old cars splattered with red clay; or the young wolf of the jukejoints blowing out his chest and sucking his belly into skyblue tights among sunbrowned camerawise boys and girls stretched out on the sand a sunny Sunday at the ocean beach; or an old foreignborn woman in a shawl waiting with scalded eyes beside other hushed women outside the high wire fence at the shafthead when something has gone wrong in the mine;*

or the boss glaring you in the eye with two fists on his desk who's bound he'll put us all through the mill;

the people is everybody

and one man alone;

senses that start in delicate tracery of fingertips, awareness of eardrums, focus of eyes, to and fro signalflashes of the sheathed nerves, stock of memories incredibly immense, words made of wind, sounds, aches, smells that tease feelings, wants, surges of need,

making up the involved where ending? where beginning? time sculptured convolutions of the mind:

each life taut in the net of lives:

*neighbors, wives, children, the postman who comes to the
door, the woman who works in the kitchen, the man higher up;
weak as the weakest, strong as the strongest,
the people are the republic,
the people are you.*

THE END